Lines in the Sky

This is a work of fiction. The events described are imaginary. Real places are used fictitiously. Any resemblance of characters and events to real life is coincidental.

Lines in the Sky

Published by Red Pill Hippie in Eugene, Oregon.

First Paperback Edition.
ISBN: 978-0-9962795-7-4
Library of Congress: 2021918962

Printed in the United States of America.

Cover photographs: *grandfailure; Gajus.* Title page image: *pandavector.* Backcover image: *boscorelli.* Flower image: *Olya Creative Art.* Fonts: Dream Catcher. **Luminari.** Logo: *Alexkava.*

FOR **DANIEL, LILLIAN, AND RIVER.**

I LOVE YOU ALWAYS AND FOREVER.

JULIE EMBERS

Shattered Roots

I LAY IN BED, STARING AT THE DARK CORNERS OF MY bedroom, waiting for them to move, waiting for the darkness to swallow me whole.

A summer breeze blows in through the second-story window, pushing at the screen. The smell of fresh-cut grass zephyrs over Frank's empty side of the bed. The recent change in President silenced the discussion of Global Warming. It doesn't exist anymore, but I feel it. Anyone without air conditioning feels it.

June bugs tap against the glass, begging to get in. The clear night sky cleanses the air of heavy particles like a fresh breath. North Carolina started seeing the same types of fires as California. By late July, smoke will choke out the air and all the windows will have to be clamped shut.

The night's heat hangs with humidity, pulling at the stars. Carter's hot, tiny fingers knead my breast as he moans in his sleep. Frank's working late and we have the bed all to ourselves. I brush his temple with my thumb and his little hand knocks it away. He doesn't like to be stroked when breastfeeding at night. His fingers ball into a tiny fist, gently and rhythmically knocking against his head. He only does that when he can't sleep.

I stare at the corner of the room, to the right of the window. Shadows fall just right to block the light from the hallway behind us, darkening its crevice even deeper. I slide my fingers between Carter's hand and his head. He grunts in tired protest and goes on nursing.

The darkness within the corner shifts.

My heart jumps. *No. My eyes are playing tricks on me.*

Carter moans and I let his fist drum gently against his head. I'm having a hard time sleeping too.

"Mom," Jackson, says from the doorway behind me. He comes into my room, slumping against my back. "Mom," he draws out the words in a whine. "Me not feel good."

A gust of hot air plows through the window screen, teasing the mosquitos and silencing the June bugs.

Jackson totters back a bit. He had been premature by three weeks. The doctors said he'd catch up, but at three-years-old, he was still petite for his age. Usually he comes running into my bedroom at some point of the night. Usually because there is something in his closet. Or so he says. I'm not going to get out of bed to prove him otherwise. Plus, I always sleep better after he sneaks into bed with us.

Another burst of air pushes through the room.

His fingers grip the thin cotton of my nightgown.

This is different.

He doesn't crawl into bed.

"What's wrong, honey?" I lean back from Carter, letting his lips fall away from my nipple. Milk drains out of the corner of his tiny little mouth.

"My head hurts," Jackson says, leaning his sweaty cheek against my back.

"Do you want to come sleep in my bed?" I pull the thin sheet covering us out so he can climb in. Since I was little, I always slept with something wrapped around me at night. Something to barricade me—protect me—from the shadows that hide in the corners. Not like there's anything in there. Not like it would provide any kind of protection.

"It hurts..." he says, rubbing his forehead.

"Okay." I scoot out of bed, sandwiching Carter's tiny, chubby little body between pillows so he won't roll off the mattress. He just turned six-months-old and has every intention of mastering rolling before July comes. "Let's go downstairs and get you some medicine."

I scoop Jackson into my arms. His hot forehead leans against my chest. His body settles deeper into my arms with each step down the stairs.

At the bottom, a draft of cool air rushes across my bare feet. It brings chills over the wooden train pieces and metal cars filling the river of my path. Our small dining area barricades any easy access to the sliding glass door opposite us. It then leads into an unfenced side yard. The door is wide open. It's the middle of the night and it's wide open.

It can't be. I swear I locked it. It's a problem I have actually: locking the door. I check it at least three times before bed. Five when Frank has to work late, like tonight.

My heart pounds. *Shit. How could I have left it open?* Goosebumps ripple like a wave over me. *I locked it. I know I had. Carter had been fussy after dinner. I hurried the boys upstairs and nursed Carter, but—*

Jackson moans.

My heart skips a beat, forcing me forward toward the open door. *Maybe I didn't lock it.*

Nothing feels out of place. The same laundry basket that sat beside the stairs to go up, is even fuller than a week ago. The living and dining rooms are clear of monsters, but I can't see around the wall into the kitchen.

Damn it. I hate when Frank works the hoot-owl and we're all alone.

I try to put Jackson down on the couch—just in case something springs out of the darkness—but he moans, clenching onto my arms. Adrenaline shoots through my veins. Carrying him towards the open door means that he'll become my shield from whatever awaits outside. That's the last thing I want. I hush him and lean my cheek against his sweaty hair. *There's no way I left the door open.*

He moans again.

I take a step. The faint sound of crickets singing comes through the screen door. *There could be some maniac out there, getting ready to burst in and slash us—* I push the thought away. *A maniac wouldn't bother pulling the screen door shut.*

The crickets stop chirping.

Unless he'd given it a lot of thought.

I grab the door handle. A half-lit moon illuminates the night. Its soft pale glow gives everything a shape. The white contrail of a plane, passing beneath the stars, is a sign that man has conquered the sky. It flies in a perfect line, parallel to our clothesline. Cloth diapers, tiny socks, and worn-out bras blow in a breeze. A breeze much too cool for June's night air. No more afraid of the sudden change in temperature than any conjured demons, I pull the door shut, locking it, hoping I haven't trapped anyone else in with us. Hoping this isn't the last day of my life.

The indoor air grows heavy. I turn around, anticipating the onslaught of an intruder, but there isn't any.

The kitchen is dark, empty.

Jackson's hand moves to my chest, the same spot Carter's falls while nursing. I head into the kitchen and grab the sugar-loaded medicine that is supposed to numb his pain. I hate giving it to the kids. It's nothing but sugar, but there's no other option. Instead of black lines on the measuring cup, they are clear, making it impossible to get the measurement right the first time. Especially when not having slept in forever. I'm already tired. When the kids are sick, I don't sleep at all. Even the thought of how much sleep I'm going to miss is exhausting.

I pour too much liquid, passing the top line, pour some back, and hold the cup up to the light. I'm numbing his pain, instead of healing it, but we both need some sleep.

Jackson moans and leans against me, knocking the cup. The liquid sugar overflows, spilling all over my hand. I scrape it back into the container and measure for a third time. He nuzzles into me again, nearly weightless. I prop him up and hold the cup to his lips. He slurps it down, but doesn't bother licking every last drop.

I lean against the counter. I'm so tired. I haven't slept since Carter was born. I got through postpartum depression without drugs, but I can feel the lack of sleep catching up with me.

Jackson's backpack on the chair, beside the counter, catches my eye. A rolled up piece of paper pokes out the side zipper. I had been too busy after preschool pickup to unravel the creation he made while away.

"What's that?" I say, placing the measuring cup on the counter, scooping him into my arms, and walking toward it. I lean him down on my knee and pull the paper out. I had hurried to make dinner, give the boys a bath, and pack a lunch for Frank. I'd forgotten to ask how Jackson's day had been. I pull him closer, unraveling it.

It's a drawing of our townhouse, situated on a forest-green hill that doesn't exist. A large tree stands to the left of our home. *A tree like that would be lovely on a summer night like this.*

Carter starts to fuss upstairs, meaning I have one minute to get back into bed. He always knows when I'm not there.

"Is this our house?" I say.

Jackson nods yes and snuggles closer.

Three white lines cross the blue sky he made.

"What are these lines in the sky?" I say.

"Death," he says, sliding from my lap.

My heart races. I kneel down to his level. "What do you mean?"

He tugs my hand and heads for the stairwell, saying, "Mommy, can we go to bed?"

I hurry after him, setting the picture on the laundry pile, scooping him up at the foot of the stairs, and leaving any hidden monsters alone. Halfway up I stop. *The garage*. I hadn't checked the garage. *Shit*. I take Jackson to my bed, maneuvering him around Carter and the pillows. He settles in. His body sinks into the mattress and he rolls onto his side, facing the open window.

Carter found his fist to suck on and passed out again. I hurry downstairs, checking the locks on both the front and side doors, then head for the garage.

A car door closes out front.

I glance at the front door—at the foot of the stairs—to the picture on the laundry. *Jesus*. It's a surprise I'm still alive: always thinking of what bad things can happen. For every moment, I can instantly think of at least three things that can go wrong. I'm trying hard not to do that. So, I convince myself the car door banging out front isn't someone trying to kill me. There isn't a monster in the garage preparing to tear me to pieces.

I meant to peek out front, but the medicine lid sitting on the counter catches my attention. I let it distract me, keep me from being brave. I pick up the lid and then the bottle. I feel ashamed, like I'd given him a narcotic so I could sleep.

The door to the garage creaks open.

My heart falls. The medicine bottle splashes to the counter. I spin around, but it's not quick enough.

Hands slide around my waist.

"No," I yell, thrusting all my weight back against him, reaching for the silverware drawer—the knives.

"Woo, woo," comes Frank's voice, ascending into a "What are you doing?"

Adrenaline eases through my veins, but the tightness in my throat squeezes out, "Jesus, Frank!"

"What are you doing up?" he says, moving closer.

I regain myself, cap what's left of the medicine, and wash the mess from my hands.

"What's got you so jumpy?" He takes off his shirt and throws it at the garage door.

If I tell him about the sliding glass door being open while he was gone, I'll never hear the end of it. I turn off the faucet and say, "Nothing."

His arms slide around my waist and pull me up against his bare chest. "You ready for bed?"

I wipe the sweat from my brow and pull away. "You're home early."

A breeze creeps through the kitchen window, cooling the phylum of sweat from my skin.

"They closed the airport for maintenance." His hand cups my breast. It doesn't take much to excite my body. His hot breath against my skin brings back the sweat, but I don't care. His lips brush my neck as he whispers, "Ready for bed?"

He'd been working swing-shift for three months. It's the first chance we had to be alone without my period getting in the way. His fingers tighten and his lips press against my neck, pushing my whole body up against the kitchen sink.

"No. Not here," I force the words. "What if the kids come down?"

He hushes me, spins me to face him, and presses his lips against mine. His fingertips push up my nightgown. The worn cotton fabric of his soccer shorts presses between my thighs. His fingernails scratch into my hip as he pulls my panties down. They fall onto the linoleum. He kisses the cotton over the top of my breast and continues down to my belly button. He breathes in the scent of my nightgown for a second before finding the soft skin of my inner thigh with his lips.

I can hear Carter moaning upstairs, sensing that I'm not in bed yet.

Frank's lips press harder against my skin, tempting me to stay in place. Carter's moan gets louder and milk leaks out, soaking the front of my nightgown.

"Mom," Jackson's voice breaks the moment. It gets louder as he descends the stairs, "Mommy…?"

Frank shoots to a stand and sprints into the garage.

I yank the nightgown down and scoop up my underwear, shoving it into the silverware drawer.

Jackson rounds the wall. "Mommy, come to bed?"

He leans his head on the counter, slumping against it. He always sleeps better beside me. It seems to heal him quicker. I scoop him up and carry him back up the stairs. I glance back at the kitchen, watching it disappear as I climb the staircase.

At the top, I set Jackson down, walking him to the bathroom, flicking the light on. "Try using the potty before I put you in my bed."

He squints. His little body sways as he moves toward the toilet. It had taken so long to get to the point of no diapers. Surely, he was only getting 75% actually in the toilet, but we were well on our way.

I hurry to peek in on Carter. He rolled onto his side, found a binky, and drifted back to sleep.

The curtains blow and the faint sound of an airplane accompanies the breeze through the screen. A chilling air.

I glance back at the bathroom.

It is empty.

I spin, scanning the small hallway at the top of the stairs. "Jackson?"

There's no answer.

My heart pounds. I hurry into the bathroom and peek around the wall that separates the shower from the toilet.

He isn't there.

I spin and hurry to his room.

His little body is curled beneath the window, almost filling his pillow.

My heart eases. I push a path through the trucks and stuffed animals on the floor, sitting on the edge of his bed, and lean to kiss his forehead. *I don't know what I'd do without you in my life*.

Beads of sweat that gathered above his brow have dried with the night breeze. It's becoming a little too cold. I kiss him, smearing the sweat onto my lips. His stuffed scarab beetle, Atum, is lodged between the mattress and the wall. Frank bought it for Jackson the first time they'd met. We had gone to the zoo. I didn't want to hit the gift shop on the way out, but there was no avoiding it. Jackson went running into the store, sprinting behind a toy shelf.

My heart skipped. I couldn't see him. It was only for a second, but long enough for someone to steal him away. He had gone straight for the beetle. It was one of those beetles that you see in ancient Egyptian texts.

Atum's shiny, black fabric is now faded from all his trips to the washing machine. I kiss its head and tucked it under Jackson's arm, taking my time to kiss my little guy's cheek.

The garage door slams shut downstairs, pulling my heart tight. Relief soon follows, knowing it is Frank.

I sneak away, tiptoeing toward the door. Everything in Jackson's room is blue. His night light barely lights the corners of the room. A breeze sweeps in and I turn to close the window, trying to ignore the corners.

Hand-drawn pictures, taped to the wall, grab my attention. One is of his fishing trip with Frank. Another of my mother's dog, Muff, playing catch with him. There are several of our new home, each drawn from a different angle. Each has parallel, white lines covering the sky. Three white lines.

I step back from the wall onto a Lego. *Motherfucker!* I grab my foot, squeezing it as I brace against the wall, trying not to make noise, trying to breathe through the vomit-induced feeling pushing up my leg.

"What are you doing?" Frank asks from the doorway.

I shoo him away and carefully put my foot back on the carpet, brushing the plastic toy pieces farther from my path.

"Mom," Jackson's voice comes as a whisper.

I turn so fast, I nearly fall.

"Mommy, I uv you," he says in his sleep.

A sick feeling pushes up from my stomach into my chest. The feeling that those are the last words he'll ever speak to me.

Coming Down

It is two o'clock in the morning when Jackson starts screaming.

My heart's pounding before my eyelids even open. It's not the "Mom, I have to use the bathroom," or the "Mom, I'm scared" scream. It is blood-curdling. I jump to my feet and jet for his room, nearly tripping and falling face-first onto the sea of toys.

My three-year-old boy is lying in his bed, facing the door. His eyes are full of tears; his hair soaked with sweat, and blood drains out of his nose.

For a moment, I can't move.

"What the hell?" Frank pushes past me into the room. "Get a cold rag."

I run to the bathroom. There's nothing but dirty clothes and a week-old hand towel that has become the perfect breeding ground for infection. I sprint downstairs for the laundry basket, reaching for the first clean piece of fabric I can get my fingers on. Jackson's drawling falls to the floor. Cold air rushes my feet, leading my eyes toward the sliding glass door.

It's wide open.

My heart chokes. I sprint back upstairs to the bathroom, shoving the towel under the faucet and turning on that fucker as hard as I can.

The fabric soaks, filling like a dead thing hung in my hands. Excess liquid drips between my fingers. I leave the water running, sprinting for Jackson's room. My heart pounds with images of my dead child. *No.* I soar around the corner into his room. *No.* I haven't had enough time. The days had gone too fast. My biggest fear, every mother's biggest fear—to lose their child, before losing themselves—floods me like a tsunami. *No.*

Frank's still on the bed, cuddling Jackson. My baby's shirt is soaked with blood. Drops of it drip out his nose onto Frank's bare arm. Fear sinks into every wrinkle of Frank's face. He looks like he's drowning in it.

Nausea pushes up my throat, but there isn't time to throw up. I run to him. Frank moves over. The color has drained from my hands and they shake as I pull Jackson into my lap, leaning his head back and pinching his nose.

He chokes on the blood. I release his nose, and sit him forward a little. It sprays into the air from his lips and nose. I cup the towel to his mouth and the warm liquid of his blood soaks through, touching my hand. I can't breathe. He leans his head onto my shoulder, moaning as his little body quivers.

Frank's footsteps pound down the stairs. His voice echoes to the second floor as he shouts into the phone, pleading for an ambulance.

The tiny vibration of Jackson's moan penetrates my soul. My throat dries out with the next breath. I can't breathe. I can feel his heart racing against my chest. I delay another breath so I can feel his chest, making sure he's still breathing. I hum, *"Hush little baby, don't say a word,"* to comfort him… and me.

Frank returns to the room. His lips spread, but no words come out. His eyes are red with tears. His words return with the sound of defeat, "There are no ambulances available."

How can that be?

He steps closer, swaying like a ghost, handing me a fresh towel. "Get in the car. I'll grab Carter."

He pauses, only for a second, but it feels like forever. He leans down and kisses Jackson on the head, then pulls away to look at me—kissing my forehead. Hot tears drip from his cheeks onto mine.

I take a breath—a deep breath. I can't breathe. *What if it's some kind of a disease? An infection? Or brain aneurysm?* I don't have time to deal with the neuroses of my brain. I have to get Jackson to a doctor.

Frank pulls back. He leans his hand against my cheek, leaning his forehead against mine like we already lost him.

No. I'm not letting that happen. I tighten my grip, clench my little boy in my arms, and head for the car. I refuse to lose him.

Broken

FRANK MAGICALLY GOT CARTER INTO HIS carseat without waking him, after heading downstairs to our beat-up 1990s Toyota Camry.

More blood soaks through the towel. I squeeze Jackson tighter, humming loud enough to calm both of us, clamping him to me, heading for the stairs. Thoughts pour through my head: the first time Jackson said, "Mama," the first time he reached up to me to be picked up, the first time he smiled and wrapped his little fingers around my thumb. All of it weighs on me as I carry him downstairs.

Jackson's drawing drifts from the laundry basket onto the floor as I hurry by. Frank has left the passenger door wide open and is ready to pull the front door shut behind me. If I move any slower, any slower at all, I won't be able to move.

Carter's baby car seat is harnessed behind the passenger seat. Jackson's car seat is on the opposite side, behind the driver. Frank hurries around me to open the door to Jackson's car seat. I freeze. There's no way I can let go of him. I can't buckle him and leave him alone in the back. *Not like this*. I can't let him sit alone. I walk to the passenger side door. I expect Frank to say something about endangering him, but he doesn't. He closes the back door and heads back to me, waiting until I've settled Jackson on my lap before closing the car door.

He hurries to his place behind the wheel and backs out of the driveway. His driving is pretty calm until we approach a red light. He slows the car.

We can't stop. Every second counts. I say, "Frank…"

He glances at the rearview mirror, grips the steering wheel tighter, and leans forward to scan the deserted street. No one. Not even a rogue drunk on his way home from the bar. Frank shots the car through the intersection saying, "Hold on."

I squeeze Jackson tighter, looking back at the baby mirror. Carter is fast asleep, sucking on an invisible pacifier.

More blood soaks through the towel, wetting my palm. We're not getting there fast enough.

Up ahead, the hospital comes into view.

My heart races with the vehicle, but it sinks to my feet when I see the curbs are lined with cars. Four ambulances clog the Emergency Room drop off area. A familiar minivan idles in the line behind them. A woman hops out, crying hysterically. It's Maria Gomez. Her son Bobby attends preschool with Jackson. Everything she says is in Spanish, which I don't understand, but it sounds like a prayer. Her husband, Ramon, jumps out of the driver's seat, runs around the car, and lifts their son Bobby out of the backseat. Their little boy's body hangs loose in his arms.

I instantly clench Jackson to me. What if it is contagious? Bobby and Jackson have preschool every Wednesday together—just yesterday.

Bobby's arms swing—limp—with each of his father's steps into the Emergency Room.

Frank slams on the brakes three car-lengths back from the van, and faces me, looking only at Jackson. He jumps out and rounds the car, just as Ramon had. He opens my door. I'm supposed to hand over Jackson.

I slid my fingers through his hair. The towel soaks more. I watched Maria crumble into pieces along the very same path I am to take.

Frank grabs Jackson from my lap.

Jackson screams.

I look back at Carter through his baby mirror, and get out of the car.

"What are you doing?" says Frank.

I rest my hand on Jackson's back and his scream lowers to a loud moan. The plan was for Frank to take Jackson in, since Carter's still breastfeeding. But I'm his mother and no matter how much Frank tries, he's not his father. If I'm not there… If something happens and I'm not there, I will never forgive myself.

"Take Munchkin home," I say, taking Jackson into my arms. "I'll call you when we're ready to come home."

He begins to shake his head in detest. The other option now is for all of us to go in. I watch Ramon and little Bobby disappear behind the ER's sliding glass doors. *Maybe it's only a new strain of the flu*. The Emergency Room doors close. There's no one else we can call. The only family we have is my mother. She lives across town, but I can't call her.

I glance back at Carter. "I don't want Carter getting this."

Frank's grip loosens. He kisses my forehead, and then Jackson's. I can feel the part of him that wants to stay by my side. Jackson's father had abandoned me in high school. Two years later, I met Frank. He was everything I needed, and still is. He makes his way back to the driver's seat, looking one last time at me before taking off, giving me one more chance to change my mind.

The fresh hand towel dampens with blood. My heart pounds, desperate to make his bleeding stop. I sprint for the Emergency Room doors.

They slide open.

An Old Friend

MY BODY GOES STIFF. THE ROOM IS FILLED WITH people. People in every seat, against every wall, pacing between the rows. Each child has someone to comfort them, but the elderly and teenage kids are all alone. More than half the people clench a bloody shirt, napkin, baby blanket, or even the blouse of a nearby old woman. It's all bloody. There's so much blood.

Ramon clings to little Bobby in the far corner of the waiting room.

The room spins into a blur. I feel sick. *All these people. Jackson will never get seen.*

"Arden!" A woman yells my name from across the lobby from where the staff slowly take people back.

What am I going to do? The room spins faster. There are so many people. We didn't get here soon enough. We'll be last to be seen. There are so many people. Their silhouettes blur.

"Arden!" says the woman. A hand lands on my shoulder.

The room comes back into focus all at once.

Theia Mulligan stands before me, dressed in scrubs. She's more fit and trim than I remember. Sophomore year of high school, we started the nursing program together, and by the looks of it, she completed the program. She squeezes my shoulder, shaking me, forcing my attention. "Arden!"

Her eyes float down to Jackson, to my baby boy breathing heavily in my arms. She nudges the cloth away from his face. Drops of blood drip onto my bare feet.

I don't look down. I don't want to look down.

A ball catches in her throat and she runs her fingers through his hair. "Wait right here." She starts to sprint away, toward those doors that could get us into the back. I'm hopeful she can pull some strings and get him seen, but then she stops midway. My heart falls deeper with each returning step.

She whispers, "Actually, wait outside."

I follow her gaze over my shoulder, taking in the rows of people waiting, coughing, bleeding. *Wait outside?* Jackson will never get seen that way.

She runs off behind those far doors.

The room starts spinning again. I catch sight of Bobby's dad. He's looking at me. His eyes meet mine. If they take us back before Bobby, he'll never forgive me. I look away from him, already deciding that, if I have a choice, I'm taking Jackson back. But Theia knows things; what's going on, or at least more than I do. *Maybe it is contagious*. I look around the room at all the people. We were the last ones through the entrance. They haven't taken anyone back since we've gotten here. It will take forever for Jackson to be seen.

I tighten my arm around my little boy and head for the exit. I stop at the double doors.

They slide open.

If I leave, it could cost Jackson his life. If I stay, the same is equally possible. Frank isn't here to help me make the right decision. I take a breath and walk through the doors.

Summer's humid night has dipped to freezing. Goosebumps entice me to step back inside—with all the others.

A Tesla peels out around the back of the building. It's fully electric—quiet. There was no warning that it was coming. Its headlights blind me and shot straight for us. My heart pounds, and I resist the urge to run back inside.

The vehicle skids to a stop behind the Gomezes' van—the same place I just stood with Frank. The passenger window draws down. Theia leans over, yelling out of the open window, "Get in!"

The towel pinned between my chest and Jackson's cheek is now soaked with blood. Defeat sinks through my body, dropping into my feet, pinning me in place. I hoist Jackson's slipping body back up against me. His head rolls on my chest. He's stopped moaning.

"Get in!" she shouts.

The ER doors slide open behind me.

Ramon comes out empty-handed. Maria flings the van door open, sinking to the ground, screaming with agony. It spreads through the town like a nuclear bomb. I feel it wrapping around my heart. Bobby's dead. He's dead and all I want to do is get the fuck out of there.

I yank the passenger door open, balancing Jackson in my arms, hoping to hell that it isn't what Jackson has.

Theia unwraps a necklace hanging from her rearview mirror and tosses it at me. It falls onto Jackson. A string of hemp feeds through a smooth black stone carved into the shape of an Ancient Egyptian scarab beetle. She pulls the car away from the hospital, hopping the curb to get out of there. Calm, she says, "Put that on him. Pinch his nose a little, but don't lean him back. It won't clot."

I shimmy the necklace around his neck. Synthetic light drifts away, with the city behind us. Moonlight takes over, fading Jackson's skin to a ghostly white. Blood seeps into my nightgown, smearing down between the breasts that once nursed him—given him life. I don't know where we are going and I don't care. I just want him to be okay. I slide my fingers through his sweat-soaked hair and rest my lips upon his head.

So many questions swirl through my thoughts. Every ten minutes I clear them with a deep breath, but they flood back in again. I don't want to talk. Not to Theia, not to anyone. I pull Jackson closer. I attempt to slow my breath and the beat of my heart, easing the vibrations I'm sending him. Each breath, I try. I try to slow the beat, but it won't ease. The pounding of my heart races harder—faster—the farther we get from the hospital.

Ten minutes turns into two-and-a-half hours. Theia drives east, to the small coastal town of Topsail Island. Marsh land and small bridges separate the town from the mainland. Another ten minutes gets us to an empty parking lot.

Storm clouds reach for the moonlight in the distance.

Theia parks the car and jumps out, but I don't want to follow. We are two and a half hours away from Raleigh's hospital. At least an hour to any at all.

I shouldn't have left. Jackson's going to die because of this idiot... Because of me...

"Come on!" Theia pulls open the passenger door and grabs onto my arm, dragging me from the seat.

Jackson's body shifts, but he doesn't moan.

"Hurry up," she says, letting go, running toward the ocean.

I follow with slow steps to the sand's edge. She makes running on the sand look easy. I step onto the beach. My toes sink like quicksand with the extra weight of Jackson and I run after her, accepting the decision I've made. I can't just sit in the car, waiting for Jackson to die. I hold his head in place as I dig my feet deeper into the sand—cementing our fate.

Theia makes it to the water's edge, waving, encouraging me to hurry up.

Calm waves rock against the shore. In the far distance, a storm stirs an unsettled sea. Its waters anger.

Jackson's body shivers. The temperature drops another five degrees.

"Come on!" Theia shouts, knee deep in waves. "Hurry!"

The ocean waves pick up. My heart decides the tide is coming in, even if it isn't. I don't see how being in the middle of fucking nowhere is supposed to help. I've read and heard that being in nature reduces stress and helps heal you, but I don't think it can fix this. Not enough to heal Jackson.

I should've asked where we were going before I got into the car. I stumble, regaining my balance where the water turns the sand firm. The tide is going out, but it doesn't feel that way. I grip Jackson, but his fingers don't tighten around my arms. He doesn't even try to hold on. His limbs flop loose, like he weighs nothing.

My muscles burn. My skin's frozen. I'm halfway to Theia when thunder spills from the distant clouds. It ripples toward us, like a warning: we shouldn't be here.

Blue streaks light up the sky. The temperature dips another five degrees and my next breath is visible, pushing out into the air.

Theia stands like a key on a kite, along the storm's edge. The strikes of color back-dropping her are breathtaking, but there are no objects—no trees—to lure the lightning away from us.

I cling to Jackson. My milk soaks into his bloody towel. I'd skipped a feeding and the adrenaline pulsing through my veins hasn't helped any.

I can't lose you. You mean everything to me. If we're making an offering to the Gods, I want it to be me. I sprint for the water's edge. *Please take me, not him. Take my life. Spare his.*

"Stay with me," I whisper in his ear. "You stay with me. Mommy loves you. I love you, Jackson."

The outgoing tide collides with the storm, sucking the water out toward the ocean.

I freeze.

"Come on," Theia pleads, wrapping her arms around her wet shoulders, chattering her teeth. "Hurry."

She doesn't want to be in that ocean, freezing, with an impending storm approaching. She's doing it for me. I pull the bloody towel away from Jackson. He barely moves. Theia runs over, attempting to take him from me.

I won't let go.

"Relax," she says, looking me square in the eyes. "Everything will be okay."

Thunder booms. Lightning tints the night sky. I want so much to believe that he'll be okay.

A wave crashes in the distance and saltwater floods in around us.

I let him go.

Theia runs into the water with him and I follow. I trip on seaweed, falling on my hands in the water. Within that small amount of time, she has taken Jackson waist-deep. She dunks him under the water. He doesn't fight for his life. His little hands float with the incoming wave, lifelessly reaching for me.

"What the fuck?" I scream, desperately fighting the water to stand up. A wave crashes into me, flooding my nasal pathway. I can't breathe. *My baby*. The seaweed wraps around my fingers as if pulling me to the ocean's floor. *No*. I refuse to let her kill him. I refuse to stand by and do nothing. I roll my hands into fists and rip the seaweed from the sand. I crash through the water to get to him.

Theia yanks him up out of the ocean.

He sits up, coughing the water from his lungs.

I sink to my knees a few feet from him. I can't believe it.

He looks at me: tired and exhausted, but he's looking at me.

Theia carries him over, placing him in my already outstretched arms.

"Hey," I say, hugging his little body to mine. "You're okay." I cup his head to my chest and gaze at the approaching storm, whispering, "You're okay."

Lightning crackles through the sky, reaching for us. My gratitude for life washes away the fear of the storm. Jackson gasps a breath of air and closes his eyes.

No. My heart sinks. *No*. "Honey?"

Fear rushes in with the next wave, attempting to darken my world like a black hole.

Jackson nuzzles into my chest. His fingers press against my breast, for only a moment, reassuring me he's okay.

Thunder tears open the sky up above.

Fear strangles any relief I've felt. He's okay, but if we stay in the storm, our chances are no better. I wait for the blood to return, to fill the ocean, to drown me and rip my heart open, leaving me to die beside him.

"We have to go." Theia looks up into the night sky.

An airplane far up above heads for the storm clouds. A thick white line trails, marking a second line in the sky.

I carry Jackson toward the shoreline. Wave after wave crashes against us. I press my lips against his wet hair, stabilizing his body against mine, trying to feel close to him. I hold him tighter and he sinks into me. I clear the water and stand on the beach, staring at the Tesla that feels miles away, only to be right there.

Theia emerges from the water, and passes me for the vehicle. Her walk—almost a run—is no doubt an attempt to warm herself more than an escape from the impending storm.

I clench my sweet boy to my chest, and make for the car. Sand clings to my feet. The air abrades my skin. Drops of water from my hair, slide like melting ice cubes down my spine.

The ocean looks as if a hurricane is approaching. Its waters shake. I no longer watch the news, but if there were a hurricane coming, the grocery store shelves didn't reflect it. No one knew this storm was coming.

The wind picks up. The air has dropped twenty degrees.

Theia hops into the car. Its headlights pop on, illuminating our worn-out bodies, casting our shadows behind us. I hurry to the vehicle. *I've got to get home.*

"Get in, get in!" Theia yells from the driver's seat.

I open the passenger door, staring at the seat. Drops of Jackson's smeared blood have dried on its cream-colored leather.

"Get in," she says.

I should sit in the back. I should put Jackson in the backseat and secure him with a seatbelt, but I can't let go of him. Instead, I slide into the front, closing the door with him on my lap.

Theia doesn't say anything. She backs the vehicle out of the parking lot and heads back over the island's bridge towards Raleigh, two-and-a-half hours away.

She turns the air conditioning on full blast.

My skin turns to gooseflesh. "Can you turn on the heater? We're soaked."

"No," she says, looking down at Jackson. "This is what's best for him."

I don't see how being wet and cold could possibly be good for him, but his nose isn't bleeding anymore, and it was her crazy notion that accomplished that. I pick up my cellphone and dial Frank.

He answers on the first ring.

I squeeze out a, "Hey."

"Babe," his voice chokes on the words. "Are you ready to come home? Is..." He stops. It takes everything for him to ask, "Is he okay?"

I look down at Jackson shivering. "I think so. I ran into an old high school friend and… she'll drive me home. Get some sleep. I'll wake you when I get there."

"So…" relief fills his voice, "he's better?"

I squeeze out a "yes," cupping my lips, restraining from crying, afraid that if I say he's okay, it will somehow take away all the magic—it will change things.

In that second, that single moment, he is better.

Undone

I KISS JACKSON'S HEAD BEFORE LEANING MY OWN against the headrest. He falls asleep with the rhythm of the empty road and the beat of my heart.

It begins to snow.

Theia sits up straight, clenching the steering wheel. She'd given us a towel from the backseat. It's the only thing barricading us from the air conditioning vent. I find myself too sitting up straight in disbelief. The towel falls to the floor, taking all the warmth with it. My sticky and sandy toes rub against the bloody hand-towel beneath it on the floor. The cold air pierces my skin, chilling the deepest parts of me.

Theia keeps looking up at the sky as we move closer to the capital. One last breath of thunder echoes at the suburbs' edge, and the clouds fade from view. We have escaped the storm—for now.

We're heading home.

"So what was that? What happened to Jackson?" I pull the towel back up, slide my hand through his hair and rest a kiss atop his head. "Is it contagious?"

Theia's grip tightens around the steering wheel. Her lips press together.

I wait two whole minutes before pressing the questions again. "Look, it isn't that I don't appreciate what you did for us back there. I do, but I have a baby at home. He's only six months old. Is this something he could catch?"

She looks down at her inner wrist—at a tattoo—then glances at Jackson. "No. He can't catch it."

Relief sweeps over me. I'm so thankful she gave an answer, I almost forget to ask, "What is happening?"

She doesn't say anything.

"Theia, what happened to my son?" I say, staring at his thin body laying against mine.

"You're going to think I'm crazy," she says, giving me no time to detest the statement. "You ever heard of chemtrails?"

"The conspiracy theory?"

"Yes," she says, leaning her head a little to look up at the sky. "Those are the lines in the sky."

"Aren't those contrails?" I say, following her gaze out the window. The lines from earlier bled into each other, clouding out the stars.

"Contrails disappear after an aircraft," says Theia. "These are passenger size planes with enormous tanks of chemicals they spray into the sky."

Part of me doesn't want to hear any of it, the other part remembers searching the clouds as a child to find shapes of teddy bears and dragons. Those types of clouds can only be seen on the rarest of days. That part has questions. "What are they spraying?"

She bites her lip and lets out a deep sigh. "Listen, I don't know yet what is going on. All I know is they used to spray the toxins: aluminum, barium, strontium, manganese, thorium, and fluoride. There are theories that this changes the ph in the environment, killing off plant life, weakening our immune systems, changing our neurochemical processes. If they were to increase the barium a little bit, it could kill us all."

We hit the edge of the city. Light pollution blocks out even the brightest of stars. Trees along the highway attempt to shield the glaring lights caused from strip malls—hide the fact that we live in a consumer society. Hide the fact that the closer we are to the city, the further we are from the world.

Theia had been my best friend in middle school. We'd drifted apart in high school. But she was still obviously obsessed with the *X-files*.

I don't know what happened. I don't really care, as long as my family's safe. Gratitude that Jackson is warming in my arms, swells in my heart.

It's easy to find our house. It's the only one in town with a full clothesline blowing in the summer air. Air that is now arctic.

Theia pulls into the driveway. I hadn't told her where we live. Yet, here we are, parking in the driveway atop yesterday's chalk drawings.

I should ask her how she knew where I lived, but I just want to be home. I want to see Carter and snuggle in bed with my boys. I pull Jackson tight as I open the car door, stepping on the chalk lines. Yesterday, Jackson had been drawing in the driveway while I hung the laundry before lunch. Just yesterday he was fine. I hold him tighter, not being able to breathe. My chest is so tight. He had been laughing. He had been fine.

Theia hops out and comes around. "Here, let me help you."

"I got it." I sweep two metal dump-trucks out of my path before bumping the door shut with my hip, and carrying him to the house. The windows are dark. Thank goodness Frank has fallen asleep. We won't be able to pay the bills if he misses any days of work. There's no room for getting sick. I try the front door. It's locked. I round the side of the house to the kitchen. The sliding glass door is open.

Thunder gives its warning in the distance and the wind picks up.

Theia hurries up behind me. "Can I hang out here until the storm passes?"

"Sure." I step into the living room. I owe her more than a dry place for the night. Jackson's breathing. He's okay. It feels wonderful to hold him against my chest, to feel the movement of life in his breath.

His body shifts in my arms. His skin is cold.

I grab a towel from the laundry basket that never made its way upstairs. Jackson's drawing floats across the floor. I set Jackson on the couch and wrap him in the towel.

He lays there limp, exhausted.

I change him into a pair of clean pajamas and underwear, and dress myself in a tank top and tights. Scooping him off the couch, I make our way upstairs. I can ask questions later. I just want to be close to my boys.

Jackson feels heavy compared to Carter, naturally. I welcome it. Jackson has been at the bottom of the pediatrics' growth chart since birth. He's finally starting to catch up. I hold him tighter, able to feel him, warm him, pull him close.

My father is dead. My mother resents me for getting knocked up in high school and making her look bad. Theia had been one of the only people in school who would still smile at me as I blew up like a balloon senior year. She didn't come to the hospital when Jackson was born though. No one did. Nothing went as I had imagined. My placenta detached early—providing the perfect reason to cut me open and get the birthing experience over and done with. I laid on the steel operating table, fully conscious, staring up at the metal sphere encapsulating the light above—reflecting the operating scene—the deep cut into my abdomen—all the blood. I couldn't feel anything from the breasts down, except the pressure—the tugging and pulling of their hands ripping the layers of my body apart. The spinal made me nauseous. I turned my head to tell the anesthesiologist that I didn't feel right, but it was too late: I barfed.

He pumped my veins full of something to stop the vomiting —a common reaction to the spinal. I suppose it was the best the universe could do at the time.

Between the pressure and the tugging and pulling, a baby's cry came into the room. It came from me, my body. I had made him. I had him, all alone. I was the only one there to greet him into this world. And nothing else mattered.

It feels like a lifetime ago.

I step into my bedroom to check on Frank and Carter. Frank lays on his side with his back facing the door, the same way he always does when he puts Carter to bed with us. I should wake him, but he needs to sleep. I peek at Carter, who is passed out beside him in the middle of the bed, his little lips sucking on a boobie that isn't really there.

My milk drops and leaks through my tank top. My boobs hurt. If I don't drain them soon, they'll become clogged and then I'll have to worry about mastitis: a horrible infection of the milk duct. It hurts to nurse; fever engulfs you and sucks out all your life—energy. There isn't much worse, except maybe a bitten nipple.

I carry Jackson to his room.

Frank has changed the sheets and cleared the toys from the floor. Normally I'd be grateful he picked up anything, but if something happened to Jackson... if he had... No. I wouldn't think about it: about how his room wouldn't have been left as I last left it—like a tomb—a memorial.

I lay Jackson on the bed. I want to see Carter, kiss his chubby cheeks, let him empty the breasts that are filling up with milk, but Jackson needs me—my warmth, my energy. I spoon in behind his little body, laying my head so that my lips touch the back of his hair. I kiss him, whispering, "I love you," and wrap my arms over his shivering body.

I stare at his bedroom closet. The door is open. The dark corners sway as my eyelids fall closed.

Eternal Sleep

I SHOOT UP OUT OF SLEEP.

The front of my tank top is completely soaked. Both breasts feel like water balloons about to burst. I squeeze the side of my right breast: the milk duct that always clogs first. *Fuck!* It's hard as a rock. *Carter must've slept right through his three o'clock feeding*. I can't go through another round of mastitis again.

I lean over and kiss Jackson's head.

He's ice cold.

My chest rubs against his arm as I climb over him. Pain gages in my throat. I bite my lip, restraining the *"fuck"* I want to scream. My breasts are too full. Once over him, I sit for a moment on the floor, resting my hand on his chest just like I had when he was a baby, making sure he's still breathing.

Softly, his chest rises.

Thank God, we made it through the night.

I tug the blanket up from the foot of his bed. Toy trucks, construction vehicles, and bulldozers roll off, crashing to the floor.

I kiss his forehead, cover him with the blanket, tuck his stuffed beetle, Atum, beside him, and push myself away from the bed. *He's so big. Both boys are getting so big.* Their childhood years will fly by way too fast and I'll soon be old.

The house is quiet.

I step out of Jackson's bedroom and into my own. No crickets creep. No early birds sing. The open bedroom window lets in a cold breeze that pushes an odd smell across the room. A musty smell, like an old basement. I go in.

The thought of Carter nursing instantly makes my milk drop more, soaking the shirt further.

Frank lays in the same position as when I first got home. That's odd. He never stays still at night. He tosses and turns at least four times, each time waking me. I walk closer. I should've been able to see Carter come into view, but he's not there. He isn't there.

The mattress is empty.

Carter?

I look at the floor. Perhaps he'd fallen off the far side of the bed. Maybe he'd rolled over the pillow and fallen down. *Carter?*

He isn't there. The floor is empty.

"Carter!" I yell. "Baby?"

The room swirls like a merry-go-round as I search for him. He isn't crawling yet, so he couldn't have gotten far. *Where the hell is he?* I rip the pillow away from the headboard and throw it to the floor. I start pulling the sheet and comforter from the bed. The rising sun tints the dark room blue. The shadows blur with panic. "Frank, where's Carter?"

Frank doesn't move.

"Frank," I start to yell as I lean across the mattress and shake his shoulder.

His body rocks, but it's limp, cold, unresponsive. A dark liquid drains out of his nose.

Blood? I jerk my hand back so fast my shoulder pops and hurts. It's the first time I've ever pulled away from him. I can't move. *Oh, my God*. I can't breathe. *Oh, my fucking God. What —?*

"Carter?" I whisper, backing away, off the bed.

A chill, like a draft flowing beneath a door, creeps up my heels. I spin, staring at the empty corner of the bedroom.

Morning's light disappears and thunder moves in.

I run for the stairs—for my phone on the kitchen counter—sprinting down two steps at a time. It's too much. *Frank's dead. Carter's gone. He's gone. He's just gone.* I miscalculate the last step and fall on my ass at the bottom. The world seems to slow down and speed up all in the same breath.

Theia stands in the center of the living room with her back to me.

My heart skips and my chest tightens. I can't breathe. I expected her to have gone home, or at least not be standing in the middle of my fucking living room with her back to me—in the dark.

I drop all fears that this is some zombie apocalypse. *Maybe she has Carter.*

She turns, but her hands are empty.

No. My heart sinks and my feet carry me the fastest I've ever moved. I almost fall beside her with defeat, but push past, grabbing the phone and pounding the numbers 9-1-1. My hands shake so bad. I'm afraid that when someone picks up, I won't be able to speak.

A thick buzz sound blares from the speaker. An automated recording repeats, "All circuits are busy."

I hang up. *Frank's dead.*

He'd been everything I needed him to be. He came into my

life when there was no one else but me and Jackson.

Jackson.

I gaze up at the stairs through a veil of tears and let the phone fall from my fingertips.

Rain drums against the window.

Theia doesn't say anything. She doesn't move. All the pain that I feel, she wears on her face as pity.

I look away, to the stairs.

Something thumps to the floor in Jackson's room.

Jackson! I sprint for him.

Thunder booms.

Jackson's on all fours beside his bed.

Drops of rain trickle through the cracked window.

His head hangs over a puddle of blood.

Every part of me screams, yet there is no sound. *Not again.*

He looks up at me. Large clots of blood drain from his nostrils.

No. Each crinkle in his face fractures my heart. I run to him, wrap my arm around his head, tilt it back, and pinch his nose. He chokes on the blood. It sprays out of his mouth. I sit him up, press his head against my chest and hum to him, rock him. *Hush little baby… don't… don't…* "Don't you leave me."

His little hand wraps around my thumb.

I could run around trying to get help, but somehow I know there is none.

There had never been any.

If I leave his side, he'll die all alone.

His little fingers let go.

I squeeze him, pull his little body up against mine. *No*. "I love you." I press my lips against his head. "I love you. I love you." If I don't stop saying it, he won't disappear. "I love you."

A cold breeze follows the rain and takes him away.

It takes him away.

"I love you." I press him against my chest. "I love you."

I love you.

Lines in the Sky

"KIDS NOTICE EVERYTHING," THEIA SAYS, ENTERING Jackson's bedroom, carrying a piece of paper—his drawing from downstairs. She glances up and stops in the doorway, studying all the pictures taped to his wall.

They are all clustered in a single area. I'd let Jackson hang them up himself. Well, he'd demanded to do it all by himself, but then needed my help tearing the pieces of tape from the dispenser. So, I sat there ever so patiently, ripping pieces of tape—ripping pieces off my time, so he could arrange them just so. I loved every single second of those minutes. I'd give anything to get them back.

"Come on, Arden," Theia says, stepping closer, chucking the paper at me. It drifts across the room, landing at my feet, soaking into the puddle of blood. The white lines in the sky settle into it. "We've got to go."

Go where? There's nowhere to go. I look at the little house sitting on top of the hill—our house. *My whole life is in this house. It's not supposed to be like this. This isn't happening.* I feel the weight of my son, limp in my hands. *My God.*

Theia heads for the hallway. "Take only what you absolutely need."

The faint sound of an airplane reaches in through the window.

"Frank's dead. My husband is dead. Carter's g—" I can't. I can't say he's gone.

She turns around, looking past me at Atum. "Is that a scarab beetle?"

I'm clenching my dead son's body and she's more concerned with his fucking stuffed animal.

She comes over and grabs my arm. I begin to pull back. She grips harder and jerks me—forcing my attention—showing me the tattoo on her right wrist—an Egyptian scarab beetle. "If you come with me, we may be able to save him."

The sound of the airplane grows louder.

She slowly and carefully pulls the necklace from Jackson, and dumps it into my hand, forcing my fingers closed around it.

"How is this supposed to help me?" I ask. "How is this supposed to help me if it couldn't save him?"

She looks away. “I don’t know. All I know is that it *does* protect you. I don’t know why your son and husband died, but I can take you to someone who does.” She looks at me. “You can’t change this. You can’t bring them back. But you can save your baby.”

“You mean find him,” I say.

“No,” she says, looking at me. “Save him.”

“Save him from what?” I say.

She glances around the room. “We have to go. We have to get out of this house.”

I want to look down at Jackson before I leave him, before I let go, but I can’t. I don’t want to see him like that. I nod yes, not looking at her, not knowing if she is even still in the room. I have to let go. *I can lay down with him and let myself die*. That would be easy. I don’t want to move. I don’t want to do anything other than cry. Somehow, through tears and an overpowering numbness, I make it into the hallway, heading for my bedroom. There’s a gold locket in the third drawer of my dresser. It had been passed down to me from my mother a month ago. She was excited about Carter’s birth; he had been more or less a ‘planned’ baby. The heart locket splits open to reveal a picture of Jackson on the left and Carter on the right. It’s the only solid photograph I have of them. I step into the room.

“No.” Theia grabs my arm, yanking me backwards into the hallway. “It’s too dark in there.”

“What?”

"I don't go into rooms I don't know…" She freezes, listening to the sound of aircraft coming in the distance. "We need to go."

Airplane engines roar closer.

She grabs my arm. "There are things in the corners of the walls."

Chills ripple beneath my skin. I let her drag me down the stairs away from that room. There's no way I could leave that house on my own. There is no way I could have walked away from him, from both of them.

Theia lets go of my hand once we reach the front door, and heads for the car.

Three white lines bleed into a clear blue sky.

Unwelcome Change

WIND WHIPS IN, PULLING AT THE CLOTHESLINE STRUNG in the side yard. Baby socks and little boy shorts swing back and forth, strangling my heart, squeezing each memory from my thoughts. All the moments of sliding on shoes, pulling up little britches, and gently tugging little chubby arms through shirts, starts to fade away. I can't breathe. I can't tuck them into my future.

Theia reaches the car, unplugs the charger she helped herself to last night, and hops in.

I can't leave. I can't leave Jackson alone in his bed, or leave Frank to decay on the bed we conceived Carter on. *Carter.* My heart jumps at the thought of him. My milk rushes to pour out.

The airplanes grow louder.

Theia leans out of the driver's side window. "Get in!"

I can find Carter on my own, or follow her. Truth is, I can't find him on my own. There is no choice but to climb into that car. Somewhere, Carter is screaming for me. *I'm not there*. I hurry to the car as the planes rumble up above. I slide into the passenger seat and shut the door. The last time I had sat here, Jackson was alive.

Theia peels out of the driveway, not bothering to look for children playing in the street.

I have nothing. I lean my head against the window, watching the clothes wave from the clothesline, regretting getting in the car. I brought Carter home from the hospital to that house. It was the house—the place Jackson took his first steps.

I watch it all sink away from me as the car speeds down the street—the street on which I planned on teaching Jackson how to ride a bike. I want to look away, but I don't want my eyes to be anywhere else. I have to watch the last pieces of my life disappear. The clothesline and all those baby clothes disappear from sight.

I throw up.

Theia rests a hand on my back.

I nudge her off. I don't want her to touch me. Look where trusting her has gotten me. My feet are covered in vomit and I don't care. I leave my head hanging between my legs. Cold air blasts across my cheek from the car vent. The image of Carter screaming alone in a dark room splits through my thoughts. I look out the window, at the houses bleeding together as we pass. *He could be in any one of them. He could be screaming his lungs out, hungry, dirty, captured by some sick pedophile-fuck. He could already be dead.* I shake my head trying to free myself from the thought. *Just like Frank. Just like... Jackson.* I try to focus on the blurred houses, anything to ground me, keep me from throwing up all over again.

The car slows. We've gone southwest of the city toward the suburban town of Cary. Neighborhoods are jam packed with half-a-million dollar houses, occupied by yuppies. We're two blocks from my parents' house—my mother's house. Dad died five years ago from a heart attack during my sophomore year of high school. He never got to meet my children.

I sit up. My toes slide through the warm pieces of last night's breakfast dinner. "Why are we here?"

"I thought you'd want to see if your mom— If she's...."

Still alive? "No."

Theia looks surprised. Why wouldn't she be? After middle school, she scored the high school quarterback, Jeff McCoy. Their relationship consumed all of her identity.

I'd forgotten how much I hated high school. I'm not going to bother explaining how much my mother hated me for making her look bad—for getting knocked up senior year. I don't owe her answers. I sink back into the seat, lean my head against the window, and wish I was anywhere else but here. Wishing I was home again. Wishing for everything to be like it used to.

The sound of a low-flying aircraft rumbles from the North. A huge jet shoots by. A trail of white exhaust lingers in the blue sky above, bleeding into the other lines.

Theia leans on the steering wheel, looking up through the windshield. "Thank Ra it's not raining."

Rain would be wonderful right now. I long for it, leaning my head against the door. A good rain can soak you to the ground and pin you there, bringing everything you need to wallow in grief or self pity.

Theia puts the car into drive and heads southwest of town, even though her parents live right around the block. Seems I'm not the only one with secrets. I don't want to talk about why she isn't checking in on them, but I need my heart to stop hurting—a break from my thoughts destroying myself.

I look for a distraction, any distraction. *The scarab beetle tattoo*. My heart skips at the thought. I carried the necklace in a clenched fist since she handed it to me. "Why the scarab beetle? Why do you have the same symbol tattooed on you as my son's stuffed animal?"

She smiles at me and returns her eyes to the road. "I'm guessing your son was very connected to nature. He knew this day was coming.... What else did he know?"

I stare out the window. It's morning and all the roads are empty.

"Did he ever say anything out of the ordinary?" she says.

"He'd talk about the monsters in his closet." *But all kids do that.*

We hit a red light, but Theia blows through it.

A National Guard Humvee pulls out in front of us from a side street, fishtailing to straighten out.

Theia cuts the car right, pulling into the parking lot of a bookstore.

The Humvee screeches to a halt.

"Shit." Theia jerks the wheel to the left, shooting us behind the building. It's lined with trees that won't hide us. She slams on the brakes and turns off the car, slouching down in the seat. "Get down."

Why would I hide from them? They can help me find Carter. They can tell me what the fuck is happening.

Theia's sunken body has squeezed between the seat and the steering wheel. Her hands are clenched together, giving the illusion of prayer. I crouch down and lean my cheek on the leather seat, staring at the dried blood—Jackson's smeared blood all over it. We're sitting there like ostriches with our heads in the ground, believing we'll never be seen. I don't care. I let the tears drain away from my body. They can't erase the stains of blood or ease the emptiness I feel.

Several minutes wash away before Theia lifts her head up to look out, opening her door. "Okay, we're going to have to go by foot."

I don't move. *Go where?*

She shimmies out of the car and runs toward the back entrance of the bookstore.

I sit up, grab hold of the doorknob, and hold my breath, ready to follow.

A plane swoops in, low overhead.

A military vehicle pulls into the alley, blocking the exit up ahead.

I duck all the way down. *They can help me—help me find Carter.* I start to climb back into the seat.

The Humvee pulls up alongside the car, blocking any chance of escape.

They can help me. My heart races. *Isn't that what they're supposed to do?*

The Humvee door creaks open.

I slide my fingers around the door handle, but stop. Something inside of me insists that I stay down, perhaps a warning from the female collective consciousness.

A second Humvee door opens and slams shut.

"Look for any new growth, any plants," says a robotic male voice.

Is it really a robot? I want to look up… See one for myself.

"Anubis," says the other guy. He's right outside my door.

If I move, he'll notice. They won't be looking for plants after that. *Shit*. I know they're carrying semi-automatics. They won't ask questions; they'll take what they want. In this shitty world, why wouldn't they?

The robotic guy says something, but my heart's beating too hard to hear it. Then he yells, "There she—"

Something happens. The sound of a fight: grunts, groans, thumps, and punches come from outside of the door. Then it stops.

I can't stay here any longer. Every minute—every second—kills me to be away from Carter. I slide the scarab necklace on and fling open the door, falling out onto the asphalt.

The alley is empty of movement. A vacant Humvee indeed blocks us from escaping. The army vehicle barricades the other end of the alley. Another airplane sprays lines in the sky up above. I want to yell for Theia, but I'm at the scene of a crime. Now a days cops shoot first, then ask questions.

Two men hang unconscious from grapevines beneath the bookstore's side-door awning. One is a man dressed in a National Guard uniform, wearing a biohazard respirator that shields his identity. The other's body is a deep, South African black. Gold and turquoise frame his toned body in an outfit fit for a Pharaoh. His head is that of a Jackal—a canine. I can't move at the sight.

The guard's walkie-talkie blares, "Unit two. Unit two…?"

Shit. I jump at the sound but still don't move. I can't do anything but stare at the Jackal head.

Theia bursts out of the bookstore's backdoor, not surprised to see the men hanging there. She grabs a grape from the vine that binds them, eats it, and nods for me to follow her. "Let's go."

I glance back at the men. It feels like I'm falling down some messed-up rabbit hole.

Voices carry from the front of the building. The hum of a walkie-talkie grows louder. "Unit two, do you copy?"

I hurry to follow Theia. She heads west, to the parking lot's edge, where a row of trees grow. We follow the tree line along the high school football field, zigzagging between tree trunks. With the next zigzag, Theia disappears from view. The trees make a single row. She's gone. I check around the closest tree and then the next. Any passing aircraft could easily target me. *Theia?* I flattened my back up against the nearest tree trunk. *Shit*. I look left and right. She's gone. There is no sign as to what way she's gone. The looming building in front of me, hints to the place I need to be. It's the one place I never wanted to step foot in again. As much as I don't want to, I run towards my old high school.

An airplane rumbles in the distance.

Gooseflesh ripples across my skin. I turn back. *Screw this*. I head for the car we abandoned. If I'm going to die, I'm not doing it in there. I clear the edge of the football field to a small stand-alone building on the parking lot's edge. The lights are off and a 'for lease' sign hints at its vacancy.

The static of walkie-talkies comes from around the front side of the building. I try the backdoor. It opens. There is nothing inside but an abandoned office space.

A bottle shatters to the floor to my left.

Someone else is in here. I want to scream out Theia's name, but I can't move a muscle—not even to scream.

Smaller aircrafts approach from the North. It's beginning to sound like a war zone outside. I can't move. Planes dive closer. I sprint away from the noise, through a set of double swinging doors, into a basic kitchen.

Someone grabs me from behind, yanking me into their arms. I try to scream. Their free hand covers my mouth. It's a man. I can tell by the hair of his forearm. He twists my arm, forcing me to face him. I know him. It's Jeff McCoy from high school, Mr. Quarterback himself.

"Arden?" he says, letting go.

His eyes scan mine and his grip on me eases. I didn't think he knew who I was. I heard he'd been attending Duke University. He sure as hell looks like he's still playing football. *Theia*. He must've been waiting for her.

He picks up a broom beside him, grabs my wrist with his other hand, and starts for the back door, dragging me along.

The sound of an airplane cuts through the sky above.

Jeff pauses to look up, listening to pinpoint its position.

I wait. Part of me wants to run into the darkness, hide until this is all over. But there is no hiding from the pain I'm running from. There's nothing that will bring back my life.

The static of a walkie-talkie blasts out from behind us. "Unit two is down... Yes, grape vines..."

Jeff's hand tightens around my arm. He flings me in front of him, out the door, and I fall on my ass.

"Jeff," says a National Guardsman, standing at the double swinging doors. He glances down at me and back at the football player, stepping closer. "Where do you think you're going?"

Jeff rolls his shoulders back and steps into the threshold, blocking it.

"We both know you can't outrun me," says the guard.

Jeff charges him, punches him to the ground, and stomps on his respirator. The back of the dude's head cracks against the asphalt. His eyes roll to the back of his head. Blood sprays from his lips against the intact biohazard shield.

"That's enough," I whisper.

Jeff clenches his fists and stomps on the man again.

"Stop." No matter how much I want to look away, I can't. Part of me wants to join in, beat some of the pain out of me and force it upon the man—as if he has any idea what is actually going on. I could run from Jeff. I could flee just when he needs someone. I climb to my feet and grab hold of his shoulder, squeezing. "Stop."

He pauses to look at me. In that moment, I see it. He hasn't lost a parent, sibling, or spouse—he's lost a child. It's written all over him, all over the blood on his shirt.

"Let's go," I say.

The walkie-talkie blasts, "Russel… Russel, come in."

Jeff looks at the man, bends down, and pulls off the guy's respirator.

The man doesn't move.

No Going Back

I LOSE COUNT OF HOW MANY TREES WE HAVE DODGED. After Jeff beat the crap out of that guard, everything blurred. I feel my heart beating—pounding in my chest—but each step has been the same. Jeff leads and I follow. We don't bother squishing up against the trees like ninjas. Now, if they catch us, they'll kill us.

Jeff takes the path Theia did, stopping every quarter length of the football field. Each time, his fists clamp and his biceps tighten like he's restraining the rage of the world.

He tugs on my hand, pulling me faster behind him, toward the high school.

I can't go to the National Guard for help now.

Jeff is the only familiar thing in a world where everything has changed.

We sprint out into the open, for the school's backdoor. I felt Jackson kick for the first time in the gymnasium behind that door. I want to let go, right there. I want to let go and fall to my knees, but I won't. *I have to find Carter. I have to become the mother I am scared as hell to be. If it costs me my life, I have to do it.*

Another airplane approaches from the North. Crosshatches of bleeding white lines cover the sky.

I can't do this.

"You can do anything you put your intention on," Jeff yells back at me, gripping my hand a little tighter.

How does he know…? How does he know my thoughts? Had I said them out loud? Did I mutter out loud that I'd rather be dead than have to fight to live this life? Every step feels like I'm walking away from Jackson. Emptiness chills me.

Jeff leans against the gymnasium wall, catching his breath.

Another airplane soars by.

I watch the 737-passenger plane from behind the gymnasium door's window. The contrail never disappears. The line is fresh and distinguished, dispersing into the crosshatch pattern that drifts so slowly with the jet stream, fading into blurred, fat lines.

Jeff heads for the school's boiler room down the hallway. I wonder if the janitor, Seth, still works here. He started my senior year of school. Rumor had it, he was the principal's nephew. He couldn't handle college, which left him mopping up cafeteria tables and cleaning up hallway tears.

Senior year, I threw up all over the hallway. He handed me his mop. I almost shoved it back in his face, told him to do his job, and keep his nose out of my business, but I didn't. The holes in his shoes and the dirt beneath his fingernails told me two things: he was no better off than me, and he didn't even have enough free time to clean his fingernails. When I took the mop, his whole body relaxed a little. His shoulders lightened, his smile deepened.

Morning sickness with Jackson was horrible. It came on from out of nowhere. I didn't really expect to throw up from being pregnant. But there it was, five feet from the bathroom door.

Someone came around the corner, down the hall. It was Stacey Quinn, top gossip bitch cheerleader.

I shoved the mop back toward him, but it was too late. Stacey had seen me mopping the floor and had disappeared behind that same corner, running to tell the first person she could.

The janitor took the mop as if it were now weightless. In one fluid movement, the evidence of my pregnancy was swept away.

I looked back at the corner where Stacey had disappeared, wanting so much to erase that moment from her memory, hold off the shit-storm that would soon follow, just a little longer.

The sound of the mop-bucket wheels rolled away behind me, leaving a clean floor.

"Ummm," stumbled out of my lips. I wanted to say thank you to him, but nothing came out.

He stopped and faced me. The edges of his embroidered name tag almost concealed the last letter of his name, reading "Set".

"Is that your name?" I said.

The smile on his face deepened. "Seth. That is what they call me here."

Here, as in here in school?

Stacey returned to the opposite side of the hallway. This time with a friend, whispering, gesturing, trying so hard not to blatantly point and fucking laugh. Gossip swept through the walls that day and stuck until graduation.

Seth only offered a smile as my uterus swelled to the size of a watermelon—while 300 students judged me.

I shoved the memory away. The boiler room door is unlocked.

Jeff enters. I stop at the threshold. He reaches back for my hand. I can see the faint shimmer of dried tears on his cheeks. His hand tightens around mine. "There's no one here to hurt you anymore."

That's easy for him to say. He had been the guy everyone idolized. I was the daddy less slut-girl who got herself knocked up senior year.

I step inside. The door closes behind me, like the bars of a prison cell. It still smells like judgement.

Stacey Quinn is sitting on an old orange couch opposite us.

I let go of Jeff's hand and step back, bumping into the wall. He reaches for my hand. I pull away, tucking my arms to my chest.

The Bitch.

Stacey dated Shawn after he dumped me—after he decided he didn't want to be a father at seventeen.

She sits on the couch, crossing her arms. Her skin is synthetically tan and she hasn't put on a single pound since graduation. "Holy shit!" she says. "So you're one of the chosen ones, huh?"

Chosen ones?

"You remember Stacey," Jeff says, "I'm sure."

Stacey ignores him, straightening up. "I see you're not knocked up anymore."

My heart races. I knock Jeff out of my way and storm her. The image of the bloody Guard's face engulfs my thoughts and I lust to feel the beating of her face beneath my fist. I swing at her. My knuckles crack against her cheek. My fingernails dig into my palm on impact. Blood drips from my hand. *Shit*. I'd wanted to do that for so long. Now, I feel like I'll barf. I bend over, flinging my wrist in the air like it will make the pain cease. But the throbbing is nothing compared to her words: *I see you're not knocked up anymore*. They stab my heart like icicles. My heart aches to feel my boys.

"Jesus." Jeff lets out a small laugh that ceases the instant Stacey gives him a glance.

She looks possessed: hunched over, pinching her nose that now bleeds. Her eyes are filled with tears and she keeps repeating, "Bitch. You bitch… You fucking bitch."

There are so many things I want to say to her. For nine months I'd listened to her shit—her attempt to make me feel like my baby—like Jackson—was a burden. *Jackson*. Tears fall down my cheeks and the corners of my lips droop. I'd endured so much from the walls of this building and never let it lessen my love for him. I can't take anymore—anymore words, anymore worthlessness.

Stacey clenches her swelling cheek.

Jeff pushes her into the bathroom at the back of the room.

"No," Stacey says.

Jeff closes the door.

Her voice muffles, "No. I'm going to kick her fucking ass —"

"She's alive," Jeff yells.

Then there is nothing. Silence.

Jeff returns to the room, guiding me back into the hallway. I lean my back against the wall, sliding down, sitting on the floor, waiting for my hand to stop throbbing.

"Did you really have to do that?" he says, sitting down beside me, folding his arms across his knees, and twirling a wedding band on his finger.

I rest my chin on my knees.

"What did she mean by knocked-up?" he says. "Are you pregnant?"

"No." I feel the sensation of my milk dropping and bury my head in my arms. My swollen breasts rub against my legs, like scraping sandpaper overtop burned skin. It hurts so bad. It all hurts so bad.

Jeff remains silent until I recompose myself and rest my head back against the wall. I hadn't noticed him take off his shirt, but there it is, extended out to me.

"Do you have any kids?" I say, taking the shirt, sliding it over my wet tank top, regaining some shred of decency.

"No," he says, tearing at his fingernails. He looks at me. Tears pool in the corners of his eyes. He clears his throat and stands. "Not anymore."

The gymnasium back door flings open.

Jeff's hands clench into fists in response.

I shoot to a stand, ready to sprint in the opposite direction.

"Oh, thank Ra," Theia says, stepping inside holding up a breast-pump. "You're still alive, Arden."

My cheeks instantly catch fire with embarrassment, but my ego soon subsides and I meet Theia halfway down the hallway, taking the pump case, softly thanking her.

I avoid looking at Jeff while making my way into the janitor's space. It's a windowless closet with no pictures. The bathroom door is closed. *God, the comments Stacey will make if she sees me with this*. There has to be somewhere else I can go to get away from her. I turn to leave, bumping into the back of Jeff.

He faces me. "I thought you were… I mean… I was guarding the door."

I smile. It's very kind of him.

"The teachers' lounge is just up the hall on the right," he says, letting me pass.

"I remember. Thanks."

While I walk to the lounge, I can't help but think about my last year confined within these walls: all the eyes of disgust and pity weighing down on me. Just when it had become too much, when I couldn't bear pulling on sweatpants any longer, Jackson started kicking. It was the same time Stacey and Shawn began sucking face right outside my homeroom class. He was supposed to be sharing those moments with me. He was supposed to be holding my hand, protecting me as I walked through the gauntlet, overjoyed to feel the kicks of his baby.

But he wasn't.

I walk into the teachers' lounge trying not to cry, setting the pump down on the counter beside a lunch tray stacked with coffee mugs. I'm exhausted. In hopes that caffeine will stimulate my mood, I stuff a filter into the coffee pot and spoon some coffee grains into it. Then I grab the glass pot, turn on the faucet, and prepare to fill it with water.

"You don't want to do that," Theia says from the doorway.

"Why not?" Typically, I only have a cup of coffee early in the morning. Any later in the day means Carter will be up all night.

I miss him.

Theia enters the room, opens the refrigerator, and pulls out a gallon of unmarked water. "They've been poisoning the water for years."

Subconsciously, I pull the glass pot away from the running water, watching it drain down the sink. It's clear and clean. There is no evidence anything is wrong with the tap water.

She closes the refrigerator door. I expect her to be joking, but her face is stern and serious. The wrinkles in her face deepen a little. I wait for her to laugh, reveal the absurdness of her statement, but she doesn't.

"What?" I ask. I'd washed the dishes, did the laundry, bathed my children, all with the city's tap water.

"You know that stuff called fluoride?" She twists the lid off the unmarked jug.

Everyone knows about fluoride. It's added to the water to prevent tooth decay. It's in our toothpaste, bottled water, and non-stick pans. The dentist lathers kids teeth with it as a preventative measure for cavities, which is fully covered by the insurance companies.

Theia grabs onto the coffee pot steadying it in my hand, fills it with water, and hands it back to me.

I take it. *Is she saying fluoride killed Jackson?*

"Trust me," she says, flicking on the coffee machine. She stows the water jug and sits down on the couch. "You don't want to drink that shit."

I dump the water into the coffee machine and place the pot on the warmer.

"If the fluoride doesn't kill you," she says, "the chlorine will."

I reach for the breast-pump, sit down on the opposite side of the couch, and piece the pump together. *This couldn't all have happened from fluoride, from our drinking water.*

Theia keeps her gaze forward, not making eye contact, giving me respect to do what I need to do.

I press the pump to my breast. It hurts. It's too full. I wince. To draw my attention away from the pain, I ask, "So you're saying it was the fluoride?"

"No," she says.

I press the rubber cup harder against my breast, creating a seal around my skin. The first ten pumps do nothing. Then milk sprays out. It sounds like a water gun being shot into a plastic bucket. The sensation of my milk dropping feels wonderful—release—but the clogged milk-duct burns, sending a surge of nausea through me. *I can't do this*. As I pump, I squeeze the side of my breast where the pain radiates. The skin's hot to the touch. *Ouch*. It isn't fair. I want to cuddle Carter, feel him up against my skin. I want Jackson to be snuggled beside us, insisting I read him a story.

Theia stays quiet.

I force myself to drain the one breast as the coffee drips into the pot. The milk stops. The baby bottle attached to the pump is full. *What a waste of milk.* I cover myself back up and go to stand.

"I'll do it," Theia reaches for the pump.

I hand it over, hanging my head low, letting the tears drip from my eyes, watching them fall to my lap. *Carter should be eating right now. What if he was somewhere at home? He'd been sleeping, hidden somewhere at home, and now he's all alone, crying and hungry while I'm sitting here dumping it all out.*

Theia pours all those nutrients—all the calories, all of the milk—down the drain. It's all wasted.

What did I do? I left. I left and he's not here. When had Carter last eaten? Shit. If I don't find him soon....

"Hey." Theia nudges me with the empty pump.

I think I took it. I mean it's in my hand and she's gone back to the coffee, so I must've taken it, but the world has gone numb. I pull the other side of my shirt up and start on the other breast. That one's a breeze.

By the time Theia returns, I'm covered up and ready to go. I take the pump to the sink, unscrew the lid, and lean against the counter. "What's happening then?" I spin, facing her. "Why are Jackson and Frank dead? Where is my baby?" I can't breathe. "Why Jackson?"

She sets her cup on the coffee table. Her eyes connect with

mine, encouraging my complacency. "I promise, we'll save him."

I turn my back to her and dump the milk—my milk—Carter's milk—into the sink. The white liquid swirls down the drain. I begin to rinse out the bottle and disassemble the pump. There's nothing to sterilize it with. Tears drip down my cheek. There's… no reason to sterilize it.

The room fills with a loud cry and I realized it is mine.

I sink to the floor, wrapping my arms around my legs. *Carter's gone. I'm never going to see him again. Jackson and Frank are dead, and Carter's gone. There's no way I'll ever find him.*

Crashing Down

THEIA FINISHES CLEANING THE PUMP AND EVENTUALLY coaxes me to the couch. She goes on about how fluoride was first added to the drinking water before World War Two. The Germans used it to make the population submissive. She cites all this research about how it calcifies the pineal gland. I don't care. I want to be left alone, but I need to find Carter. Something tells me these people have a good idea of where he might be. The scarab beetle hanging around my neck reminds me of that.

I can feel Stacey in the doorway, looking at me, judging me. I want to sleep, sleep forever, but Jeff comes into the room and scoops me up. I let him, not caring where we are headed. He carries me out of the lounge and down the hall toward the gymnasium.

I watch the worn ceiling tiles blur by. He passes the girls' locker-room. The only thing beyond that is the boys'. I attempt to sit up in his arms, but he lifts them enough to sink me back down.

"Jeff?" I say. "Where are we going?"

His steps quicken.

I wrap my arm around his neck, trying to jump out of his arms. I wiggle out to a standing position, two feet from the ground, with my breasts pressed up against his face.

He tightens his grip and uses my back to push open the boys' locker-room door. Blue tiles line the walls. His pace slows toward a row of shower heads on the far wall.

"Jeff...? No." I try again to get free, out of his grip. I'd spent so many nights worrying about an intruder when Frank was away. I'd never imagined it'd be someone I know. "No."

His arms tighten harder.

I can't breathe. If I wiggle, my spine will snap. "No!"

He sets my feet down and loosens his grip. My eyes connect with his. He withdraws his arms and brushes his thumb across my cheek. "You're safe here."

Part of me believes him and the tightness in my shoulders eases—a little.

He looks around. "Try to pull yourself together."

"What's really happening, Jeff?" I sink onto the bench. "Why are they dead? Why can't I find Carter?"

"You're not ready yet." He turns and walks out of the locker room.

What does he mean: I'm not ready yet? I'm all alone and I let it drown me like a tsunami, knocking me down onto the bench, pinning me against its metal. I stare blankly at the lockers across from me. *How the hell am I going to get through this?*

The faint sound of an airplane flies into range.

Then a second.

They're coming—but it's louder, lower, faster than anytime before.

A bomb explodes, taking out the front side of the building. The walls shake. Tiles pop off the wall and smash to the floor. The lights flicker. I fall off the bench.

"Arden!" Jeff's voice muffles with white noise from the door.

The lights go out.

"Arden!" Jeff screams. "Watch the corners!"

Another explosion shakes the building.

Jeff grunts like he's fallen over. He yells into the locker room, "Stay away from the corners of the room!"

Across from me—in the corner closest to the showers—darkness moves.

I climb to all fours.

It moves closer.

"No!" Jeff charges into the room at it. The shadow shifts away from him, like he has thrown it to the side. Jeff grabs my hand, yanks me off the ground, and pulls me through the dark room towards the door.

Before I can clear the threshold, something grabs hold of my hemp string necklace.

Jeff jerks me out into the gym. The string brakes. We fall to the floor and I land beside him. The glass roof of the gymnasium has shattered. Broken glass cuts into my back. Jeff stares at the locker room door, holding an arm across my body, blocking me from whatever the fuck that thing is.

"What the hell?" Stacey's high-pitched voice comes from the hallway.

Another explosion drops on the far side of the building.

Jeff nudges me up, glancing at her. "They're here."

Another explosion goes off, this time closer.

Stacey yells at him, "No shit, they're here."

"No." Jeff motions toward the locker room. "They're here!"

She takes a step back. "What do we do?"

"Plan B," Jeff says. He gets up and heads toward her.

I glance back at the door. It cracks open.

Jeff glances back at me. "You coming?"

I hurry to follow him, unsure if they are trustworthy, but fearful of the shadows.

The planes circle back.

I look up through the broken ceiling. Plumes of dark grey smoke pocket the white lines in the sky.

We head for the boiler room.

Theia jets out of the teachers' lounge with the breast-pump. "Looks like we're heading out early."

Jeff leads the way, past the boiler room for the back door, and flings it open. It hits something, and ricochets shut. He falls backward onto the floor.

The door jerks open. A National Guardsman blocks our exit, carrying a big-ass gun, wearing a biohazard respirator.

Familiar Faces

"THEIA?" SAYS THE GUARDSMAN. HIS VOICE IS muffled behind the respirator, but familiar. I know I know that voice, if only I could see behind the mask.

Theia stands stern beside Jeff as he climbs back onto his feet.

The Guard lowers his weapon.

Theia runs into his arms, hugging him. Stacey pushes past me, getting in line for the next embrace.

"Not this way." He nudges her away, looks back behind him, and shoos us back inside. His voice is hoarse, "We're sweeping the school next."

Airplanes stoop down overhead, but there is a break in the gunfire.

"I don't know how," the Guard looks at me, "but they knew you'd be here."

It's Shawn, Jackson's dad.

He glances over at me. He isn't screaming, or telling me how much he doesn't want to be a dad, that he doesn't want to marry the first girl he fucked.

I should say something, tell him Jackson… *Jackson's… Our baby's dead.*

Aircraft engines grow louder, coming down from the north.

"Go," he says. "The bombers are coming in ten minutes. Go. Go!"

Theia, Jeff, and Stacey start off down the hallway, back toward the gymnasium. I take one last look at Shawn.

His eyes search for our son. I was responsible for keeping him safe. He'd left Jackson in my care and now he's gone—because of me. I couldn't keep him safe. I choke back the tears and run after the others, digging my heels into the floor, mostly running away from my guilt, wishing the pain in my heart would dull.

I catch up to the others in the gym. We make it halfway across the room when a group of guardsmen march into the building from behind us.

"Halt!" yells the man with the Jackal head—the ebony man dressed as elegantly as an Egyptian Pharaoh. It is the same robotic voice as before. He is their ringleader. None seem surprised or terrified of his canine head. He raises his hands, and his obedient followers aim their guns at us. Each is armed. Each wears a respirator mask.

Theia halts first.

I try to stop, but slide into the back of her. Pieces of broken glass settle into the bottoms of my feet. I throw up my arms, wanting so badly to die, but not being able to ask for it.

Jeff lets out a deep grunt and faces them, drawing fists at his sides.

The ringleader, Anubis, takes a step towards us. "You have the right—"

"We have no rights!" Jeff shouts, stepping in front of us. He looks up through the broken ceiling at the sky and screams, "We've never had rights!"

Far above the plumes of smoke, a 737-passenger plane flies, filling the sky with more lines.

Jeff looks back at the men, yelling, "You're too blind to see that."

Anubis steps closer. "Sir, put up your hands—"

"I will not allow you to kill us anymore," Jeff says, clenching his fists tighter.

"Sir," Anubis says, tilting his head to the side, "I will not ask you again."

Jeff swings his arm like he's pitching a baseball. A tomato rolls out of his hand and smashes into the canine-face.

Where the fuck did that come from?

"Shoot them," yells Anubis, wiping the seeds from his eyes.

Stacey grabs my hand and pulls me, sprinting for the back door.

Gun shots rip through the gymnasium. A bullet blasts over my right shoulder and hits the wall. I try to duck my head, like it will help.

Stacey flings open the door. For all we know, a firing squad awaits us on the other side.

Sunlight races across my skin as we cross the threshold. She pulls me toward the backside of the football field bleachers, along the trees. I spent several of my early high school years under those bleachers during football games.

Stacey lets go of my hand and crawls on the ground, deeper beneath the bleachers, toward the lowest seats.

I follow behind her, trying not to think about how disgusting it is. My hand slides through a big wad of gum, a cigarette butt, and some gooey shit I don't even want to think about. Dirt cakes beneath my fingernails.

Stacey pivots so her legs squeeze under the lowest bench, toes facing the field. She lays her cheek down on the ground, smearing it into what looks like a hocked-up loogie. She whispers, "Get down!"

I back my ass under the lowest bleacher, with my head facing the trees. If anyone looks beneath the bleachers, we'll be easily seen.

"Jeff's shirt," she says, "take it off."

I do as told. Small grains of sand stick to the damp tank-top covering my breasts.

She squeezes closer to me and pulls the shirt over our heads.

My heart pounds against the dirt. It feels like an elephant bounces on my back, pounding me repeatedly into the ground.

"Search the concession stand," a voice comes down the path. "They couldn't have gotten far."

I stop breathing. The weight of the elephant holds still.

Stacey grabs my hand and stares directly into my eyes. At that moment, the past doesn't matter. We're about to be ripped from the bleachers, raped, beaten, and killed.

Her grip tightens, and I can't tell if I squeezed first.

Fighter jets tear through the sky and swoop lower, closer, up above.

The gymnasium explodes. The ground vibrates. A high pitch rings in my ears. I want to cup them, stop the noise, but if I move they'll notice us.

We're still alive, for now.

Closer

ONCE THE ADRENALINE WORE OFF, I PASSED OUT. There wasn't anything else to do but get lost in my thoughts, or drift off to a world where everything was right again. *I want so much to return to my life, the life I took for granted—a simple life—one where I live in a crappy little house with my boys, with Frank, as a family.*

"Hey, we better get going." Stacey nudges my hand and pulls the shirt off our heads.

It is dark out. The high school burns in the distance. Night masks the smoke's pollution and accentuates the flames. I'd dreamed about this day—the school burning to the ground, but it wasn't anything like I'd imagined.

We crawl back through the filth.

Stacey looks around. "You know the gas station three blocks from here, the one that sells cigarettes to the high schoolers?"

I know the one. Shawn stopped there before we went to see this zombie movie about Yosemite. No doubt he stopped there with her too.

She glances at my shirt—the dirt smeared down my breasts—and hands Jeff's shirt over. I slide it on. My milk has come back in. Without a pump, I'll have to empty them soon or they will be too hard to express by hand without a warm shower. My cheeks itch from dry tears. I scrape at them, flinging an escaped teardrop away, smudging in the dirt.

Moonlight glistens off the lines in the sky.

Stacey grabs my hand and searches the perimeter. She looks down at her wrist. A metal watch glows slightly in the dark. The second's hand tick.

Every line counts.

Not everyone has what it takes to care for a child. It is a long, hard road to feel like you're not screwing it all up.

I need to find Carter. Who knows what kind of person has taken him.

"Shit," Stacey says. "We're late."

The words draw me out of my thoughts and into worse ones. *Too late to save Carter?* "Late for what?"

She heads toward the row of houses hugging the school property, on the other side of the trees.

"No. I'm not going." I stop at the tree line, raising my voice, "I'm sick of these games. I need to find my baby."

She turns around. Her face has hardened. "You'll never find him without our help. You have no idea what..." She glances around and stares at a nearby shed. Her voice lowers. "You have no idea what's going on."

"Then tell me," I say.

Her voice softens even more, "Not here."

She continues on her path, pausing to make sure I'm following.

I do, running along the trees' edge until clearing the length of the field. Stacey heads for a little blue house butted up against the property line. Its lights are off. No doubt its inhabitants are dead, their stench of decay already filling the confines of its walls. Stacey heads for a 1970s shagging-wagon parked in its driveway. An orange and yellow stripe wraps around the van's chipped brown body. Stacey approaches its side door, slides it open, and hops into the back. Wall-to-wall shag carpet brightens up the black walls and curtains. Trippy mushroom and pot-leaf drawings alternate between blacklight posters glowing in the purple hue.

"Dude," a guy whispers from the passenger seat, "what took you so long?"

"It's been crazy out there." Stacey plops onto a beanbag chair behind the driver's seat. "Didn't you hear the air raid?"

"Is that what that was?" he says. "I've been in here for hours."

I try to lean over and catch a glimpse of the guy's face, but he slouches deeper in the seat.

"Shut up," Stacey says. "I'm sure you found a way to occupy yourself."

Their bickering carries on as I stand outside, examining the van that could have easily pulled up outside my house, parked, and stolen my baby.

Carter.

"Arden,"—Stacey reaches for me—"get in here."

I step back.

"No, shit. Arden?" the guy's voice perks up. It reminds me of Brad: a pot-head, wannabe guitar player who had been a grade below us in school. After my so-called friends started talking behind my back and avoided walking with me to class, Brad started walking with me. We didn't talk and most people wouldn't have noticed he was there, but I did. On the last day of high school, he handed me a piece of clothing and walked off. It was the last time I'd seen him. It was the only gift anyone had given me for Jackson—a black onesie with the phrase 'rock'n life' on it.

And that had been it.

I had taken so much shit in high school. It would have been easier to have an abortion. If I had, I wouldn't know what it felt like for everyone in town to despise me, look at me, judge me.

I climb into the van, mainly to sit down. The mere thought of abortion popping into my head while Jackson's corpse lays in his bed makes me sick. I'd give anything to have him back.

Brad stares at me, but I don't focus on it.

How the hell did I end up here? I should be out looking for Carter. Carter should be in my arms, clinging to my breast. His little fingers should be kneading my skin as he nurses. Fuck my boobs hurt.

Stacey moves over, making room for me behind the passenger's seat.

Brad climbs into the back, leaning over me to pull the door shut.

Stacey spills onto a mattress in the back. "Have you talked to Nephthys?"

"No." He slouches into the beanbag chair. "They cut the cell service."

"Shit. I guess we'll have to drive out there then." She pauses and looks at me. "She's been waiting to meet you."

What? Me? Bullshit. "I'm not leaving town. Not without Carter."

Brad starts, "You don't seem to understand the importance of all this—"

"I don't give a fuck. I don't care what's happening. I just want to find my baby. I want to not have my whole fucking life falling apart." I look at him for the first time.

His whole right arm is robotic. A faint mechanical noise

accompanies the movement of its fingers—his fingers. He catches me staring. "I joined the Army after graduation. They sent me right over to Afghanistan. I thought the war was over, that it would be a safe place to be. But the things our government was doing: the opium, the experiments on the people who used to have everyday lives, like us...

"There was an explosion. All I remember is waking up strapped to a cot in the middle of the fucking desert. Some doctor told me everything was going to be okay, stuck me with a big-ass needle, then everything went dark. When I woke up, my arm was gone."

"Assholes," Stacey says under her breath.

"So they fixed you...?" I ask.

"There was never anything wrong with me," he says.

Someone pounds on the backdoor.

"Open up!" a male voice bellows. "Open up or we'll blow you up."

"Ready?" Stacey says to Brad.

He nods. His metal fingers swirl a seed in the flesh of his left palm.

Stacey flings open the doors.

A single guardsman stands outside. A respirator covers his face and a rifle hangs loosely over his shoulder.

"Show me," Stacey says to him.

Theia steps out from behind him. "Does he really have to show you?"

"Both of you." Stacey puts her hand up, stopping them from entering. Her free hand digs into her pants pocket, clenching something. "Now!"

"You really need to stop being such a tight-ass." Theia holds out her right arm, palm up—revealing the black tattoo—the scarab beetle—on her wrist.

The guardsman pushes back his sleeve, revealing an identical mark.

I glance around, at Brad. He's back to a relaxed state, swirling the seed in his palm. The veins of his left arm appear to faintly glow a fluorescent green beneath the black light.

Stacey and the guardsman climb in. The doors shut like those on a prison cell.

The guard pulls out a zip-tie from his back pocket and waddles on bent knees toward me. It's Shawn.

I push back, trying to get away, but there is no room to move, so I turn my back to him. I don't know what three years has done to him, and I don't want to be that close. I don't want to be stuck in a Goddamn van with him and his whore.

"Hold her down," Theia says.

What the fuck?

He wraps his arms around my waist, pinning my arms to my sides, and yanks me back into his lap. He holds me there with one arm and covers my mouth with the other.

"Arden, this has to be done," Theia says. "Relax. We're not going to hurt you."

Fuck this. I don't want his arms around me. I don't want to be around these people. *I don't want to be here*. I squirm, trying to throw my head back into his face, missing.

"Brad," says Theia, with all her attention on him.

He looks up from swirling the seed in his hand and gives me a look I don't quite understand—one of excitement and concentration. He shrugs. The robotic shoulder rises to his ear and falls at the exact same time as his natural limb. He closes his hand around the seed in his hand and looks up at me.

Shawn's arms tighten over my mouth. I can smell the morning's soap on his fingers. It's still the same scent as senior year.

Brad's face scrunches, like he's concentrating. He opens his hand. The shell of the seed has split open. A white tail—a primary root—slithers out. It grows. Secondary roots spit off from the central one. The seed coat falls off and two leaves roll out in perfect symmetry. They grow into large, beautiful cannabis leaves.

My body goes limp. *How did he do that?*

"Jesus, Brad," Stacey says, "you're such a pot head."

He shoots her a glance and she shuts up. The tips of his fingers curl up and the plant grows larger. Buds form.

Outside the sliding side-door comes the hiss and static of a walkie-talkie.

Shawn's hand tightens over my lips again. Whoever is outside wasn't expected.

Brad looks past me, at Shawn, and nods.

Shawn's hand loosens from my mouth. His other hand unwraps from my waist, brushes my hand, and squeezes it before pulling away. Then he takes out a knife.

Brad sets the roots on the carpet. The fresh green leaves wither, brown, and dry.

Shawn cuts the tie from my wrists and nudges me toward Brad.

Brad pulls out a lighter and ignites the dry leaves. Smoke swirls into the confined space.

We're going to suffocate. I go for the side door.

Brad grabs my arm and shakes his head in protest—not to open it. The hiss of the walkie-talkie ceases outside and a loud, constant beep sounds.

The smoke takes over quickly. Brad disappears like he's been swallowed by a dragon. Maybe he has. Maybe I'm lucky and this whole world is a dream—a nightmare.

My breasts start to leak. *Shit*. A laugh begins to crawl out of my belly. I'm sitting in a pot-filled van and my breasts are leaking. I start to cry.

The backdoors fling open.

Smoke floods out into the night. The cold, unnatural summer air rushes in and rips the intoxicant from the air. For a moment the smoke conceals us.

Gunshots fire.

I can't hold my head straight; it's too damn heavy. Gravity

pulls it to the side. *I should get up, move, do something. Why bother?* It's so warm and comfortable hunched against the back of the passenger seat. The shag carpet is soft beneath my fingers.

Brad pops out of the haze. His robotic fingers wrap around my wrist. He's yelling something, but the gunshots mask the words. Bullets splash against the van's bumper, making their way toward the front—toward us. He jumps over me, yanks the side door open, pushes me out of the van, and jerks me to my feet to follow him.

They shot at us. *They're shooting at us.*

Several guardsmen round the back of the van, to the side where I struggle to regain my stance.

A lone guardsman comes from the opposite side, behind us. It's Shawn. He yells through the respirator, pleading, "Go!"

Brad pulls me as he sprints past Shawn, in the opposite direction of the guards.

Gunshots whiz past us.

Shawn cries out in agony.

I turn back in time to see the bullet shoot through his left shoulder. Blood sprays into the air. A guardsman punches him to the ground. *Shawn!*

The guard unholsters a pistol, looks me square in the eyes, and shoots him in the back of the head.

Shawn! I slip from Brad's grip and fall to the ground. "No."

Brad disappears, fleeing behind me.

The piece of shit guardsman storms me. Grapevines spread out from underneath the van. The guard's eyes shift to the movement.

Brad grabs me, pulls me to follow him so fast I almost miss seeing the van flip into the air and land on Shawn.

No.

Brad tugs me into the backyard, to a tree. A weathered ladder reaches up the trunk, to a kid's treehouse. The makeshift door looks like it was cut for an eight-year-old child. We'll never fit.

Brad pulls me around the backside of the tree trunk, pushes my back up against the bark, and pins me to it.

Gunshots light up the van wreck like a war zone.

Brad grabs onto a small branch to my left and pushes it down. A section of tree trunk opens like a door and I fall backwards, into the tree.

Falling Into It

I SINK INTO THE DARKNESS. IMAGINING THAT I'M falling to my death. A wooden platform catches me. My spine absorbs most of the impact.

Brad jumps down into the hole, reaching to help me up. I pull away and scoot back. He gasps.

I fall backward, further down. Air shoots up around me. For a moment, I am completely weightless. I expect my spine to shatter into a million pieces, but something soft, like a mattress, saves my fall. My head lands wrong, whacking something hard like a headboard. I roll onto my side, cupping the pain, pressing my palms against the back of my head, not being able to sooth it.

A door slams up above. The light at the top of the tunnel disappears.

The darkness begins to glow green.

Am I dead yet? I long to be with Jackson and Frank again. I miss Carter so much.

The walls blur with the pounding in my head. I can see Brad wiping his hand around the room, against a curved wall. Pixels of green light illuminate beneath his fingers. The dim light hurts to look at. The blood in my head throbs against my skull. I close my eyes, letting tears ease the burning sensation.

"Jesus, Arden," he says.

I feel for the pain on the back of my scalp. A warm liquid seeps through my fingers. I'm bleeding.

Brad grabs my hands, pulling them away.

A bump swells beneath the wound and blood pulsates beneath the skin to gush out.

Fuck.

Brad moves across the room. I hear him banging around drawers, but I can only see his blurred silhouette. He returns and sits on the edge of the mattress.

I press my palm against the bump, trying to ease the pain—the throbbing in my head—but it doesn't help.

Brad inches closer and pulls my hands away again. The metal of his fingertips is cold against my head. With the other hand, he stabs a sewing needle through the gash.

I dig my face into a musty pillow, balling it with both hands, screaming into it as he continues to stitch the throbbing wound. Its sharp tip slides through my flesh, dragging the plastic thread through to the other side. It burns as he pulls it tight. He stitches it through again and again, until the weight of his robotic fingertips lifts from my scalp.

I lay there, staring at a wall covered in bioluminescence. Its soft glow drums in the darkness as my head throbs.

Down the Rabbit Hole

"HEY." BRAD NUDGES ME. "HEY. HOW YOU feeling?"

I let out a groan and open my eyes. This isn't a dream or a nightmare. All I want to do is sink into the mattress and disappear into the dark. I close my eyes again.

"Mom." I hear Jackson's voice. *"Mommy."*

I squeeze my eyelids tighter and force all the air out of my lungs. My breasts have filled. I'm all Carter has left. I push myself up and notice Brad has moved across the room to some sort of filing cabinet.

The bioluminescence gives enough of a glow to reveal the curved walls of the room, like a blacklight would. I lay on a full-size bed beneath a staircase that hugs the wall. At its top, before the door to get out, is a landing. There are no stair rails and I had fallen a story-and-a-half down onto a mattress.

"Brad," I say.

He stays still, staring at the cabinet with no answer.

"Brad."

"Yeah?" he says.

"I need a bathroom." My breasts hurt.

He faces me. His eyes scan the room. "Um, there's a trashcan over there…"

"No, I need to…"

"I know. I won't look." He gestures to the metal can and sits down on the ground, facing the cabinet. "You had a boy, right?"

I nod even though he can't see it. *I don't want to talk about it*. I pick up the trash can. Another round of breastmilk is about to be wasted. My whole life, wasted. I fought endless sleepless nights, for what? To have nothing—nothing to show for any of it? *It's too hard. This is too hard*. The image of a respirator breaks into my thoughts. I see Shawn. His face is covered in blood. I shake the image. Pressure rolls around in my head like a marble. I look at Brad. "What was Shawn doing here?"

Brad sits, silent, staring at the bottom drawer of the filing cabinet.

I pull the front of my shirt up and cup my hands on both sides of my right breast. It's always the first to clog. I squeeze harder than usual. It's only a matter of time before I lose my milk. The skin burns beneath my fingers—mastitis is setting in. I suck in a bunch of air, trying to keep from throwing up. Milk sprays into the trashcan, like the milking of a cow on a colonial farm.

Brad clears his throat. "You guys didn't talk much after your baby was born, huh?"

Tears roll down my cheeks. Shawn pressed me for an abortion, screamed about how I ruined his whole life. What about my life? Everyday I'd run out of homeroom to throw up. Girls would walk into the bathroom, talking about how they wished so-and-so would kiss them, while I clenched the edge of a dirty fucking toilet. There I was, knocked up, in all its glory. Once my stomach started to fill out, Shawn couldn't take it anymore.

"His name was Jackson." I empty my breast and move on to the other.

"I'm sorry," Brad says, pulling the cabinet drawer open.

"You were the only person who was kind to me back then." I let the silence carry as I finish the other breast. I tuck it back beneath my shirt and set the trash can down. "Thank you."

He nods his head, grabbing what looks like packets of seeds from the cabinet and shoves them into a backpack.

"Theia said she'd help me find my baby," I say. "His name is Carter. I don't know how long he's been gone. I don't know where he could be. I don't know what the fuck is happening."

Brad comes over, sitting—sinking—onto the mattress beside me. He wraps his arm around me and rocks us back and forth, hushing me, calming me, letting me know I'm not dead yet.

I slink out of his embrace and lay on the mattress, letting the tears drip from my eyes.

He joins me, propping his head with his hand. "I ran into Shawn a year after high school. Well, to be honest, he came looking for me. He reeked of alcohol, and looked like shit. He started drinking senior year and never gave it up. He came looking to score some coke. I don't know why people think that if you smoke weed, you're some huge drug addict." He lets out a heavy sigh. "I invited him in for a smoke and then he lost it. He broke down and told me everything about you guys."

I sit up. *What things?*

"I mean… everything that happened senior year." Brad tries to look away, but his eyes come back to mine. He clears his throat and lets out a deeper sigh. "He didn't know how to make things right with you. So, I gave him a job."

"You gave him a job?" I say.

"He cleaned himself up and joined the National Guard. In those two years, he never accepted who we were—who we are. He always called us freaks. But he did it for you."

I stand up, pacing the room. It doesn't make any sense, none of it. All I want to do is find my baby. All I want is to be home, to kiss my boys goodnight, to fall asleep next to Frank.

Brad stands up and blocks my pace. He grabs my wrist. "You're one of us."

For a moment, I think I see a faint glow in my veins, an almost nonexistent green glow. I yank my arm away from him. *No*. I look back at my arm, waiting for the mirage—the faint glow—to disappear, for my eyes to go back to normal, but they don't. "What did you do to me?"

"Arden," he says. "It's okay."

The room is spinning.

"Arden, look at me."

The green pulsating through my veins blurs with the bioluminescent glow of the walls. I can't breathe. My head spins with thoughts I can't control.

"Arden," his voice is soft, yet he's screaming.

I can't do this any longer. What's the point? There's no point. Frank's dead. Jackson's dead. Carter's….

"We'll save your baby." Brad's voice slices through my thoughts. He walks away, scooping something off the floor and tosses it over.

It's a Nirvana tee-shirt so worn out it feels like silk, with a pair of Batman boxers. They're probably dirty, but why care? I switch out my clothes with the new ones. For some reason it reminds me that my underwear is still in the kitchen drawer.

"If your baby's missing," Brad says, "he's still alive."

My heart drops and a sigh bursts from my lungs, filling the room. I slouch further into the mattress.

"It's not going to be easy to save him." He returns to the filing cabinet, grabbing more seed bags and stuffing them into the backpack.

I drag myself off the bed and join him, staring at the veins of my wrist. There's no glow. I'm ready to find him. He's the only thing that means anything in this world anymore.

Brad thumbs through row after row of plastic bags filled with seeds, filling the backpack.

"What are you...?"

He pauses to look at me. "We are the last of humanity." He returns to scooping out the packets. "We are Earth-walkers."

"What?"

An alarm clock on his watch goes off.

"We've got to go, or we'll miss the next check-point. Nephthys can tell you everything when we get there." He glances at me. "I shouldn't have told you."

Ascending

BRAD LEADS THE WAY UP THE STAIRS THAT HUG THE curved wall, tunneling up to the top. I have questions about who he is and who I'm supposed to be, but there is no time for conversation. He leans his ear against the door, listening for sounds of the outside world.

I can't hear any voices, gunshots, or airplanes.

He stands up straight, cracks the door open, and motions for me to follow.

My feet are pinned in place, waiting for me to wake up from this reality. I take a step. I don't want it to be real. *I don't want to live this nightmare.*

The door creaks, despite his care to ease it open. A wave of cold air blows in. The sky is still dark. The night is quiet. No insects sing. Brad exits and disappears into the night. I step out into the backyard, closing the hidden door behind me, pressing my back up against its bark. Nausea pits in my stomach. I don't want this life, but I can't escape it. I lean my forehead in my hands. The faint lines of my veins don't glow; there is no hue of green. I close my eyes, wanting to concentrate on the pain building within me, distracting me from the idea that I'm some kind of freak. I had spent my whole life not wanting to be different.

I can't help but think about Jackson, about Carter. *I should be at home tucking Jackson in for bed, reading him a story. Carter should be lying beside me, pulling at my breast, giggling with pure contentment before latching*.

I look at Brad, but he's gone. I gasp, holding my breath. *Shit*. I had let my thoughts distract me, numb the urgency. I search the surrounding yard: the van explosion, the house. *The house!*

A silhouette moves past the kitchen window that overlooks the driveway.

Brad? I glance back at the van, expecting an army of guardsmen to gun me down.

The coast is clear.

I sprint for the house—for the flimsy storm door that overlooks the backyard—pull it open, and go inside. It bangs shut behind me. *Shit. I should've eased it closed.* I crouch down. My heart tightens like a slingshot about to impale. I'm not sneaking up on anyone now.

Two or three houses down, trash cans clamor to the ground.

"Brad?" I whisper. *Brad?*

Someone—something—moves in the adjoining living room.

Maybe it's not Brad. But in the window… I saw… I assumed it was his silhouette, but what if it wasn't? What if it was that thing from the locker room? I climb to my feet, but before I can stand, something hits my cheek—punches me—knocks me back down. Pain slingshots through my head. Blood seeps through the stitches.

"Get up!" says a strong, female voice. A muscular woman stands overtop of me. Her fists are tight. She's wearing solid-black tights like some sort of a ninja outfit. Fabric wraps her head, exposing only her eyes. Her eyes—they're like a snake's or dragon's. Fucking snake eyes that shimmer with night-shine. Her pupils draw into vertical lines.

I scoot back from her, bumping into the cabinet behind me.

She steps closer. Light ripples across her eyes as she reaches down for me.

I wince, closing my eyes. Maybe it's all a dream—a bad fucking dream.

She grabs the front of my shirt, bends down, and shoves her nose against mine. "Are you Arden of Earth?"

I can't move. My cheek throbs from her assault. My heart's weight pins me to the ground.

"Get up!" She stands and kicks me in the stomach.

My abs crunch in reaction and air spits from my lungs, leaving me hunched and breathless in the prison I have created for myself. Nothing helps. I can hear someone start to cry, and realize it's me. *It isn't a dream.*

"I asked you a question. Are you Arden of Earth?" She grabs a fist full of my hair and begins to yank me up off the floor. She shoves the hemp necklace Theia gave me into my face. It had been her in the locker room.

A gunshot breaks through the kitchen window.

Her fingers release from my shirt. The necklace falls to the floor and she follows. Her head whacks the floor. The vertical lines of her pupils dilate into circles—like ours.

A red laser beam moves across the kitchen window, from outside, centering on my forehead. I try to hold up my hands, but pain shoots through my ribs.

The guards storm the house. The biggest one of all shoves a gun to my face, yelling at me to "Get down!"

Get down. I laugh, even though it hurts. *I've got to be dead now. This must be hell.* I had premarital sex and now am in hell for it—for not keeping my legs closed—but those are my mother's thoughts, not mine, and I am allowing them to shape my reality.

The ringleader grabs my arm, twists it back behind me, and rackets a pair of handcuffs on my wrists. They're way too tight.

I give up laughing to fight the urge to barf.

The guard standing over top of me, blabbers on about something.

My eyes return to the corpse of my attacker. Nothing is funny anymore. I'm not dead, and I'm not dreaming.

He yanks me up. The handcuffs dig a trench into my skin. I force all my weight away from him, but he yanks me back. The cuffs shift, carving deeper lines into my skin. Nausea pits in my stomach. He shoves me toward the front door. His full attention is on me. The rest of his minions stand armed—cautious—nervous, pointing their guns at the corners of the room.

I step outside. The walkway is lined with guardsmen on both sides, all armed, all wearing respirators. I stop, digging my heels into the porch step. The man tightens his grip on my arm and yanks me closer, demanding obedience. He shoves me off the porch.

I lose my footing and trip forward, about to fall face first onto the pavement. The ringleader yanks the handcuffs backwards, countering my fall. My shoulder blade muscles tear with the momentum. He allows no time for me to absorb the pain. He pushes me forward again, toward a police-style van, the kind they transport prisoners in. It is parked along the street with its backdoors already spread open.

Stacey is in the back. Her body lays limp across the left-side bench.

Shit. Even if I claim to have nothing to do with her—with them—she can make up any lie. We have a past because of Shawn. I can't deny that even if I want to.

The man pushes me into the van's back, like I'm some criminal. I fall to the floor, landing on my shoulder. He closes the door.

Great. I wiggle like a caterpillar to sit upright. The van takes off and I fall back down. The cold, metal floor bounces beneath my cheekbone, banging against the bruises on my face.

Moonlight streaks through the windows, dancing on the ceiling. Stacey's body flops with each turn.

I look away and close my eyes. So many nights I'd wished for her to be dead.

Strangers

"ARDEN."

My jaw throbs. My head aches.

"Arden," Stacey says. "Wake up. Get up."

I open my eyes.

She shakes me, grabs onto the handcuffs behind my back, and helps me sit up on the bench. Her fingers reach for my cheek. "Shit."

I pull back, knowing how much it will burn if she touches me.

The van screeches to a halt.

"Don't tell them anything," she says, fidgeting with her hands. She looks around the enclosure for something.

The interior light turns on.

"Don't tell them anything. They'll kill you."

What does she mean, they'll kill me?

"Arden." She looks me square in the eyes. "Don't tell them anything."

The door opens. The beefy guardsman stands armed and ready, still wearing a respirator, concealing his identity. The other is the black man with a Jackal head.

Stacey leans over and whispers in my ear, "Umstead."

The ringleader grabs her.

"Don't tell him anything," she says.

He yanks her out and they disappear from view.

"Don't tell him!" she yells.

The Jackal-man, Anubis, reaches for me, and I let him. Instead of pulling me out, he climbs in.

Shit.

Another guard comes up behind him and shuts the door. He pounds on the roof of the vehicle and a hiss of fresh air fills the cabin. The armored van begins to drive on. He holds out a hand to me. His voice is calm and stagnate beneath the robotic tone of his mask, "Hand."

"What?"

"Give me your hand," he says.

I lean against the wall, pinning my cuffed hands behind my back.

"Arden," he says, "I'm not playing with you. Do as I say and I won't hurt you."

How's he know my name? Won't hurt me, yeah right. A deep breath escapes my lungs. *Won't hurt me? As if this could hurt anymore.*

His eyes shift to my breasts.

Blood rushes to my cheeks from embarrassment, filling the bruise on my face. I turn my back and hands to him, letting him unlock the handcuffs.

They fall to the floor with a thud.

I don't want to face him. If I stay still, perhaps he'll go away. I ease my hands in front of me, keeping my eyes down, rubbing the handcuff's indents on my skin.

He grabs my right wrist and yanks it, spinning it, examining it. "Where is it?"

"What are you talking about?" I say.

His lips pucker together. "The mark." He jerks me closer. His eyes run up my arm. "Where is it?"

The scarab beetle. He's looking for the tattoo.

His eyes lock onto mine and widen with intensity. "Strip."

"What?"

"Take off your clothes." His voice deepens. "Right. Now."

"No." I yank my arm back.

His grip tightens and he pulls me closer. His strength is crippling. "Now."

"Why?"

"Because I said so!" he screams.

I lose my breath. My body jumps, tightens.

His chest falls as he exhales. He releases my arm, grabs my shirt, and rips the silky old Nirvana shirt straight down the middle. I try to turn, to move away, to kick him, but he's too fast, too strong. He throws my hips to the side and rips my boxer shorts. I fight to sit up, get out of that position as fast as possible, but he takes out a glass knife and comes at me, jabbing the blade through the loose pieces of my clothes. He flips me over, tearing the fabric from my body, then lets go, clearing his throat, and backs off.

The metal bench is cold against my thighs. I try to wrap my arms around my body, but there's too much exposed.

He sits back.

The hiss of air kicks on again. Goosebumps ripple across my skin. Milk drips onto my upper thigh.

He sits up straighter. His canine lips curve into a faint smile.

I scoot back. I have questions, but I'm afraid to move, let alone ask anything. If I speak, if I move, it might entice him to rip my thighs apart and take whatever he wants.

The door opens. A bright light—a spotlight—fills the van's cabin, warming it.

"Get that fucking light out of my face!" yells Anubis.

"Yes, Sir," says the man holding the light. "Sorry, Sir." The light swiftly points toward the ground. The guy's eyes dart to me.

Salt air fills my nostrils. I can hear the ocean.

The Jackal-man, Anubis, grabs hold of my arm and scoots out of the van, dragging me along with him. Rows of military personnel, still armed and in respirators, line a different walkway. This one leads to a two-story colonial mansion. The white paint has faded cream and a bright white sheet wraps around the front porch, creating a biohazard tent. Floodlights wash out the stars up above.

Anubis shoves me forward.

The brick path beneath my feet is still warm with the day's sun. I make it halfway to the porch before my knees buckle. I can't go through something else—anything else. I can't go on anymore.

He steps past me, grabbing my arm, forcing me to follow, then stops at the entrance of the tent.

"Clear!" yells the guard to his left.

Another guardsman, inside the tent, pulls back the entrance sheet. He nods at Anubis, then stares at the controlling grip he has on me. His respirator fogs. A disgusted "ugh" slips out, like I repulse him somehow. He stands there, judging me, making me feel like some sort of freak, through the plastic barrier of his respirator.

We step inside the tent. A burst of air rushes down from the ceiling. The guardsman nods at Anubis. Air floods the front door and it opens to a dark living room. Beyond is a kitchen with a wall full of windows that overlook the beach.

A man stands with his back to us in the kitchen. He rolls his shoulders back, standing up straight. His voice is deep, "Leave her."

Anubis obeys and disappears back the way we had entered.

"What's your name?" the man says, as if asking the ocean, gazing out of that wall of windows. His voice crescendos with the repeated phrase, "What is your name?"

I tightly fold my hands in front of me. I'm alone and naked. My name seems unimportant.

"How is it that you're still alive?" he says.

"I don't know," I say.

He turns around, leaning his back against the window. It's Seth, the janitor who once showed me so much kindness. His suit looks expensive—custom tailored. There is no evidence he'd once worn a faded and worn-out name badge.

"Seth?" I say.

He pushes away from the window and storms toward me, pausing when he realizes I'm naked. His approach slows. He stops a foot from me, straightening his shoulders back. "Arden, why are you alive?"

I press my lips together and try to control my breath. *After all I've been through, he's asking me this question—like I'm supposed to be dead.*

He grabs my right arm.

How dare you? I tear it back.

His eyes weigh on me. There is a hunger behind them that I have never seen before. He grabs again, this time clenching my right wrist, twisting it, no doubt looking for the tattoo.

A scarab beetle tattoo sticks out beneath his right cuff.

"So, you're one of them?" I ask.

"No." He follows my eyes to the tattoo and tugs the sleeve of his suit down. It has only been three years, and yet all his empathy, all his compassion has gone. He takes a step, cups my face, and slides his fingers into my hair. His grip tightens and he takes out a knife—a small dagger—from the inside lining of his blazer. It's shaped like an Egyptian cross, carved out of a pure, clear crystal. The bottom tip is sharpened like a blade, that he presses against my neck. It begins to glow green. "But it seems you are."

Stacey's warning, *"Don't tell him anything,"* pounds through my thoughts. I insist, "I'm not."

He stows the dagger and returns to the kitchen.

"Will you help me?" I ask, sinking to the floor, burying my head in my hands. Sobs escape my pleas. "Will you help me find my baby?"

A pile of clothes lands beside me.

"Get dressed," he says. "Bathroom is down the hall. On the right."

I scoop up the clothes and head down the hallway off to the right of the kitchen. Another right takes me into the bathroom. It's a half-bath the size of a closet, containing a toilet and sink. The small privacy window blurs the military lights out on the front lawn. I ignore my reflection in the mirror, and slowly express the milk from my breasts, watching the liquid drain—waste away—down the sink.

Once my breasts are empty, I slump onto the floor. *This world—this piece of shit world—has taken everything*. The tiled walls echo with sobs I no longer try to control. I have never felt further away from finding Carter as I do now.

The door eases open. Seth steps in, closing the door behind him.

I hold my breath. I should have locked the door. The throbbing pain of my face intensifies.

He sits down opposite me, leaning his head against the door. "Arden you have to help me. If you do this for me, you'll get your baby back."

I look at him. *How the hell can you promise that?*

"You'll have everything you've ever wanted," he says.

I wipe the film of bogies from my lip onto my knee. He looks like a man who can get whatever he wants—buy whatever he wants. I ask, "What do you want?"

"I need you to find the people you were with."

"I don't know what you're talking about."

He stands up and opens the door. "Get dressed."

I pull the pile of clothes closer as he walks out. The blouse and pants are something I'd never be able to afford. I pull my hair back into a ponytail, but I have no tie, so it falls back into a mess. As much as I'm disinclined to, I join him in the kitchen.

He leans against the counter, staring into the living room.

Someone is… moaning.

I follow his eyes to the noise.

Stacey is on the couch, squirming. Her mouth is duct-taped and her hands are cuffed behind her back.

Seth straightens up from the counter and snaps his fingers.

A woman steps out of a dark corner to the left, out of a closet. Her pupils narrow and shine like a night animal—vertical lines like a snake—like my attacker. She has a baby in her arms. My baby.

Carter! My stomach pits. I run for him. His little arms reach out for me. The pacifier in his mouth falls to the floor as he coos. *I can't believe it*. The creature lets go. I squeeze him into my embrace. He nuzzles his head between my breasts and rubs his eyes. I walk with him over to a lounge chair and begin to lift my shirt.

"No," says the man.

I freeze, not really believing the words, and look back at him.

He clears his throat. "From what I understand your milk is on the way out. You've missed how many feedings?"

"What?"

Seth nods at the woman—the freak. She melts back into the corner's darkness and vanishes. He comes closer.

Carter turns his head, rooting, trying to find my breast to comfort and ease the flood of emotion flowing through him.

"You will bring me Nephthys, or you will never see him again," he says.

Stacey starts to scream in protest, but the duct-tape does its job. She throws her body onto the floor toward him.

He walks away, down the hallway, and disappears from sight.

A guard enters from the porch and drags Stacey away.

Carter begins to whimper.

I look down at him. He smiles, a great, big, toothless smile, and I let the rest of the world sink away.

A Mother's Choice

CARTER NURSES TO SLEEP. MOST OF THE MILK HAD been wasted, expressed down the drain, but what was left felt good to get out. The clogged duct has worsened. When he nurses, it burns. I endure the pain, grateful. Once the first minute of latching passes, the vomit-inducing ball in my throat eases. I nuzzle deep into the couch, drawing Carter as close to me as I can. I can't take my eyes off of him.

His little lips fall away from my skin as he drifts to sleep.

I pull the blouse down over my breast and stroke his chubby little cheek with the side of my finger.

Daylight glows between morning clouds.

I want to stay up, watch him some more, but my eyes drift and the weight of my eyelids grow heavy.

Seth approaches from down the hallway, wearing nothing but silk pajama pants. Money afforded him ample time to work out and eat right. His physique had changed since I last saw him. A large snake tattoo wraps around his right shoulder and slithers down his arm to the beetle. Genetics gave him a great smile and he uses it. "Hungry?"

I look away from him, over at the closet.

"What happened to his father?" he says.

Frank? "He's dead," I whisper.

He laughs.

What an ass—

"If he were dead, that baby wouldn't be alive."

What the hell is he talking about? I hadn't been with anyone since Frank. *How dare you—*

"It's a recessive trait. Both parents have to carry it," he says. "It's very rare."

There's no way. I hadn't been with anyone else. I look down at Carter. He is still alive and his father is dead. It cannot be genetics that caused Jackson to die, his father is dead too. In image of Shawn wearing a respirator pops into my head. Franks dead. There is no way Carter isn't his. His tiny fingers twitch as his eyes chase dreams beneath delicate eyelids. "I—"

He snaps his fingers.

The woman from last night appears out of the same corner of the wall. Her snake-eye pupils dilate with dawn's light, almost appearing human. She heads straight toward me and Carter.

I squeeze Carter tighter to me. He squeaks and wiggles, still asleep. I look at Seth. "What the fuck is this?"

The woman stops halfway and looks back at him for instruction. He nods and she continues closer.

"This is Bastet," he says. "She is your son's wet nurse."

All the air from my lungs aspirates. *No*. I got him back. There's no way I'm handing him over to anyone, let alone some creature—some freak of nature.

"The faster you bring me Nephthys, the sooner you'll get him back." He grabs something off the kitchen counter, steps around the woman, and points it—a gun—at me. "You know it will be harder after he wakes up."

"What are you going to do, kill me?" I say.

"Why wouldn't I?" His face doesn't change with the words. There is no reaction, no feeling behind them.

I don't know what he did to get to where he was, but something told me I would only live if I obeyed. I look down at Carter. I'm so tired. I want to find a bedroom, curl up with him, and sleep, feel his warm body next to mine, listen to him coo in his sleep, feel his little fingers wrap around mine, squeezing tight. Just one more hour. That's all I want.

Seth clears his throat, urging my compliance.

I look up. Bastet reaches for Carter, but I can't let go.

Her pupils tighten into lines and she scoops him from my hands. My heart drains with emptiness as I let go. Seth steps back, holding his aim at me, guarding her as she walks toward the closet—toward the darkness.

"Wait." I push past him for Bastet—for Carter—his little body limp, completely asleep in her arms. He moans. I lean over and press my lips to his cheek, take in a long breath—his smell—and pull myself away, looking at the floor. *I can't do this*.

Bastet places her hand on my forearm. I look at her, hoping to hell she'll take care of him.

I give her a nod and close my eyes, turning back to face Seth. I can't watch him disappear. I feel the emptiness behind me, the emptiness of my arms, the nausea pitted in my stomach. A tear runs down my cheek, but I stand taller in front of him. "Who are you really? And who is she?"

He grins. "You should've demanded those questions before letting go of your baby."

What an asshole. He's right. I just let him go. *What have I done?*

I turn for the closet and run into it. *I'd rather die than be without him another minute*. I hit the wall, with my face, and fall to the floor.

"My real name is Set." He looks at me like I should be surprised, impressed, know what the fuck that means.

Maybe it's a pop culture thing. It had been over a year since we threw out our television. I hadn't want to do it, but Frank insisted it would be the best thing for our family. Once I adjusted, it was amazing. What little care of celebrity gossip I had, withered away into nothing. I started focusing on those who were present in my life and cared about me. For once, my life was headed in the right direction. *Now look at it*. I don't ask him why he thinks his name is important. Men like him always make sure you know.

"I own Tekk Corp," he says.

I don't give a shit what company he owns. But what is Bastet? She isn't human, that's for damn sure. "Who is she?"

"She is a Shadow-walker." He heads into the kitchen and pulls out a frying pan and some eggs.

What the fuck is that supposed to mean? I follow him, stopping at the kitchen counter, keeping my distance. Maybe I can wrangle the gun away from him and demand that he give me back Carter.

The black snake tattoo wrapping around his shoulder almost shimmers beneath the stove lights. Its scales spiral down his arm to a cobra head, its mouth wide-open to attack the scarab beetle on his wrist. The beetle is more faded than the snake.

"Cut the bullshit and small talk," I say, glancing at the corner Carter had disappeared in, rubbing my head. "Let's get this over with. I don't care who you are or what you want."

He laughs. "I've always liked you."

He picks up a walkie-talkie from behind him. "Anubis, get your ass in here."

The hiss of the air kicks on outside the front door and the Egyptian creature enters. His eyes meet mine, and lower to the floor. "Ma'am."

"Whip us up some breakfast," Seth says to him, glancing at me. "We need to talk."

My body stiffens. I liked having the barrier between us, the distraction of his focus.

He rounds the counter, heading for the living room. "Make some for yourself too."

Anubis takes over behind the stove.

Seth says nothing. He sits on the couch and watches me, waiting for me to join him.

I do join him in the living room, taking the oversized lounge chair across from him.

"Bastet is… they… well, you'll see soon enough. As for your task. We'll get you to the rendezvous at Umstead State Park."

"How do you know—?"

"They'll take you to Nephthys. You have to persuade her to enter a house, any building with corners. I'll take care of the rest."

"Why me?" I say.

"You're alive," he says. "And you're not one of them yet."

I look down at his wrist—at the faded scarab beetle. "Were you one of them?"

"There's one thing you need to know about these people," he says. "They distort reality. They'll attempt to distort yours."

"What if I say no? What if I can't get her to go?"

"Walk with me." He stands and walks back to the kitchen, stopping before the wall of windows, overlooking the beach.

I follow, keeping my distance.

The sun crests over the ocean, caressing the sand with its rays. The waves pulse at the beach's edge.

Seth speaks into the walkie-talkie, "Bring the girl to the beach."

I glance back at Anubis. His shoulders drop a little as he whisks a bowl of eggs. I look back, out onto the ocean.

A man is dragging Stacey across the sand to the water's edge.

"What are you doing?" I ask, stepping closer to the windows.

"You want to know what will happen if you fail?" Seth presses the button of the walkie-talkie. "Now."

The man in the distance throws Stacey to the ground, pulls out a gun, and shoots her in the head.

Fuck. He's crazy. This is crazy.

"I don't play games." His fingers touch my face, gliding along my cheek.

I coil away from him, bumping my head into the windowpane.

His hand cups my cheek, like he's going to kiss me.

I tighten my lips, restraining any possible contact, daring not to move.

"Arden," he says.

I relax them, holding my breath, trying to think of how the hell I'll get out of this fucking mess—away from this crazy place. *How am I going to get Carter back?*

"You don't have to do it for me," he says. "You have to do it, to get your baby back."

I face him, pushing his hand away from my skin, and spit at his face.

He backhands me.

It hurts, but it's worth it. My cheek throbs and traces of blood stimulate my taste buds.

He grabs my arm and pulls me closer, forcing me to look at him.

"You shouldn't push it," he says. "Not in a life where I control what happens to you: where you sleep, what you eat, who gets to fuck you."

I look away, anywhere else but at him—out to the sheet of sand. There were nights when I was pregnant with Jackson that I wished for Stacey to be dead. But the blood from her body washing into the ocean only fills me with sadness and guilt. My wishes were granted too late. I'd forgotten I ever placed them.

Anubis scrapes a fork against a metal bowl, beating the eggs —the dead chicken fetuses—destroying them so that we can live.

Seth yanks on my arm, demanding my attention again. "Was that enough of a test? You want to push me? See how far I'll go?" He motions to Stacey's corpse outside, but I won't look. "Fine," he says, grabbing hold of me, dragging me through the living room, and opens the front door. Sunlight illuminates the white tent and the hiss of clean air showers us from the ceiling. "I have a whole army out there. You ever been gang banged?"

I yank my arm away from his grip and step backward, back into the living room. "You're crazy."

He shuts the front door, grabs my arm, and drags me down the hallway, opening the door opposite the bathroom. Then throws me in. "Watch your step."

I lose my footing on what must be stairs, tumbling down them, stopping when my head hits earth at the bottom. What light there is turns dark.

"Are you ready?" A male voice comes from my left. It is cold and damp, likely the basement. A hand grabs mine, lifting me up with one swoop, and pulls me into the darkness.

Another World

IT IS DARK.

I hold onto the man's hand, afraid if I let go, I'll disappear into an abyss. *It'd be easier to just let go*.

We've gone only a few feet before he whispers, "Steps."

My foot slams into an unexpected bottom step. He squeezes my hand harder, stabilizing me before continuing up a set of stairs.

There is no sun. No light. He flings the door at the top of the steps open. Moonlight trickles down the hallway to meet our feet.

Moonlight? The sun had just dawned. *How the hell is it night? Where the fuck am I?*

The hallway looks the same as the last house, but there are no pictures, no furniture, no fresh air. The man, Anubis, lets go, and walks into the kitchen—a kitchen identical to the last. I follow him, glancing back at our footprints tracked across a dusty floor.

"Would you like something to eat?" he asks, still carrying the spatula.

I run to the window—to see Stacey's body lying lifeless on the shore. I can feel Anubis watching me—staring, observing me like I'm some lab rat, some sick experiment.

Her body isn't there. The ocean is calm, mirroring the moon perfectly. The coastline is empty. The sky is clear of lines.

"Where are we?" I ask. "What is this place?"

"Relax," he says. "See, Seth has a hard time transcending worlds. So, he had both houses made identical to one another. It softens the transitions."

"What are you talking about?" None of it makes sense.

He walks to the front door and opens it.

Instead of a vinyl tent, an empty lawn looks out on a distant city—a city that isn't supposed to be there. The lawn shows no evidence the military or guard have ever stepped foot here. The small beach town of Topsail Island, that's filled with two-story condos and townhouses, has been replaced by a cleared field. A white metropolis stretches into the skyline in the distance. A single emerald pyramid sits at its center.

Anubis walks out onto the porch. I push past him, running down the steps, digging my toes into the sandy lawn, looking up at the moon. Part of me expects there to be two of them. *I don't understand. This can't be..., this can't be happening. How am I going to get back? How—?* I fall to my knees. "Where the fuck am I?"

Blades of grass wave in the ocean breeze, taking me back to the beach with Theia. With Jackson.

"Time..." he says, walking back into the house.

I stare at the blades of grass stretching for miles, focusing on a single blade, watching it wave—welcoming me to its world.

It isn't fair that the grass is alive, that Jackson and Frank are dead, that I let Carter slip through my fingers. I lay back on the sand, letting tears drain from my eyes.

The stars blur into sharp images of light, hanging in the cold, dark universe.

The porch boards creak behind me. Anubis has returned.

"Where's the sun?" I say.

He sits down beside me with two plates of bacon and eggs, offering one out.

I take the plate from him.

His eyes shine with the moonlight, but they don't look real. He looks away. "I'm not supposed to talk to you."

I let out a soft laugh. *This just keeps getting better.*

"But since you are in my world, you should know." He reaches for the necklace around his neck, but stops before touching it, then forks his food portions onto my plate. "You know that feeling when you're all alone: like something—someone is there. Something brushes your shoulder, a whisper behind your ear? That's where our worlds touch. This is a parallel world to yours, separated by night and day—a few hours."

I look at my plate. It's filled with eggs, bacon, peppers—the carcasses' of dead animals and remnants of vibrant plants.

"Within the corners of the Earth, they meet." He puts the plate down beside him and rubs his palms together, as if warming them. "That is my gift. I can transcend our worlds." He opens his hands, revealing nothing. "What's yours?"

"I don't know what you're talking about."

He smiles. "If you're supposed to bring back Nephthys, you must be someone." He looks down at my right wrist and back at the city.

My stomach growls and I fill it as we sit in silence.

"We'll head into town at dawn," he says. "Your eyes won't be so noticeable then."

Tekk Corp

THE LAST GLOW OF MOONLIGHT ILLUMINATES THE CITY, reflecting off its bright white buildings. No building has a corner. They are all rounded, curved, twisted with the dirt of the earth, like mud-huts painted with white plaster. Vehicles are silent, similar to electric cars. There are no fumes, no exhaust. My lungs take in the freshness of the air, craving it. The streets are bustling, shoulder-to-shoulder. The people are all thin, healthier, happier in a way.

Anubis hurries to the center of town, toward the pyramid. Blocks of emerald Aventurine stone are stacked to the sky like the Great Pyramid of Giza. The doors are gold, carved with hieroglyphics, large like giants live there. Anubis opens them. I'm about to follow when a man in a black cloak flashes in the corner of my eye, disappearing down a nearby alleyway.

Anubis grabs my arm, yanking me into the building.

I glance back as the door closes.

It is bright inside. On the far wall behind the receptionist's desk is Tekk Corp's logo: an airplane flying above a cornfield. It takes up the entire far wall. Beneath it is the tag line—Modifying Fate.

"Identification," says the receptionist. She is a middle-aged woman dressed in a white monk's robe. She looks normal—human—except that her canines are slightly longer than they are supposed to be. Her eyes dilate like Bastet's—like a snake's or dragon's.

I face Anubis.

He presses on his necklace.

Nothing happens.

"Identification," repeats the receptionist, sliding her hand beneath the desk. Her pupils dilate into thinner vertical lines.

He presses the necklace again. The form of the Jackal-head melts away, into the thin gold necklace. He's an older, fit black man with human eyes.

A laser shoots out of the wall behind the receptionist, scanning Anubis' retina.

An alarm sounds.

The receptionist reaches beneath the desk and draws a gun, pointing it at him.

Anubis slowly raises his hands in defense.

I don't dare move.

"Relax," he says to her. His voice is smooth without the Jackal's head.

The logo on the wall parts. A man in an identical white robe steps out with a bigger gun. The Robes protect Tekk Corp.

"Jesus," says Anubis. "I can explain." He rubs his eye on his sleeve.

Both guns cock.

"Fuck!" he says. "What is wrong with you guys?" He reaches into his right eye socket, pinching at his eyeball. He grunts, bends forward a little and digs harder, pulling something out. He flings it at the receptionist. It is a contact lens.

The Robe stays steady, glancing at her for instruction. She nods. Reluctant, he lowers the gun. The laser scans over Anubis' eye again. The receptionist keeps glued to the computer monitor. It pings with approval.

"Let's go," says the man, waving for us to follow him beyond the same secret doors the Robe appeared out of.

Anubis digs into his other eye, dumps a second contact lens onto the front desk, then glances back at me. His eyes are bloodshot. The pupils of his eyes narrow like a snake's—like a dragon's—like the others'.

I stop in my tracks. I expected him to be one of them, but part of my heart fills with disappointment at the realization. Part of me hoped he'd end up on my side.

He reaches back, grabbing onto my wrist, and I have gratitude that I'm not doing this alone. He leads me past the receptionist, into a small room. Stairs tunnel and twist up, like those of a lighthouse. It's made of old stone, like a castle. He lets go and ascends the steps.

And so, I follow, expecting nothing less than a beast at the top.

Long Way Down

THE STAIRS GO ON FOREVER, TO A PENTHOUSE AT THE top. A wall of windows spans a glass pyramid tip. There is no one there to greet us, no one to reassure me that what I'm doing will get Carter back.

Anubis heads straight for a rounded closet in the middle of the room. He walks faster toward it, sliding the door open. Four corners frame the interior space, it is a closet.

"Are you ready?" he asks, reaching for my hand.

I look at the corner he stands closest to—the one to the far left—and hold my breath.

"Relax," he says.

I try to, exhaling an almost painful breath.

"Get to the rendezvous site." He flicks the light switch off. Darkness fills the room. For a second, the light piercing the doorway behind us shines across his eyes, reminding me he isn't human. He's a Shadow-walker. "Get Nephthys back to a house —any house—near the dark corners of its walls."

I take his hand and pull the door closed behind me. Darkness swallows the remaining light, deepening as we walk.

Moonlight stretches through a window up ahead. We are no longer on the top floor of a pyramid. The place smells like funk and the carpet looks stained, even in the dark.

Anubis lets go of my hand, pressing the necklace around his neck. His Jackal-head returns, sheltering him from our air.

I step to a window, wiping the glass with my sleeve. Pieces of chipped paint flake off.

The run-down remnants of a roaring 1950s neighborhood hugs both sides of an urban street. It's the part of town I grew up in. It's my world. It is home.

Airplanes shoot through the air and roar above the dead houses. Summer's breeze drifts in through an open window down the hallway, bringing the smell of death with it.

"Goddamn it, he didn't clear the corpse of this one." Anubis storms down the hallway, toward a bedroom, and never comes back.

Escape

I follow Anubis' footsteps and find a set of car keys on the kitchen counter. They go to an old Volkswagen Jetta in the driveway. I take the vehicle and head for Raleigh. Static fills the radio and I let it play as I grip the steering wheel, trying to fight my memories.

It was warm the day I told Frank I was pregnant. I had purchased a "big brother" tee-shirt for Jackson. He was wearing it when Frank came home from work, but Frank didn't notice. It was one of those days: work had beaten and worn him down. Jackson ran up to him, like we practiced.

Frank flopped on the steps and unlaced his shoelaces. "Is dinner ready?"

I didn't say anything; I was too nervous. We weren't planning on a baby, not yet. Jackson was a handful and a piece of me already felt guilty that Frank was paying for him. He wanted to, I know that, but he took on the responsibility of another man's—of Shawn's.

"Arden, is dinner ready?" he said. Anger or annoyance vibrated in his words.

Jackson reached for him, stretching his little arms up around Frank's shoulders. Frank nudged him away, to finish undoing his shoelaces. Jackson's head hit the stairwell behind him and he started to cry.

My heart sank. *It wasn't supposed to go like this.*

I expected Frank to yell, stomp away, leave us, but he didn't. He let go of the laces and scooped Jackson into his arms, clenching him to his chest, pressing his lips against Jackson's cheeks and cuddling him closer.

Jackson's cry faded to a moan.

"I'm sorry," Frank said. "Shhh," he rocked him, "I'm sorry. You're okay. I got you. Shhh, Daddy loves you."

I walked into the kitchen, out of view.

It was nothing like I imagined.

I grabbed the ice pack from the freezer, but by the time I turned around, Jackson was running in for it. He leaned his head against my leg, clinging tight. It was only for a moment. Then he returned to the living room where we'd been practicing the night's scenario.

Frank walked into the kitchen. His eyes looked at mine and then to my stomach. There was no expression on his tired face. He stepped closer.

I backed away, not knowing why or what was coming. The refrigerator held me in place.

He slid his hand around my waist, pulled me close, and pressed his lips against mine. A smile puckered out of the corners of his lips and a laugh pierced the moment. It grew into a thunderous giggle and he pulled me closer, rubbing his hand across my belly.

So much for fighting off memories.

I grip the steering wheel of the Volkswagen, passing the gas station known for selling cigarettes to under aged kids.

Lines crosshatch the sky.

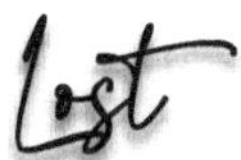

HOW THE HELL AM I GOING TO FIND THE PARK?

I've heard of it. My father used to jog on the multi-use trail most Sundays, but I have no idea where it is.

I need to get this over with as soon as possible—get Carter back as soon as possible. I can stop at a house—any house—for a phone book, but there is no way to tell which houses are empty.

A few cars sit dead on the highway. Most have coasted off to the shoulder before their owners had bleed out.

I take the beltway around the capital. There is no traffic. I'm still too far from the city for that. An old 1950s style Diner sits at the edge of the highway entrance, up ahead, on the opposite side of the street.

I turn off the radio—the static—that numbed my thoughts. I continually scanned through all the FM stations, hoping something would play and dull the torment of my mind. Then I gave up. All the AM stations are out too. But the static had been as hypnotic as the music could've been.

I jerk the car left, heading for the diner, but give it too much gas, nearly rolling the vehicle. I jerk the wheel, ease off the gas, and level back out. All four tires touch down. I let the engine idle and stare at the "open" sign blinking in the diner window. The building looks old enough to have a payphone and a paper phonebook.

An airplane flies overhead, rumbling, swooping closer towards the earth.

The diner regains my attention. If someone is alive inside, they'll be armed. It is North Carolina after all.

Three other cars are parked in the diner's parking lot.

I cut the engine and get out.

Clouds build in the distance. Theia's fear of the rain has followed me, encouraging me to run to the building. The door gives easily. An old couple sits to the right, hunched over with their faces drowning in spoiling food. To the left, is a fat man stuffed into a booth with his head resting against the windowpane. Another body sits at the end of the counter, taking up two stools, having fallen over. The faint smell of death floats like a thick fog on the floor. There is no phone booth. In old movies, the server always pulls out a chunky address book and a landline phone from underneath the counter.

I have to pass the dead man laid out across the barstools to get behind the counter. I push through the hesitation and make for it, trying not to look at him as I pass, but I do. His wide-eyes stare motionless at me. I hold my breath, like I'm not already breathing the same air as them.

Behind the counter, a woman's body lay on the floor.

I halt, but my bare feet keep sliding, almost stepping on her. My toes coast into the edge of blood pooling beneath her face. It is sticky and cold. I pull my foot back, trying to wipe the liquid off my toes, onto the floor tiles.

The cash register drawer is open and empty.

A metal pan crashes to the floor in the kitchen that is hidden behind a set of swinging double doors, beyond the server's corpse.

My heart jumps. There's someone else inside, moving around back there. I glance around the diner. There is nowhere to hide.

The murmur of a male voice seeps between the only barrier separating us.

I step back.

The voice gets closer—louder. "Grab the fucking meat and let's go."

I glance back at the front door. *I might have enough time to get back to the car before they come out.*

"Now!" he says. "Or I'm leaving you."

I take another step back, bumping into the dead guy at the counter. *Oh, God.*

His corpse shifts, teetering closer to the stool's edge.

Where? Where can I hide? The fat man beside the door is big enough to hide me. I run to his booth.

The kitchen door bursts open.

I dive beneath the table and scrunch up against the wall, squeezing behind the dead man's bloated legs, drawing my feet in as close as I can get them.

A man steps out through the kitchen doors. "I don't know why you have to take so long with everything."

I wiggle a little farther back, trying to conceal myself behind the dead guy's cottage cheese thighs. His skin stretches over swollen blue veins that reach like roots toward his feet. His fat toes hang over the sides of his flip-flops. His big toenail is long, split at three places.

"Let's go," says the man.

A 12-year-old girl follows. Her arms are pale and thin, stuffed with food. She has a boy's haircut, but it doesn't take away any of her femininity.

"Hurry up," the man says, heading for the front door—toward me.

I lean harder against the wall behind me, but there is no farther to go.

The girl stops at the dead body now shifted on the stool. I can see her fully from where I hide. She bends a little, looking beneath the table.

The front door swings open. The man yells back into the Diner, "Come on, what are you doing?"

"There's…" Her voice is shaky.

"Let's go!" he says, disappearing with the swing of the door.

The girl takes a step for the door and drops a bag of chips. She bends to retrieve it, locking her eyes to mine. Her words come like a whisper, "Follow Atum."

The front door flings open again.

"Get in the fucking car," the man yells. "Right now!"

The girl scoops up the chip bag and stands up, running for the exit.

The door shuts and silence sweeps through the diner.

There's no way she just said that. Instinct urges me to save her, but I can't. I can't take that guy. I've already wasted so much time. So much time away from Carter, while he's trapped with those freaks. *Fuck*. My stomach pits. *How could I have left him?* The thought strangles me. I can't breathe. I inhale, taking in a breath full of the dead guy's toes.

A car starts outside.

I vomit all over his feet. How can I help her? I can't even help myself.

Tires screech as the car peels out of the parking lot.

I can't. I look down at the cracked toenails, the spent bile seeping between his toes, and crawl out from beneath the table. My knee scrapes through the vomit, bumping his bloated foot. I climb to my feet and look out at the parking lot.

They are gone and I'm left with the dead.

Umstead

THERE IS A PHONEBOOK BENEATH THE COUNTER, FROM 1967.

Hopefully Umstead's an old state park.

I thumb through the pages. In a dead world, each one weighs heavily between my fingers. I flip through them so fast I have to backtrack.

There it is: northwest of the city, close to the Raleigh airport.

I tear the page, and before I know it I'm leaving the diner in the past, taking the beltway. Every lane in front of me is empty.

I should've helped that girl.

I watch the restaurant fade behind me, disappearing behind a row of trees that hug the highway.

I get off at the Glenwood exit and take a left. There is a red barn restaurant on the right, at the top of a hill. Not long after is a wooden sign labeled: William B. Umstead State Park. Its entrance gate is drawn, blocking the asphalt road that could have taken me to the heart of the park.

I park, hop the fence, and walk from there. The old me would have let the gate stop me. *The faster I get this over with, the faster I get Carter back.*

I left that girl with that horrible guy. The guilt repeats through my thoughts, torturing me. I long for pieces of regret to fall off as I walk down the road.

A small ranger house sits back from the road on the left. It's old. Not as old as Seth's house, but old enough. Chills shoot up my spine and I keep going, deeper into the woods, down the river of asphalt.

The road opens up to a clearing. A modern-style Visitor Center is on the right. I try the glass double-doors at the front of the building. They are locked. Of course they are. I yank on them again, but they only shake with reluctance.

Thunder rumbles in the distance.

Shit. Theia's fear of the rain pierces through my thoughts. A storm is building and the urge to get inside crushes me. I peek through the door's glass. There is no one in the lobby.

I jerk on the door handles.

The sun begins to fade from the sky. The clouds build,

choking out the light. I run to the left side of the building. Windows frame the entire section. Inside are desks separated into two rows.

A man sits at the farthest desk, opposite a side door. His head is down, tucked into his arms. His light-grey shirt is embroidered on the sleeve, designating him as a park ranger. A matching green baseball style hat rests beside him on the desk. *He must be dead.*

I look around, searching for something to break the window of the door. There is a large rock to my left. It's likely to have been used to prop open that same door. I pick it up. Flakes of dirt break off into my palm. If I'm going to get Carter back, I have to become someone different from who I am. I chuck the stone at the glass of the door and turn, shielding my face.

Its window shatters. The stone thumps to the floor inside, giving me an "it's all clear."

The man lifts his head.

Jesus! I step backward. *He's not dead.*

He stands, pushing back the desk chair. It screeches at the force. He is fully dressed in a park ranger uniform, complete with a law enforcement duty-belt and holstered gun.

I wait for him to make the next move, after all he is the one with the gun.

The rain is coming.

Letting him make the first move means he isn't reacting to anything I do. Maybe it will indicate something about him: how nice he is, how much fucked-up shit he's gone through.

He doesn't smile, greet me, or introduce himself, but he does open the door. "I hope you're going to pay for that," he says.

Are you kidding?

He leaves the door open, walks toward a nearby refrigerator to his left, and withdraws a paper bag, tossing it to me.

I catch it.

"You look hungry," he says, looking me over. His eyes flow over my curves before he heads back to his desk.

I clear my throat, hoping it will spark conversation, but it doesn't. So, I take the desk adjacent to his and open the bag. Inside is a peanut butter and jelly sandwich on wheat, a pack of sliced carrots, and homemade cookies. I don't care if Mr. Park Ranger is going to talk at this point. I'm starving and my body is still making milk. Once the sandwich and veggies are gone, I pick up a cookie, staring at the other. I look at him. His head is back down in his arms. "Hey, do you want one?"

He lifts his head to look at me.

Rain pelts the roof of the building.

I gaze out the window. Water pours like a white sheet from the sky. Raindrops clink against the windowpanes behind us. White liquid flows down the glass like milk.

The Ranger stands, moving to the broken side door, turning its knob.

"No, don't," I say.

He looks at me and lets go of it. His hand moves to his holster and his fingers rest on the gun. "What do you know?"

I stuff the cookie in my mouth. I don't know what the hell I know.

He steps closer.

I don't know who he is. I have no idea what he's capable of. I'd pegged Seth as a good guy but he's not. Stacey's words haunt me, "*Keep your mouth shut.*"

"What"—he slams his hands on the desk, leaning in—"do you know?"

"I don't know," I say, leaning back from him. "One of my friends… this girl I know… she said not to go into the rain."

He lets go of the door knob. I can tell by his face that the answer isn't satisfactory. His cheeks are too stained with tears and his eyes are too red from crying. I know how much those tears don't wipe off, how they itch, how only more tears can wash the feeling away. I know what it feels like to cry so much that your eyes feel like lava, burning down to your skull.

Rain drums on the roof and thunder booms.

I jump, startled. The storm grows closer.

He chuckles and walks toward the lobby. "Come on. Let's sit somewhere more comfortable."

There is no place to run, so I follow, stuffing the other cookie in my mouth as I go.

He leads me to the sitting area in the middle of the room. Two wooden benches face each other in front of an empty fireplace. Its stone mantel stretches up the wall, begging to get out. He has taken the bench on the left, facing a dark hallway that leads into the opposite end of the building.

My whole life I felt like something lived in the darkness. There was no way to know when or if one of those creatures was coming. I take the opposite couch, leaving my back to the hallway and my nerves on end, laying down. I'm tired and dizzy. The clouds rain white water.

The Ranger sits on the edge of his bench, not bothering to sit back. He rubs his palms together, staring at me. His hands clamp together and his body tightens. His gaze shifts from me to the darkness beyond. He reaches for the gun in his holster, jerking it free as he stands.

Behind me, Jackal eyes pierce through the dark hallway. Anubis steps into the room.

"No!" I scream, jumping onto the couch—blocking the Park Ranger's aim.

He knocks me out of his way. I fall from the bench, whacking my head on the floor. Before I can look up, Ranger-boy is lying beside me.

Anubis steps onto the guy's hand, forcing the gun from his grip. The Ranger screams. Anubis scoops up the gun and steps off the guy's wrist.

The Ranger rolls to alleviate the pain—crying.

Anubis offers out a hand to me, helping me up. "He's getting anxious. You need to head out of here and find her."

"What about the rain?" I say.

He looks at the front doors and back at me. "After the rain." He turns, walks back toward the dark, then stops, retracing his steps, and hands me the gun.

I take it.

He pulls a hemp string—necklace—from his pocket and slides it over my head. The weight of the stone-cut scarab beetle weighs against my chest.

Anubis disappears.

"What the fuck was that?" Ranger-boy says, cupping a swollen wrist and sitting up.

"I don't know," I say. I should tell him something or explain what happened, but how can I? I don't know what he is. He's some kind of gatekeeper—Shadow-something or other. *I don't know what the fuck he is*. Though it is obvious he had come for me. I find Ranger-boy's eyes locked on me, waiting for more. "Listen," I say. "I'm supposed to meet some people here, but I don't know where they are. How big is this park?"

He begins to laugh. "I'm not helping you, or that freak."

I look at the gun in my hand. I don't want to have to force him to help me. I don't want this world to change who I am, but it already has. "They have my baby," I say. "If I don't do what they say, I won't get him back."

He says nothing.

I sink down onto the bench across from him. "I don't know what else to do."

"Over 5,000 acres. That's how big this park is. But there are only a few places they would meet up." He heads for the side door I threw a rock through.

Oh, thank God. He's going to help me.

"One deal," he says, stopping at the refrigerator. "You give me the gun."

I stare at it. I don't know how to use it, or even unlock it. But it is leverage I have and he doesn't. Granted, he could take it from me by force, and based on his size, would easily succeed. But the clock has already started ticking. The longer this takes, the longer I'll be away from Carter. I hand it over and force the word, "Deal."

He takes it and smiles, but it isn't friendly. It's the kind of smile a serial killer would give you.

I step backwards, bumping into the sofa. I handed him the gun. It's a stupid move and I regret it the moment the metal has left my fingers.

"One more thing," he says.

I cross my arms. Now that he has the gun, he can force any deals he wants.

He holsters the weapon. "The necklace."

The necklace had been important enough for Anubis to track me down and return it. My attacker in the house—the woman asking if I were Arden of Earth—tore it from me. Theia had mentioned it was for protection. I take it off, watching it spin as I hand it over. It isn't worth my life, or risking never seeing Carter again.

He takes it and heads for the door.

And so I follow Atum—the scarab beetle—as the girl in the diner had said.

Poison Drops

I FOLLOW RANGER-BOY TOWARD THE DOOR, BUT slow, keeping a few steps back. The clouds have lifted. The rain ceases as quickly as it poured.

He makes his way through the broken side-door, to a white Park Ranger pickup truck outside.

The engine ignites and idles.

I observe the sky, safe behind the building's window. Grey clouds have faded, leaving it blue. Rain covers the asphalt like white pebbles. I push the door open, not wanting to find out the reason Theia had feared the rain. I sprint for the passenger side door. Beads of rain coat the truck. I don't want to touch it—open it. I stand outside the door, staring at the raindrops bleeding together, dripping down the side of the vehicle.

The power window draws down. The Ranger who had never given me his name, yells from the driver's seat, "Get in. It's unlocked."

I look at the white drops pooling on the bottom of the door handle.

The door flings open, hitting me. He opened the door from the inside, pushing it outward toward me. Rain soaks my blouse. I gasp, expecting death, or at least pain. Nothing happens. I don't feel any different, but wet. I slide into the truck and pull the door closed.

Ranger-boy backs out of the parking lot and heads deeper into the park, flooring the gas pedal. I grab the Oh Shit Handle and lean against the door. He begins to laugh, a weird and mad laugh. The truck speeds through the parking lot to another, then skids to a stop at the bottom of a set of stairs. They led to a building, no doubt a bathroom. He fidgets with his belt—with the holster—and withdraws the gun.

I let go of the Oh Shit Handle and sit up, waiting for him to abuse me. I wait for him to confirm all my fears. Instead, he holds out his free hand. "I'm Ranger Steve."

I nod and shake his hand, giving him my name, "Arden."

"Come on," Steve says, hopping out of the vehicle.

I get out and stand beside the truck. *This is a bad idea.*

He takes a trail leading into the woods, disappearing behind the trees' leaves. It sounds like he's talking to someone.

Maybe they are here, and he isn't luring me into the woods to hack me into pieces. I run up the trail after him so fast I don't see him coming back down. We collide and I fall backward onto my ass. Mud cakes my pants—wet, cold mud. *Great.*

He offers me a hand, but I'm already dirty, so what the hell, I push off the ground myself. My hands press into the muck. I wipe them off onto the sides of my pants. He stares at me for a minute, so I shoot him a dirty look to get him moving.

Humidity weighs down the leaves of the trees, holding their wet branches back from us.

The trail goes on for a while. I could start a conversation, but Ranger Steve doesn't seem like the talkative type.

That's the one thing that drew me to Frank. He loves… loved to talk. I was working at Topsail Diner when I met him. It was autumn. Leaves were falling from the trees, raining down color, splattering, rolling, sticking to the sidewalks. Frank stumbled in with a group of men at three o'clock in the morning, reeking of beer. I'd been fighting with Jackson's dad, Shawn, for two years, and I hadn't had sex since his conception. Frank was supposed to be a one night stand, a release of frustration. He talked his way into my pants, into my life, and into keeping Carter. I loved him for it.

The leaves are now green and sunshine glistens off the white rain drops.

Life was finally getting good, and then this shit happened. *I can't do this.*

"Hey!" Ranger Steve yells back at me. "You coming?"

I snap out of my thoughts, letting them drift away. I can't breathe. *This mission's impossible.* I'm lost in a forest that is dripping with white rain. We come to a wooden platform in the middle of the trail—a wooden deck with a bench.

Ranger Steve leans on the guardrail, looking out at whatever it is the platform was built for.

The soft colors of evening begin to take over the sky. An airplane in the distance spills fresh white streaks that bleed into fat brush strokes.

Steve starts down a set of steps, moving further into the woods, further down the trail.

I don't want to go on anymore. I could stay there, rest on that bench, wait for the clouds to empty on me—wash away what's left of this life. I have nothing, nothing but the thought of getting Carter back. It isn't much, but it's enough for me to follow a stranger, deeper into the woods.

The steps are wet and a film of slickness coats them, leaving me teetering down each one.

Steve's disappeared in front of me. My heart jerks at the thought of being out here in the woods alone, but there is a path—one direction—I have to keep on. It isn't fair. The whole thing isn't fair. I have no choice. There is no choice. If I want Carter back, I have to play the game, fill a piece in their puzzle.

Steve's light-grey shirt gives away his location up ahead.

I hurry to catch up and then slow enough to keep me a few steps back, leaving that safe buffer for escaping.

He continues along a swelling stream, until he stops at a

cluster of cabins tucked between the trees.

I hesitate at the edge of the thinning tree line. It's an abandoned campground.

He yells toward the cabins, "Anyone out here?"

My heart sinks. He gave away our location. I'd seen every *Friday the 13th* movie there is—even the impossible-to-find number four. The last thing you do is head for the woods as night sets.

The leaves above us rustle, dumping their remaining raindrops on us. Their branches stretch—grow—reach down, and wrap around our torsos: restraining all movement.

"Who are you?" comes Theia's voice. "How did you find us?"

The screen door of a large building—a mess hall—at the campground's center creaks open. Brad emerges, gives me one look, and runs over, swiping his natural left hand across the branches binding me. The branches loosen, returning elegantly to their place, hanging above our heads.

Steve takes one look at Brad's robotic arm and wiggles to get to his holster.

Brad swipes his hand over Steve's branches and the tree flips the Ranger into the air, hanging him like a basket. He scoops me into his arms for a moment, then holds me out, looking at me. His eyes brighten. "You're alive. I thought I lost you."

The tightness in my shoulders eases. It's nice to see someone who instantly comforts me. I don't have to worry about doing this on my own.

A young black woman steps out of the rundown building. Her hair is kinky and dark. She looks like she's just been at Woodstock.

Nephthys? It can't be. She's so young. She's my age.

"It is funny you know me, Arden." She walks straight to me. "Even though I'm not what you expected."

Brad sets me down, and steps aside.

She reaches her right hand out for me to take it. A black scarab beetle is tattooed there, like the rest, but almost hidden against her skin tone.

I take her hand.

Black Magic Woman

We leave the campground in the Ranger truck. Brad drives, with Nephthys in the passenger's seat. I'd taken the seat behind him, and Theia shoved Steve in the back, pushing him in the middle between us.

His hands are still bound with entangled branches. The tires hum beneath us. We stay quiet, listening for the sound of aircraft —the sound of pursuit. The weight of the air and silence is suffocating. Brad takes the freeway to a destination no one will diverge, heading west for the Blue Ridge Mountains.

Nephthys twirls a rifle between her legs. Steve sits pissed-off that his hands are still bound. Theia had taken a seed from her pocket, coaxing a vine to grow—to split through the seed—and twisted it around Steve's wrists, intertwining around his arms.

I lean against the window. Airplanes soar overhead, cross hatching the sky with white lines. Four hours drifts into bouts of dozing off. The truck has climbed into the mountains where the forest thickens.

"Tell me what happened to my son," I say, staring at her—staring at Nephthys. She is the one I'm supposed to sacrifice. She is the one who knows why.

"Have you ever heard of a decan?" she says, leaving her eyes to the road ahead.

"No," blurts out Steve, like he'd been invited into the conversation.

"Are you an Aquarius or Capricorn?" she asks.

"She's an Aquarius," says Theia. "We almost have the same birthday." She looks at Ranger Steve. "You must be a Capricorn."

"You see," says Nephthys. "Ancient Egyptians studied the decans almost religiously. There are 36 of them. Each zodiac contains 3 decans. So the sign of Aquarius has three. You were born under only one of those."

"You're saying this is all because of my horoscope?" I can't believe that.

"You are alive because your ruling planet allows you to be," says Nephthys.

Brad looks at me through the rearview mirror. "I think it's been a while since we've gone through this." He glances at Nephthys. "They started spraying the skies over a decade ago. The conspiracy theory about chemtrails has, just recently, started to make its way into the mainstream.

"They've been spraying us with toxins for years." His eyes return to me and back at the road—to the sky indeed being painted with lines. "We didn't know what it was: heavy metals, bacteria, nano-technology."

"First it was a way for them to dispose of toxic waste at a low cost," says Nephthys. "Then the military conducted their typical research into bio-warfare."

"This time it worked," says Brad. "This time they took out all but the second decans of Aquarius and Capricorn."

"Why not all of us?" I ask. *Why not kill us all? Why save some?*

"We are easier to control," says Brad.

Theia, who has been silent beside me, speaks, "They *thought* we'd be easier to control." She gives Nephthys a look like they have been expecting this to happen.

Brad turns the truck down a hidden driveway, off the beaten highway, leading into the outskirts of Asheville, North Carolina—snuggled within the Blue Ridge Parkway.

The tires splash through deep puddles.

A small house rests at the driveway's end. I only have enough time for one more question. Instead of asking who sprayed the world with toxins—assuming it was likely a corporation or evil man—I ask, "Why have they sprayed the skies? Why did they kill my son and husband?"

"Too many people were waking up," Nephthys says. "Too many people were following the feeling that there has to be something more. That there is something more than what we've been led to believe."

Brad stops the truck outside of the house. Moss covers its roof and old glass windows frame its right side, creating a greenhouse effect.

Theia pulls a seed from her side pouch and wiggles her fingers. A vine emerges from the seed and wraps around her fingers. "If we only knew what we are actually capable of, it would change the world."

"Both our worlds," Nephthys says, glancing back at her. Her pupils don't dilate, but her irises shimmer like a cat's night-shine.

They all hop out and flood inside, taking Ranger Steve with them. I haven't awakened from anything. The world still carries a heaviness to it—a fog. Wall-to-wall indoor plants lift the atmosphere of the house. The floors are all dirt and the walls are all curved to create rooms with no corners. A dining room and kitchen are to the left. A living room furnished only with a circle of pillows, is on the right. It smells faintly of the woodstove at its far wall.

Nephthys heads to the circle. The plants move a little as she passes. She takes the pillow in front of the woodstove. It is by far the warmest place on those cold mountain nights. Her eyes shine as she turns. I swear her pupils draw into vertical lines for a second.

I sit down two pillows away with my back to the windows. *Is this how Judas felt as he kissed Jesus?* I am the one who would deliver her to death. I am her Judas. *Does she know I am to betray her?*

She smiles at me.

"Nephthys…" I say.

She raises her hand, refraining further conversation. "That's what they call me." She glances at Theia and Brad with Steve in the kitchen. "Call me by my birth name: Chastity." She laughs. "Though, that hasn't held up too well."

I look past her, at the trees outside, at the leaves beginning to blow against night's returning breeze.

"Theia brought a breast pump with her," says Nephthys. "It's in your room. Why don't we talk later?"

My cheeks burn and I feel the fabric of my shirt dampen as my milk drops, releasing a little at the mention.

"Jordan!" she calls towards the kitchen.

A young girl, maybe 12-years-old, emerges from a side room opposite the kitchen. It is the girl from the diner. She has a new nose-ring, the kind a bull wears, and a streak of blue in her hair. She enters the room with interlaced fingers, giving Nephthys a slight bow.

"You'll be bunking together," says Nephthys. Her gaze is on the plant beside her. She waves her fingers near the leaf's tip. The plant stretches and grows. "We'll talk more after dinner."

The pre-teen leads me down the hallway, to the bedroom. It is stuffed with two sets of bunk beds and an end table. A small circular window sits above the table, overlooking a backyard garden. Jordan flops down on the bottom bunk to the left, and grabs a pen off the end-table.

"You know when shit went down the other day? I was sitting in my room and started bleeding—down there," she says, pointing to her pants. "What a time to get your fucking first period, huh?"

I sit on the bed across from her and try to cover the wet circle expanding across my blouse.

"My mom never had the *birds and the bees* talk with me. Why would she? She was too busy doing lines of coke with her boyfriend…" She looks out the window. "He died not long after we left the diner."

Gusts of wind pound against the windowpane. Her eyes drift up to the noise.

"A storm is coming." She sits up and leans toward me. "It's going to be worse than you can imagine. They're all looking for us. They won't stop till we're all dead."

There's a knock at the door.

I jump.

The girl smiles and begins to draw on her wrist.

Brad peeks in around the door. “How’s your head?”

I reach for the stitches on the back of my head, stopping short, already feeling the swollen skin around it. I wince.

“Let me take a look.” Brad joins me on the bed and parts the hair with both hands: his mechanical and real fingers. The robotic parts don’t make noise, which surprises me. The parts in his arm move up and down as he moves the hair back from the stitches. “We should cut that and clean it better.”

I hang my head and nod in agreement. I’m surrounded by strangers and I can’t help thinking about last night: holding Carter, smelling him. *The breast pump*. I shoot to a stand, whack my head on the top bunk, and fall backwards onto the mattress, holding my head in pain.

Jordan and Brad stay silent.

I moan and sit up.

Brad takes a seed from his pocket and swirls it in the flesh of his palm. A sprout curls out and flows into two leaves which continue until a full female cannabis plant buds from it.

“Awesome,” says Jordan as she slides off the bunk.

Brad sets the plant on the floor. Its roots are white and clean. He tears a bud off, cups it in his hand, then opens it to reveal the dried flower.

Jordan brakes off a piece.

Brad hands me the remaining part and takes out a glass bowl, for smoking, from his pocket. He looks at Jordan with disapproval. She hands over the piece of bud without having to be asked.

He looks at me. "Well?"

The tips of my ears burn. I look away—out the window. "Oh, no thank you."

He lights up, inhales, and exhales a thick plume of smoke. "I heard you gave it up when you were"—his voice drops—"pregnant."

It's true. The best part about smoking was the great sex that came with it. I'm a control freak and the only time I can let go—completely—is when I'm stoned out of my mind. That precise thing landed me knocked up. For the past few years I was too busy trying to survive to care about great sex. Who needs it anyway?

Brad lets out another puff and passes it to Jordan. "You know it was the Rockefellers who pushed to make pot illegal? Before that, it was a common remedy in every doctor's medicine bag. When Ford made the first car, it was powered by hemp. Anyway, have you ever asked why? Why a plant, part of nature, was made illegal? Yet pharmaceutical companies push synthetic man-made chemicals instead of the natural compounds found in plants—the precise thing they are derived from? Marijuana isn't just illegal, it's classified as an opiate."

I laugh. "What are you talking about?"

He takes the bowl back from Jordan and puffs, holding his breath. "It's not because of intoxication." Smoke floats out between his lips. "Shit man. Alcohol is fucking horrible in comparison. You ever drive on weed… you drive slow as shit."

I start to feel lightheaded.

"No." His eyebrows lift. "They made it illegal for a reason. You'll see."

Theia enters, carrying a black case—the breast pump. She makes eye contact with me and hands it over.

Jordan stares at the case. Her eyes shoot to me, then to my breasts. "I know what that is."

The atmosphere shifts. It tightens.

"I had a brother… just a few days ago. Mom thought she'd try breastfeeding. Turns out you forget shit when you're snorting coke all the damn time."

Brad begins to laugh. "Shit Jordan. Don't kill my buzz."

Jordan smiles and sits back against the wall. Her voice lowers, "Your baby is the one missing?"

I get up and take the case from Theia, scooting past her into the hallway. No way am I going to talk about it.

Voices carry from the living room.

I walk closer until the conversation becomes clear.

"So what are they?" Ranger Steve asks.

"Aliens, humans in an alternate dimension," says Nephthys. "Or my favorite is the people of Duat. You pick what conspiracy theory you want to believe in. They are all the same thing."

I lean against the wall, trying to peek into the room while remaining hidden. Nephthys' eyes shine as they shift to me.

"Come on in Arden," she says. "Your friend, Steve, here is learning all about the things that hide in your bedroom corners as you sleep." She laughs.

Steve shifts on the pillow beside her. His hands are free, yet close enough to his duty belt if needed.

"Relax," she says to him, "you're safe here. There are no corners. No dark places to hide. No portals to creep out of."

"What do they want with us?" I say.

"It's not us they want," Nephthys says.

"What are we?" I say.

"His last hope," she says.

What the fuck's that supposed to mean? "That's not an answer."

"You didn't come here for answers," she says.

The tips of my ears burn. It's true. I hadn't come for answers, but how does she know? I cross my arms. I would've been offended, but she's right. The only reason I'm here, is for her—I came for her.

"Come sit down with us." She gestures to the empty pillow on her other side.

I search her eyes, waiting for them to shine again, reveal how evil she is—like those creatures that have stolen Carter. I want to see her pupils dilate into lines, proving that I'm doing right by sacrificing her.

They never do.

I take a seat. The plant behind Nephthys catches my attention. A single, bell-shaped, purple flower hides in its full green leaves.

She too turns her focus to it and smiles. "It is called belladonna."

Steve glances at me. A grin spreads across his lips and he takes in a deep inhale. "Deadly nightshade."

"Let's begin," says Nephthys. "You are what is left of the human race. You are the life givers. Have you ever noticed your house plants still live after not watering them for days? Do you notice your front lawns need to be mowed twice as much as your neighbors'?" She looks at me. "Did you ever notice that your children hated to be inside?"

My weight shifts with unease. Jackson spent so much time outside that my house looked like a dump. I hung clothes outside to dry, not because it saved us money and drew less energy from the electrical grid—those things were just extra benefits. I hung the laundry outside as an excuse to get the boys outside more. On summer nights, Jackson insisted his bedroom window be open so he could hear the bugs. In the winter, I could only bear it being open a quarter of an inch. There were no bugs singing then, but trees whispered bedtime stories, and a neighboring owl would sing him to sleep.

I look down at the rug. In its center is a swastika. My heart jerks. I look at Nephthys. She follows my eyes to the symbol, looks back at me, and smiles. I don't get it. Why would she be sitting around a swastika? She's far from white or what I expect a Nazi to be. Her eyes narrow like she's reading my thoughts. Maybe she is.

"Hey," Theia says, startling me. She appears like a ghost out of nowhere behind me, taking the empty pillow beside me.

Brad and Jordan join us.

"Where the fuck is Osiris?" Nephthys yells over my shoulder, toward the hallway. She straightens her spine and rests her wrists on crossed knees, like she's going to meditate. Brad and Jordan have already taken identical positions. Steve looks to me and we both loosely mirror them, like we're in some yoga class.

Nephthys closes her eyes and the others follow, lightly tilting their noses toward the sky. Each lets out their own tone of "Ah-Ohm."

Nephthys' chest inflates with a deep inhale.

I glance over at Steve. He's already attempting to fit in.

"Hey guy…s…" A man walks into the room. He notices the mediation circle and shuts up, glancing at me. He wears a black cloak, identical to the one worn by the fleeting pedestrian outside the pyramid. Dirt covers most of his face, but he's easily the most attractive person in the room now. He smiles. My jealousy melts off and I can't help but reciprocate a smile.

He moves across the room, disappearing behind me—out of view. I could see him if I turned my head. Instead I convince myself he's taken a seat somewhere behind me, not preparing to stab a knife through my back. I hope these are only fears my mind is conjuring. He's probably just sitting behind me, getting ready to join whatever trip they're all taking.

I glance around at them.

Nephthys stares at me. She's been sitting there watching me, but for how long?

The thoughts in my head had drowned out being present in the moment.

She lifts her arms to the ceiling in prayer pose, takes in a deep breath, lets out an "Ah-Ohm," and centers her hands in front of her heart, whispering, "Namaste."

"Namaste," the man, Osiris, says from behind me—directly behind me. If he leans forward, I'll be able to feel his breath against the back of my neck. He moves to the pillow beside Theia.

"This is Steve and Arden," Brad says in an almost whisper. "They are with us now."

Steve says hello, but Osiris ignores him, staring at me.

He begins, "The guard is—"

"No business," Nephthys' voice comes soft, but stern. She grabs a ceramic bowl sitting beside her, dumping its contents—an assortment of seeds—into her hand. "Choose one."

The shapes and colors take hold of me. Some are long like black rice. A few look like beans. There are little black dots: the smallest balls I've ever seen. The one that catches my eye is something I've never seen before: a small star-shaped seed.

Nephthys offers out her open palm to me.

I pin the seed beneath my nail and drag it closer, pinching it, rolling it out of her palm into mine.

Then Steve takes one.

Nephthys dumps the rest back into the bowl and hands Brad a pouch at her hip. "Brad you go first."

He digs into the pouch, withdrawals a seed, and rolls it in the flesh of his palm. Its shell splits open and the tiniest sprout spins into a pair of leaves. Within a blink, he has turned the seed into a bushel of potatoes, hanging from full green leaves.

Jordan follows, ending up with carrots. Nephthys forms celery that grows twice as fast as the others. Brad's seed turns into a small, short plant that looks more ornamental than edible. He notices me staring at it—trying to figure out what the hell it is—and plucks a leaf off, offering it to me.

I take it.

"You know that smell?" he says.

I put it to my nose. *Oregano*. It is oregano. I'd never seen it before being dried, crushed, and stuffed into a shaker.

The room is silent.

"Steve," Nephthys says, "let's see what you can do."

"What do you mean?" he asks, holding out the tiny seed in his palm.

"Just cup your hand around it," she says, "and picture it growing in your mind."

He tightens his fist around the seed and squeezes, looking more like he has to shit as opposed to creating something. Sweat beads on his forehead. He opens his hand. Failure fills his face. The seed looks the same. He groans with frustration.

"Your biggest problem will be impatience," Nephthys says.

Her eyes move from him to me. She nods.

I close my hand and open it. I don't expect anything to happen and it doesn't. I look down at the seed. Nothing has changed. Part of me expected it to grow, for something—anything—to happen. *What if they figure out I'm a fraud? How will I ever get Carter back?* Sweat builds in my palm.

"Your biggest problem," says Nephthys, "will be believing in yourself—finding worth. You must realize that this will take time and—"

"I don't have time for this shit." I clench the seed in my fist. *I should grab her and drag her down the driveway, into the dark corner of a room, get it all over with*. Every moment I'm here, I'm not with Carter. I have to get back to him. *This is taking too long*. I stand, throw the seed to the floor, and storm back to my room.

What does she know? She doesn't know me.

I spent the remainder of the day's light in endless thoughts and bouts of letting my eyes drip with tears. Thoughts of how I'd get Nephthys to do what I needed. Maybe if I got Brad to help me, we could tie her up, drag her down the mountain, find a house, and enter its shadows. What if he rats me out instead? I don't know him that well. He's just some guy who was nice to me in high school. And that was years ago.

The sound of airplanes rumble outside, barreling closer.

Stranger

"WAKE UP SUNSHINE," JORDAN SAYS, SITTING BESIDE me on the mattress. She sets a seed on the end-table. "You ready to try again?"

The mattress bounces as she stands up.

"It didn't work," I say. "I'm not like you"—I look at the doorway—"like any of you."

She smiles, heads for the threshold, and waves for me to follow.

It has been another night away from Carter and I feel it in my breasts. They ache with fullness. I swing my legs over the bed's edge, letting them hang like the defeat I feel. I don't want to be here, with strangers. I want to hold Carter. My soul aches.

I make it into the kitchen before realizing—noticing—that my feet have moved me, that I'm still alive.

Theia hurries toward me with a cabbage leaf in hand, pressing it to my breast.

What the—? I back away. *What the hell?*

"Chill," she says, grabbing my hand to replace her own, atop the cabbage leaf. "It'll help bring down the burning."

I take the leaf. It is cold. I slide it down my shirt. It's really cold. I absorb the pain, letting it thaw against the burning mastitis infection starting.

Nephthys is in the kitchen with Jeff, who's cooking at the stovetop beside her. They are in their own world. He's smiling and she's pushing her hair back in a way that demands he notice. She catches me staring and goes back to it—no judging, no jealousy, no second glances. Jeff had been that guy in high school—the one you desperately picture yourself with every night before bed. The one you masturbate to.

I close my eyes and, for a moment, I'm back home.

Frank's warm hand glides around my waist from behind. His lips press against my right check. It's a Monday evening. He's getting dressed for work as I crack an egg on the stove. We started eating breakfast for dinner once Frank began nightshift. Jackson would pretend we'd all just woken up, that our lives weren't slaves to a modern society of unnatural rhythms.

"Good morning, beautiful," he says as his lips pull away. "How'd you sleep?"

"Why?" I ask. "You don't really care."

He smiles. "Wow. Where did that come from?"

I don't reply. I sift the eggs and dump them onto a frying pan.

"Why don't you go to bed after I've gone?" he says. "You look like you could use some sleep."

"Are you saying I look like shit?" I don't mean to say it, but I'm so goddamn tired. So tired of him working during bedtime routine. So tired of his side of the bed being empty.

"Why would I say that?" His arms wrap tighter around me. He spins me, staring into my eyes. "You're safe with me."

"Arden…." Frank's voice disappears into Theia's.

I open my eyes. She's holding out a plate piled with eggs, bacon, and cantaloupe. Nephthys, Jeff, Brad, Jordan, and Ranger Steve have taken seats at the table. Brad smiles at me, but I tuck my head down to my plate, and squeeze in at the far end of the booth, away from everyone.

Nephthys stands, pushing back the chair, and screams, "You're safe!"

What the—? Her words cut into my heart. *Carter?* My whole body jerks to see what she's referring to.

She sprints for the front door, reaching it before it swings open.

A man stumbles into the house, covered in black tar.

My heart sinks. It's not Carter. His empty hands drip with some sort of melted asphalt.

"Jesus, Osiris," says Nephthys, waving for the others to do something.

Brad, Theia, Jordan, and Jeff scatter like cockroaches: grabbing towels, stove mittens, and even a house coat beside the door.

Ranger Steve remains at the table, eating, staring at me.

The group returns, and one by one take to their seats. Nephthys serves up another plate. Osiris enters the kitchen, wiping the tar from his face with a white towel. Nephthys offers a plate to him.

"No," he says, heading toward the hallway. "I should get cleaned up first."

The group roars in protest, coaxing him to the table.

"It's warm now," says Nephthys. "Eat, and then you can do all that other stuff."

He slides in beside me. Nephthys places the plate in front of him and goes back for another. He scarfs the whole thing down before she returns with a second helping.

"Did you find it?" says Nephthys.

Osiris shakes his head no and devours the food. He picks up a napkin, wiping his mouth, smearing a blotch of tar across his cheek.

The cabbage leaf grows warm and limp. I pull it from my shirt and set it on the table.

He looks up from his plate.

Embarrassment sweeps through me.

"What were you looking for?" Ranger Steve perks up with the possibility of adventure.

Osiris looks to Nephthys for approval before saying, "The Dagger of Anubis."

My heart races. I'd just been with Anubis... *The dagger.*

"It's made of a clear crystal," says Nephthys. "It's shaped like the Ankh. The symbol of life. The Egyptian cross. The crystal forms a dagger at the cross' bottom. Its hilt is a crystal tear-drop."

"What does it do?" I say.

Ranger Steve's gaze turns attentive, letting his eggs turn cold.

Had he heard me call Anubis by his name?

"It takes away life." Brad gets up first, and heads into the living room. Jordan, Jeff, and Theia funnel behind him. I don't want to follow. I want to grab Nephthys and get the hell out of here—get it over with already.

"That's the purpose of a dagger," says Steve. "To kill someone?" He gets up and places his plate in the sink. It clunks to the bottom.

"It traps the soul," says Osiris, sliding out of the booth.

"Isn't that what death is?" I say. A release of your soul.

"Not even close," says Nephthys, moving into the adjoining room with the others.

Osiris begins to follow. He hesitates—about to say something—then continues on.

Steve comes back toward the table, diverting from the others path, nodding in the direction of the hallway—like I'm supposed to follow him.

I grab my plate, taking it to the sink.

Steve intercepts my path, grabs my arm, and yanks me down the hallway to my bedroom, leaving a trail of egg bits on the floor. He throws me into the room and closes the door.

"I'll scream," I say.

"That wouldn't be too smart of you." He lifts his shirt, tapping his holster.

"What do you want?" I say.

"Turns out you've made a deal with the devil," he says.

"Fuck you." I go for the door he guards. He pushes me back. I stumble, hitting my head on the top bunk bed and fall onto the bottom mattress. The plate still in my hand, falls to the floor, spinning in vibration.

"You have a secret," he says.

Rain begins to drum on the roof.

He starts to undo his belt buckle. "I'll keep your secret."

"No," I say.

"Or I can tell them… that you were talking to those freaks… that you have a plan. I assume it's not in their best interest." His pants fall to his ankles and he steps closer, out of them. "It's your choice."

I lay back on the bed and stare at the wall, wishing there was a corner—wishing the walls weren't round.

The mattress sinks as he climbs on top of me.

I'd give anything to be with Carter. *How important is the choice of sex? How much could it change my life? How much could it matter in this fucking world?*

He kisses my neck.

Tears roll down my cheeks. *How much could it matter?*

His hands slide beneath my butt and pull my pelvis closer to his. I feel the stiffness of his skin press against my pants.

No. How can you just lay there, and not at least fight? How can you just give it away? No. I push him off with all my force.

He falls to the floor.

I duck my head beneath the top bunk and go for his pants on the floor—the holster—the gun. I fumble through the fabric, spinning the duty belt, looking for it. I find the holster and pull on the gun. It doesn't budge.

He laughs from the floor behind me and stands up.

I tug the gun harder. It still doesn't budge. He steps forward. I have one more chance. I loosen my grip and then yank, hard and fast. The gun frees. I aim it at him and pull the trigger.

Nothing. Nothing happens.

Shit.

He comes at me full force.

I glance at the gun, tighten my knuckles around it, and punch him in the face with it. He stumbles backward. I sprint for the door, clear it, and glance at the living room full of people.

They won't help me. Why would they? I run down the

hallway, to the door at the end of the corridor—the bathroom—and burst into it, slamming it shut. I go to turn the lock, but there is none.

The shower is going. Steam circles me like a dream. Osiris' tar-soaked clothes are in a heap outside the shower. My heart pounds with the stillness of movement. *Is he still in here?* He has to be.

There's no time. I press my back against the door and dig my heels into the tile, bracing for the impact coming.

The shower stops.

Confession

RANGER STEVE RAMS THE DOOR.

It pounds against my back, opens a crack, and then slams shut.

"You fucking bitch!" Steve screams through it, "I'm going to fucking kill you!"

The metal hooks scrape against the shower rod as the curtain draws back. Osiris steps out, dripping wet. He looks at the gun in my hand and raises his arms like a zombie, stepping closer, unafraid.

I close my eyes. Tears pour out of them. I can feel his breath. I can feel his energy. I open my eyes to find him leaning inches away, bracing the door with his right arm.

"Fucking bitch!" Steve pounds on the door.

I flinch.

Osiris stands calm, quiet. His eyes scan mine.

I look away to the fogged mirror, trying to escape the anger from outside the door and the full on male nude pressed up an inch from me.

The faint voices of the crowd erupt down the hall, coming closer. Steve silences. Ivy leaves stretch—grow—beneath the door, entangling my toes.

"Everything okay in there?" Nephthys says through the door.

"Yea, we're cool." Osiris smiles, releases his hand—his weight—from the door, and makes his way for a towel hung beside the shower. A winged scarab beetle tattoo takes up his entire back.

A rush of blood flows through my veins and milk drips out of my breasts, wetting my shirt. My cheeks burn and I cross my arms. The gun hangs heavy in my hand . I clear my throat, mustering up a, "Thank you."

"You're welcome," he says.

"Don't you want to know?" I say.

He wraps the towel around his waist and faces me.

My knees grow weak. "Don't you want to know what happened?"

He steps closer.

I turn my eyes to the ground. I don't know what to look at. I'd seen movies with guys whose bodies looked like his, but I'd never actually been so close to one. My body's screaming things I don't want to think about.

"Do you want to tell me?" he says, sliding his fingers alongside my cheek and into my hair.

I look at him. He leans closer. His pupils dilate into vertical lines. I gasp, try to push myself into the door—through the door—away from him.

"I don't understand..." I say. He's one of them. He's the cloaked man outside Tekk Corp's green pyramid. He'd seen me with Anubis. My face must say it all. I push him away and raise the gun to his chest. *He'll give me away.*

He places his palm over the barrel's end and steps closer. "I'm sorry. Sorry that you lost your child, your husband, your... baby."

Chills rip through my body in one wave. *He could help me: get Carter for me. Then I won't have to waste my time here.* "Will you take me to your world? Help me get him back?"

"No," he says.

"What do you mean, no?"

"You don't know my world. Evil controls the corners. Very few know about your world. Those who do, do not allow passage to just anyone. There is a reason our world has few corners and yours is filled with them." He sits on the toilet seat. "The people who have your baby have control. You don't know how many years I've had to plan this, what I've had to do to get here." He looks at the floor. "What I've given."

I step toward him, breaking the vine tangled around my toes, and kneel before him. "Please."

"What is it he wants?" Osiris' eyes relax back to circles.

I bury my face into the towel of his lap. I can't tell him. He'll never help me. None of them will. "I'm not one of them. I'm not special. I don't have any powers. I'm not one of them. I just want my baby."

Before I can lose all control, his weight shifts, nudging me up. He grabs my wrist and drags me out of the bathroom. The hallway is empty. Light conversation carries down the hallway from the living room. Osiris drags me into that room. All their eyes fall on him as we enter—to me—and then to the gun. He flings me into the circle, onto the swastika, and lets go. I fall on all fours before them.

"Tell them," he says. "It will set you free."

I look back at him. *What does he know about freedom?*

He crosses his arms and stands firm.

The weight of the rain drums heavy on the roof. White liquid splashes against the windows. I can't leave now even if I want to. My fingers brush the fabric of my shirt. A rash has developed where I fell in the rain the day before. It's begun to blister.

I look at the floor. Tears drain from my eyes, but I refuse to cry. I won't let them see how weak I am. At least Steve will have no control over me. I draw in a breath and force it out of my lungs. Theia said they'd help me, but that was before she knew I was a fraud, worthless, different from them. I look at Nephthys. "If I deliver you to them, they'll give Carter back to me."

The room is still.

Nephthys leans forward, setting her clenched fist on the floor in front of me. My tears drip, seeping through her fingers. They fan open.

There is that rare seed—the star seed. A small sprout has curled out of its cracked shell and begun forming a primary root.

"Don't you see?" I look at her. "I'm not like you."

She grabs my hand and drops the seed into my palm, closing my fingers around it, softly saying, "It's yours."

It's impossible.

"I can teach you how to harness it," she says. "Then we can go get Carter."

There's no evidence she's lying to me. I wait for her eyes to dart away, to give me the sign she should be sacrificed as quick as possible, but they don't.

The sound of distant airplanes comes into earshot.

I can't waste any more time here. *I want to go now.* A tear drips onto my hand and drains into the curve of my palm. The sprout grows leaves.

The airplanes roar closer. They sound lower, more dangerous than before.

Nephthys looks up at the ceiling, as if peering through it.

The rumble gets louder—closer. The ground vibrates.

"Basement!" she screams.

Everyone darts for the hallway, including me.

The window beside the wood stove explodes. A hole blasts through the front wall, throwing the dirt foundation.

Theia falls. I'm pushed past her by the person behind me. The roof cracks and rain pours in. She screams. I stop, turning to go back for her, but am pulled back down the hallway by someone else. Another explosion wipes out any noise that is left. My eardrums ring with a high-pitched hum. I follow whoever is in front of me down a dark stairwell. The wooden steps shake with the explosions.

Brad swipes his hand around the room, stimulating lichens—illuminating the hole we are in. It is a dug-out basement in the earth. I huddle against the wall, hugging my knees in. If the earth caves in, perhaps the fetal position will save me.

Jordan stumbles down the stairs. Her eyes widen as she searches the small space. "Where's Nephthys?"

Osiris slides down the steps, knocking Jordan off her feet, catching her as she falls.

A bomb explodes overhead, shaking the ground above us.

A dark silhouette rushes down toward us, through the cloud of dust. It's Jeff. He's dragging Theia's motionless body behind him. Her feet touch the ground and he lets go, collapsing in tears.

Brad runs over to her, digging around in his pouch. He dumps a handful of seeds on the ground, rolling his fingers through them. Jordan reaches over, resting her hand atop his, shaking her head. It's no use. Theia is dead.

Brad hangs his head and grunts, barely holding back the pain of his heart ripping into two. Jordan squeezes his hand, but he doesn't move.

She's been my friend. I can't move. It had been years since she came over to my house for slumber parties, years since we passed notes in English class. My body numbs. I've lost so much that reality is losing its grip—its power over me.

Another explosion shakes the ground. Light penetrates the stairs from above. There is nothing left of the house to cover us. Rainwater won't fill the hole enough to drown us, but I'm already suffocating in grief.

Black Hole

WE'RE DEEPER THAN SIX FEET BENEATH THE GROUND.

The bombs stop, but the rain drums.

Jordan conjures up some strawberries and Jeff grows carrots. We eat and let reverence fill the void of conversation. The bombers have pulled out. We only have to wait for the rain to stop. Brad sits beside Theia's body and cries. It feels like hours in the cold, dark hole. And the rain refuses to stop.

A helicopter approaches from the West. The sound of its blades cut through the rain like a bullet, piercing each of our hearts.

"Shit." Brad stands, staring at the staircase, then looks at Theia.

We should have braved the rain.

"Soil," says Osiris.

Brad nods, climbs what steps remain, and raises his arm to the hole in the ground—the only thing supplying us with oxygen. A tree grows from his palm and stretches for the opening. Its branches unfold into buds, and leaves spread out, shading the entrance. The trunk reaches up and the roots entangle his hand. As it grows, he braces his left hand with his robotic right. The light penetrating the opening disappears. He sets the roots on the ground and they dig in, like they've always been there. The leaves and branches compensate for any vulnerabilities, cutting off the opening completely.

The sound of an approaching helicopter amplifies, despite the enclosure. The ground vibrates as it touches down up above.

Brad wipes the illumination from the walls.

Muffled orders carry out over top.

This will be my grave. I'll suffocate down in the dark, never make it to see the clouds again, never see my baby, never smell the air again. I gasp. I can't breathe. There is no air. I sink to the ground, pushing my back harder against the wall. There is nowhere to go. My fingers brush Osiris'. I inch them away, but he takes my hand, squeezing it. I hold on. I take a breath. *I can get through this*. I have to. I can breathe, it's just my stupid mind telling me I can't.

Something explodes up above. The roots of Brad's tree shake.

Light cracks through the top of the stairs.

"Brad," Jeff whispers.

A small portion of the wall illuminates.

Jeff digs around in his pouch. Another explosion goes off. Dirt crumbles from the ceiling. He squeezes a seed in his hand until it grows, filling the gap between the stairs and us, setting its roots on the ground.

It shoots into another full-size tree.

Osiris pulls me to my feet. Brad presses his hand against the trunk, encouraging its growth so we'll have a larger barricade. Jordan leaves the wall, taking cover behind the tree trunk, to the backside of the basement. Jeff moves around it, front and center before Theia's lifeless body.

Osiris pushes me behind the tree with Jordan. "Stay here."

I clutch Jordan in my arms, lean against the tree trunk, and peek around it. Brad has wrapped vines around Theia, propping her up like she's standing at the foot of the steps, like a scarecrow.

The ground vibrates with another explosion. White noise, dust, and light flood the basement.

Shit. I squish myself up against the tree, against Jordan. Gunshots splatter into the earth all around us. Jordan pulls me closer.

Footsteps clamber down the steps.

A deep voice, masked by a respirator, descends the basement, "Sir, they're not here."

"Make sure," says another.

They light up the basement. Bullets splatter against the bark.

"Ouch!" Jordan grunts in pain, cupping her arm.

"There!" says one of the men.

The onslaught ceases and a guardsmen reaches around the trunk, tearing Jordan away from me, throwing her to the ground on the opposite side of the tree. Bright white gloves of a Tyvek biohazard suit grab for me. The rubber gloves skid across my scalp, gripping the stitch of my hair, and throw me to the ground beside Jordan. The guy points a gun at my face.

"Wait," says the other man. He steps closer. His face is bloody and bruised. The cut in his lip oozes as he says, "You!"

It's the Guardsman Jeff nearly killed behind the bookstore.

"Where's your friend?" He grabs my cheeks and squeezes as hard as he can. Then presses the gun against my forehead.

Where is he? I try to look around, but the man squeezes harder. *Where's Brad?* Where are any of them? All three men have disappeared.

Jeff jumps out of the darkness beside the steps and hammers down on the man. The guard's rubber gloves slip from my cheeks and the gun swings away. Ivy vines fling from Jeff's fingertips and wrap around the man's neck.

Briers twist from Jordan's hands. Thorns wrap around her attacker and tighten like a cobra. Holes poke through his biohazard suit, letting in the air.

Osiris appears from the opposite wall and snaps the guy's neck.

A shot fires.

Jeff falls to the ground, groaning.

A third guardsman, suited in biohazard gear, stands at the top step, holding a gun. Bullets rain down the stairs.

I roll toward the edge of the basement room.

Jeff throws a vine of ivy at the guardsman. It wraps around his neck. The man drops his gun, trying to free the vine with both hands.

I stand, grab the bottom of my attacker's respirator, and rip it off. He gasps, trying to fill his lungs, trying to hold his breath. Shots spray down the stairwell and across the dirt toward us. A bullet cuts through the guard's leg. He screams and starts to choke. Blood sprays from his lips and drips out his nostrils. He looks at me like I'm some kind of a disgusting, repulsive monster.

I look down at my fingers gripping the respirator so tight they have turned white, and let go. The dark veins running up my arm give a faint green glow. I release the respirator mask. It thuds to the ground.

"Arden!" I hear Osiris' voice, but it's too late. The man at the top of the stairs has cut the vine and fallen down the steps, now aiming a rifle at me.

Jordan comes from the left, tackling me to the ground. Something surrounds us, encases us in complete darkness. Gunshots drum against its outside.

A man grunts—it's muffled—outside of whatever is encasing us.

The gunfire ceases.

The scent of Jordan's lavender shampoo fills the space. She's huffing to catch a breath, to slow her heartbeat. She wiggles her fingers. "Come on…"

We're stuck in some sort of a tube. I can't hear anything except her breathing.

A single shot fires.

Panic radiates from the muffled dialogue outside.

"Come on!" Jordan cries.

I twist my fingers around hers. Her palms are sweaty.

"Sorry," she says. "I'm claustrophobic."

"Can't you just…" I think back to Brad in the van: he had grown the bud and withered it, "just kill it?"

She starts to breathe heavy again. "Oh, God…"

The faster and heavier she breathes, the sooner we'll run out of air.

I close my eyes.

There's Jackson, crying out from his bedroom. I shoot out of bed and into the hallway. There's no glowing nightlight coming from his bedroom. I'd forgotten to turn it on. I kneel at the edge of his bed and scoop him into my arms. "I'm here. Mommy's right here."

"Mommy, I'm scared," he says. "There's something in my closet."

Chills creep up my spine. Being the grownup, I'm not supposed to get scared. But I am. The corners of the room have always made me uneasy. I cling to him and press his cheek against my chest.

"Close your eyes. Are they closed?" I feel his little head nod yes against my breasts. "Keep them closed." I stand up with him secure in my arms and walk to the nightlight. "All you can feel is me. You're safe. I won't let anything happen to you." His arms tighten around me. I lean, flicking on the nightlight. There's nothing in the corners. I return to the bed and set him down. "Okay, Jackson, let go."

He shakes his head no.

"I'm right here. I'll always be right here."

He lets go. His eyes follow the rays of light on the ceiling to the choo-choo train nightlight. He says, "You were gone."

"I'd never leave you," I promise.

"I'm scared."

"Just close your eyes." I pull Atum, his stuffed scarab beetle, from the bed crack, tucking it in his arms. "You can be anywhere you want to be with your eyes closed."

He snuggles Atum closer, closing his eyes. I kiss his forehead, closing mine.

Only to return to the dark.

Jordan's fingers squeeze mine. Her heavy breath blows against my face.

I squeeze her hand. I'm the grownup. It's my job to comfort her. I squeeze harder. My hands shake. I lean my forehead against hers, saying, "Close your eyes."

With Time

A CHAINSAW STARTS OUTSIDE THE ENCLOSURE. I HAVE calmed Jordan down to long, steady breaths as the sound penetrates deeper. The blade breaks through our encasement and I squeeze her hand. This time—as the chain cuts closer—she squeezes back harder. The enclosure vibrates. Sawdust sprays against my leg. There's no place to move.

My God, it's going to cut into me. I clench my lips. Sweat builds between our palms.

The teeth of the chain eat into the side of my calf.

I bare down on my teeth, trying not to scream. That doesn't work. Blood throbs through my body and swells at the wound. Vines slide up along my leg, wrapping up my torso, and twisting up to my head, yanking me out of the bottom.

Fresh air brushes my face.

Without darkness, I can stop focusing on the pain. It lasts a full second before demanding all my attention again. *Oh, God, it hurts*. I have to barf. *I have to barf*. My stomach tightens. *It hurts so bad*. The breeze passes and leaves me crippled on the ground.

Jordan stands up, ripping the vines away from her body, pacing the room, staring at all the dead guardsmen. And Theia's corpse.

The tube had been a tree. Jordan had encased us in a tree. We nearly died.

I look at the gash in my calf, fall to the ground, and scream at her, "Why did you do that?"

She stops pacing. "To save your life!"

"You could've killed us!" Spit sprays through my teeth. My leg throbs. Warm blood drips from the wound.

She storms toward me. Brad blocks her, kneels beside me, and presses his hand against the cut.

"Why didn't you let us out?" I say to her.

"This doesn't look good," Brad tries to whisper to Osiris, but it's no whisper.

I lay back, pushing my head against the ground, trying to absorb the throbbing pain.

Brad whispers to Jordan, “What happened? Why couldn’t you control it?”

“Stop fucking whispering,” I say.

He clears his throat.

“I was scared!” Jordan yells, kicking the ground. “Okay? Happy now? Jordan’s defective! Happy?”

The fluid in my stomach retches. *Oh, God.* Nausea sweeps through me again. I’m going to barf, I need to barf. It hurts so much.

Osiris kneels beside Jeff, handing him something. “Here.”

Jeff puts his hand out and clenches whatever it is. I doze off. When my eyes refocus, Osiris is holding a handful of little white flowers. The pounding—throbbing—in my leg intensifies with each breath. He crumples the flower in his hands and presses it against the wound. “Good thing it isn’t deep.”

Brad puts his hand on Jordan’s shoulder. “I’m sorry.”

She jumps into his arms and rests her cheek against his chest, like he’s her big brother.

“There,” Osiris says, letting go of my leg. “How’s that?”

It still throbs, but the blood has clotted. “How…?”

“You’d be surprised what plants can do.” He smiles. “It’s time for you to learn.”

“Learn what?”

"Your place in this world." He offers out a hand.

I take it, standing at the bottom of the stairwell. There's no way up. It's too far, too steep.

Jordan sinks to the ground beside Theia's body, placing a seed on her, cupping her hand over it. A rose bush emerges and engulfs Theia, dragging her down beneath the soil. Jordan withdraws her arm. Scratches from the thorns bleed.

Brad steps up beside me and smiles, rolling a seed in his hand. "Need a lift?"

Vines slither out between his fingers and reach for me. I let them. Leaves brush my skin as new vine twists around my body and spreads up the walls, pulling me up over the broken stairwell.

"Don't touch the ground with your bare hands!" Brad shouts.

The ivy continues high enough to set me on my feet.

There are no walls. No shelter is left. The demolished home looks like a broken crushed gingerbread house.

White puddles of rain cover everything.

A door lying on the ground moves. Someone moans beneath it.

Nephthys? I run over and grab onto the plank of wood. My fingers slide through the white raindrops sprinkled on top of it. I throw the door. Green pants led to a grey shirt. *No.*

Steve's face is bloody. His skin hangs in loose pieces from sitting in the rain—the white liquid.

My fingers begin to burn. I look down. Little blisters start to form. *Fuck.* I search the area for something to wipe them on—something dry.

The others emerge out of the basement behind me.

I face them, palms open, hoping for an instant suggestion.

"The pump!" says Jordan. She sprints for the backyard, to a garden with an old-fashioned iron well-pump, and wrenches the lever up and down until water flows out. She sticks her hands beneath the pump, scoops a handful of water, and dumps it over the pump handle itself.

I run over, shove my palms into the cold water, and rub them together, gagging at the pain of the blisters chafing.

"What were you thinking?" says Jordan.

I have to find Nephthys. If I don't—

She lowers the pump handle.

The water slows to a drip over my hands. The blisters fill out and puss pools beneath the skin.

"Shit, man. That looks bad." Jordan heads back to the group.

They huddle around Steve, who's still lying on the ground, moaning.

Jordan nudges Jeff's shoulder, nodding back at me. "Burns."

Jeff digs around in his bag and takes out a handful of random seeds, picking one out of the mess. The right side of his shirt is bloody and torn. The same white flowers pressed against my calf clot a bullet hole in his torso.

Brad calls out, "Nephthys?"

Osiris calls out, "Nephthys!"

They take turns calling her name, kicking through the rubble.

A cactus-type plant starts to grow in Jeff's hand. He stops it mid-size and snaps-off its thickest leaf. A clear-goo seeps out and he squeezes it into my hands—over the blisters.

"What is this?" I say.

"Aloe vera," he says, smiling, returning his attention back to the application.

"Like the green stuff you use on sunburn?" I say.

"Well, yes and no. That stuff in the store is a synthetic man-made chemical. It's based on this plant." He holds out what is left of the thick leaf. "This is the natural substance, the free one, the one our bodies evolved with."

"Why isn't it green?" I say.

He chucks the empty leaf to the ground. "You mean why is the stuff in the store green? It's supposed to trick your brain into associating it with the primitive thought that expects it to come from something green."

Steve moans.

Jeff breaks off another leaf and offers me the entire plant. "Try dripping it on his skin. Don't wipe it in. Not with dirty hands, or an infection will start." He peeks into his bag. "I don't think I have what I need for that." He glances over at the garden's old well-pump—the garden blossoming with life—now beaten to death from the white rain.

I bend down next to Steve and snap off a leaf. He's been a piece of shit, but I feel sorry for him—for the world which was left to us.

He moans and chokes, "You're fucked."

Aloe plops on his cheek.

"What's he saying?" says Jeff. "Ask him if he knows what happened. Where Nephthys is."

I look at the guys: Osiris and Brad, now on the opposite side of the house, sifting through rubble. The empty military-chopper sits on the front lawn. I stand up, backing away from Steve's blistered and burned body.

"What are you doing?" says Jeff.

"Fuck him," I say, letting the aloe plant fall to the ground. "I'm not wasting my time. He's an asshole." I step past him, searching the area. I have to find Nephthys. *She's my only hope*. A tree on the edge of the garden catches my eye.

Pink bulbs fill the tips of its branches, unraveling into flowers before my eyes. The petals wither brown and crumble, falling to the ground.

"There!" I say. *She's there*. She had been in there longer than we had been in Jordan's tree. There is no way there is any air left.

Osiris sprints for her. Jordan and Jeff follow, but I get there first. I pound against the tree trunk, pleading that she be in there. "Nephthys?"

The branches begin to crumble and fall to the ground. The top spills down, decaying to reveal her. She's still alive.

The clouds overhead shift and, for a second, sunlight blinks across the landscape. A knife at my feet flashes with light. It must have come from the kitchen. I look back at Steve. One way or another, he is set to destroy me. If he does, Carter will be left with no one. I won't be there to see his first steps. *It would all be because of this fucker.* I pick up the knife. *I'm not a murderer.* I take a step toward him, kicking the aloe leaf with my foot. The knife's hilt squeezes into the blisters as I tightened my grip. I shove the blade down, plunging it into his eye.

He screams.

I rip the blade out and thrust it back down. I'm not going to let him take away my baby. I tear it out and jam it back down, until he stops screaming. I tell myself it's to set him free, but that isn't the real reason.

Traitor

"NO!" JEFF SCREAMS.

Osiris sprints toward me. Brad throws a line of ivy at me, binding my hands, pinning me from moving. The vine continues around my legs and binds my ankles. Osiris grabs my arm, whispering in my ear, "You shouldn't have done that."

Why the fuck not?

Nephthys' voice raises as she hurries over, "Release her."

"But—" says Jeff.

Nephthys' eyes flash a gold color as the clouds drift back in overhead. "She doesn't know any better. She doesn't know the consequences."

Tell them. Tell them why you did it. He was going to ruin everything. It's what he deserves for earlier anyway. I look around the group. Their eyes hang to the ground, to the stranger that was no different from myself.

Jeff rips the rest of his shirt off and lays it overtop Steve's face.

Thunder rumbles in the distance. The wind blows strands of my hair across my view.

The sound of aircraft comes closer from down the mountain.

Another burst of thunder erupts. I jump. There is no telling what will come next.

Nephthys looks to the sky and steps toward me, pulling the knife from Steve's flesh. She presses it an inch from my face. "I don't know what secrets you keep, but they will not serve you. Not in this life, or the next."

"I'm here for you," I say.

"That's nice—"

"You don't understand. I'm here to take you to him." I glance at Osiris. "But you already know that, don't you?"

The way she smiles says everything.

The group stays silent. It's what allows us to hear them coming. Helicopters approach.

"Brad," says Nephthys. "Under the chopper. Everyone else, climb inside."

None of them—not one—look like they can actually fly a helicopter. Jordan wastes no time climbing into the back.

Brad hunches underneath it, where the ground is dry. His

robotic fingers dig into the soil. His other hand reaches into the pouch of seeds.

Osiris climbs into the back with Jordan. I hurry over, grabbing the handle to pull myself in. Jeff steps in front of me, blocking my entrance.

"You are no better than her if you don't let her in," says Nephthys.

Jeff moves aside.

I climb in, taking a seat among the group of people who think I deserve to be dead. They aren't wrong. *What have I done?* I sit down beside Jordan. I'd taken a life, a life that wasn't mine to take.

"She'll let it go," Jordan says. "We've all done something we're not proud of. And it's not over yet."

Jeff squeezes in beside me, becoming my own personal prison warden. Nephthys takes the bench opposite us, with Osiris, and pulls the door shut. Osiris and Nephthys eyes glow like the creatures that have my baby.

Carter.

Rain taps on the ceiling.

The helicopter lifts into the air, yet there is no driver. It sways back and forth like an unbalanced giant has hoisted it up. Thunder echoes through the sky and shakes its metal frame. It tips to the left and I grab onto Jordan's hand. She doesn't pull away or wipe her hand off onto her jeans like I'm some disgusting monster—a freak—a selfish freak who only cares about herself. She lightly holds on.

Approaching aircraft rumble through the sky. Gunshots fire from a distance. The helicopter shifts to the opposite side. I grab onto the seat and keep myself from sliding. Jordan lets out a soft grunt and clenches my fingers. Momentum squishes us together.

My legs lift off the seat. For a second, I'm weightless. Then I slam back down onto the bench, hard.

The helicopter launches like a football over the treetops and sails down into the trees, clearing leaves and smashing through branches. The windshield cracks. Pieces of bark slide across its windowpane. The floor beneath our feet skims through forest canopy. Centrifugal force throws us like rag dolls.

Jordan and I land on the metal floor. The roof is dented and a branch flings into the cabin, crushing the wall where Jordan and I had been sitting.

Gunshots continue, but they are well into the distance now.

Brad. My head pounds and my body hurts everywhere. I shoot to a stand. All the blood rushes to my head. The wound in my leg throbs and my calf gives out, knocking me back down. The corners of the helicopter spin. *Corners.*

"Woo," Osiris says, grabbing onto my arm, settling me down onto the bench. "Take it easy."

"What about Brad?" I'm surprised at the volume of my voice, the frantic scream that escapes.

"He's a big boy." Osiris' attention turns to the sound of a grenade going off. He glances at Nephthys. She holds her side, gritting her teeth. His head hangs low. "He did his job."

My heart tugs at the words.

"What now?" Jeff whispers.

Rain sprinkles through the canopy and trickles down the branch that broke through the windshield.

"We wait," Nephthys says.

Jeff sits beside Nephthys, digs a hand into his bag, and combs through the seeds.

"Shit." Nephthys lifts the side of her shirt and sucks in a breath of pain. A deep bruise has formed beneath her skin.

Jeff presses his fingers against the bruise.

Tears drip from Nephthys' eyes. "I'm not going to make it."

"Quiet…" Jeff says.

Nephthys grabs his hand. "You have to finish this."

His eyes move to the floor.

Nephthys looks up, staring at me. Icicles shoot through to my heart. She says, "Take me to him. It is time. Carter is the only thing that matters."

Jeff glances at me and back at Nephthys. "We can find a doctor. We can fix this."

Nephthys squeezes his hand, forces a smile, and pats his leg. She closes her eyes and says, "When the rain stops."

No one says anything.

I'm getting what I want, but it feels so wrong, so unfair.

Osiris grabs my ankle and pulls my leg towards his lips. He presses his tongue below the wound of my leg, licking it like a dog. I pull back, but his grip tightens.

"Relax," says Jordan. "You'll thank him later."

His tongue flattens against my skin, scraping like sandpaper along the edge of the bloody, dried yarrow leaves. Saliva washes the wound clean, but it burns. He sits up, lets go of me, and hocks a loggie to the floor.

I stare at him.

His eyes have dilated to vertical lines, that begin to recede back to round irises. A smile crosses his lips. "You'll thank me in the morning."

Sacrifice

NIGHT FALLS ACROSS THE FOREST BEFORE THE RAIN stops. The clouds open up to a velvet sky painted with twinkling stars.

Twinkle, twinkle. Little star…. No. Little star. No. Not tonight. I stare through the broken windshield, into the dark forest. *Jackson would love this.*

The woods are silent: the tree frogs don't croak. No crickets sing. Even the mosquitos have vanished. An owl hoots in the distance, but it sounds more like agony than any song.

The group is asleep, each leaning on the other. I sit in the corner, alone. Maybe Anubis will grab onto me and pull me back to the other world—the one still oblivious to ours. Then again, most of us aren't even aware of our world before death forces us to be. All the time I spent checking statuses and messages, I yearn to get back, to relive those minutes to use my time wisely.

Jordan mumbles in her sleep. She wiggles and turns to the opposite side.

Osiris lifts his head. His eyes shine in the lunar rays. He tilts his chin up. "How's your leg?"

I hadn't thought about his tongue pressing against my skin since he… he… My cheeks blush, burn. The chainsaw wound is swollen, but it doesn't hurt, there is no blood. Thick scabs have formed. I look at the aloe leaf beside me, the one Jeff had offered prior to conking out. Thoughts of Osiris' sandpaper tongue flood me. I address him, "What are you?"

He lets out a half-ass laugh and softens his voice, "Why not ask what you are?"

I don't know what the hell he's talking about, but I'm getting sick of this shit: sitting around doing nothing. I look at Nephthys. Jordan had grown some bud. I don't know what type it was, but it knocked Nephthys out. She lay down in a way so that her head rests on Jeff's lap. His hand lays on her abdomen.

"Evolution," Osiris says.

What? That doesn't make any sense.

"Evolution," he says. "That's what you are."

"You mean like Darwin?" I say. "Natural selection?" That can't be, because I'm still alive and Jackson's dead. We share half the same genes.

He laughs.

My heart jerks.

The others stir in slumber.

"There are other theories of evolution, you know?" He eases into a chuckle. "Like Elaine Morgan's Aquatic Ape Theory."

Jordan flops back over.

He reaches for my hand.

I hesitate, drawing away from him, then let his fingers slide over mine. He gently pinches the skin between my thumb and pointer finger.

"It explains this." He lets go, sitting back. "Your world is too easily persuaded. You believe what your rulers want you to believe. History isn't written by the oppressed."

"What makes your world so holy?" I say.

"Do you know what the ones who control my world say about yours? What they call it?"

Of course, I don't.

"It is called Duat," he says. "It is the world of the dead."

That's not true. I shake my head in detest. He's lying. Anubis said the other world—his world—was Duat. "What do you call your world?"

"Earth," he says.

No. I'm not going to believe it.

"Is it so hard to believe? Your government allows toxins to be disposed of into the air, ground, and water. Corporations pay for a permit. The state, county, city: all allow a certain amount discharged into the water source you drink from. Does this not sound like the land of the dead to you?"

I don't want to believe it. I'll never hold Jackson again. He's gone. These people are fucking nuts. But what if they aren't?

He stares out the broken windshield. "It isn't your fault. We all want to believe the stories we are told. We want more than anything for there to be a Santa Claus. And yet there isn't."

I want to cling to my old storyline. I want it to be easy. I don't want to be where I am.

"It was only a matter of time before they killed her," he says.

"Nephthys?" I say.

"No," he says. "Your Earth."

"Who's they?" He can't possibly get any crazier.

He nudges Jordan off his shoulder and stands up, leaning over toward me, grabbing my hand and yanking it toward him.

My fingers clench into a fist.

He pushes the back of my hand against the tree branch that has penetrated the window. "They are killing her. Do you feel it yet?"

My heart pounds. My fingernails dig into my palms. My jaw tightens.

"Do you feel it?" he says.

My fingers loosen, shaking as they flatten out against the branch. My fingertips slide across the deep, rigid groves of the bark. My pinky brushes the leaf. Its tip caresses the back of my hand. Its outside edge is dry, crispy, wilted. Real rain has rapidly become a luxury. My eyes follow the branch, to the forest of trees waving in the wind outside. The green of the forest is lush. A single, limp leaf hangs toward the ground, parched but still flowing, playing with the wind. I can feel it, from all the way across the forest, pulsing through me.

"I don't understand," I say, drawing my attention away from the leaf to look at him. The pulse fades until I can no longer feel it. "This is because I'm an Aquarius?"

"No. Tekk Corp hasn't figured out how to wipe you all out yet." He glances away. "Everyday people are offered the ability to wake up—are tested." He sits down beside me and leans against the wall. "It's like switching on a light. Most haven't stopped staring at the white wall to even notice that there is a light switch. You find the switch—you can activate your dormant DNA."

"And everyone has this?"

"Yes," he says, looking at Nephthys. "At least in your world." He looks at me. His pupils dilate into vertical lines for only a second. "What made you look for the light switch?"

My heart swells. I don't know the answer to that question, but my heart does. I didn't have anyone when Jackson was born. My dad would have been there—no matter what—but he wasn't. He was dead. *Jackson's dead.* It's because of me Jackson is dead. I know it. I felt the guilt eating away at me the moment I let go of him. I stand up.

The small metal interior of the helicopter blurs with the night's shadows, and sways in the branches with my movement.

I yank open the side door. Cold mountain air blows in.

The helicopter had landed in the branches of a tree, hanging over the edge of a cliff that is at least ten stories high.

"What about Carter?" he says.

"Jesus," says Jordan rubbing her eyes open.

"He'd be better off without me," I say. I don't want to say it. The words burn as they come out. I don't want to believe it. I don't want to believe that someone else would be better for him than me. Bastet's snake-eyes flash through my mind—the image of Carter nursing at her breast makes me nauseous. I bend with the urge to vomit, lose balance, and stumble over the helicopter's edge.

Osiris grabs my arm and yanks me back.

"Get off me!" I say.

"Are you trying to kill yourself?" He looks down at the treetops below.

I lean back into my place on the floor, keeping my eyes on the open door. I don't want to have to live.

He sits down beside me, looking out at the night sky. "They managed to wipe out everyone but their target."

"Who is their target?"

"You," he says.

I'd give anything to trade places with Jackson. "They killed my son?"

"Ever wonder if the separation you felt from nature was on

purpose? That the fluoride in your water is a sedative. That the mercury fillings in your teeth leaches out, causing brain fog, spreading toxins throughout your entire body. Don't even get me started on pharmaceuticals. All of it, all of this, is to keep you away from the only thing you've ever been looking for."

"I don't understand," I say.

Nephthys grunts, trying to stand up. Jeff braces her as she gets up, hugging her waist. She looks at me. "You were their target."

"What do you mean, me?" I say. This is making no sense and getting us nowhere closer to getting Carter back. "What about the others? Like Jordan. Why do you say me?"

"They didn't take her child," she says, sitting back down, grabbing her side. "They took yours."

"You knew? You knew all this time… that they took him?" Why hadn't they protected him? "What do they want with him?"

"You," Nephthys says, laying a hand atop mine.

"Then why not keep me? Why send me after you?"

"You do not have what he wants yet," she says. "Now, we must go."

There is a break in the clouds and dawn is lending us its first light. There is no way to get down from the helicopter.

"Can I do it?" Jordan says, reaching for Jeff's seed bag.

"Let's see what you got, kid," he says, handing her the bag.

She slides it on and steps to the edge, cupping a seed in her hand. Her shoulders droop and her breath relaxes into a deep exhale. A bright green vine pushes out between her fingers.

Large leaves form. A yellow flower emerges, transforming into a tiny green ball, then a large pumpkin.

Its weight pulls on the vine and Jordan's fist tightens around its end. It begins to descend toward the earth. The leaf node grows roots that long to ground themselves in the soil. Once it gets there, they dig themselves down, fast and deep.

Jordan presses her palm against the helicopter door, twisting the vine's end around its handle. She lets go, swiping her fingers one last time across the primary roots, making them mold into the metal.

"Who's first?" she says.

Nephthys stands. She sucks a breath of air in-between her teeth, baring the pain of another step.

"I'll go," I say. *If she dies, I'll never see Carter again.*

The space goes silent.

I join Jordan at the helicopter's edge. I can't see the bottom. The morning landscape is still colored in deep hues of blue. *Fuck. I'm just going to die.* I grab onto the vine and sit with my legs dangling ten-fucking stories in the air. The helicopter shifts a little and my body slides over the edge. I grab onto the vine tighter. My legs whale to find it. *This was a stupid idea.*

"Here," says Jeff reaching out his hand.

No. I don't want help. *I'm doing this alone.* I grip the vine harder. It's only ten stories high. Sweat builds in my palms. I can't find the vine at my legs. *Where is it?* I fling one foot to the right and the other frantically searches the left. *Where is it?* Sweat cakes my palms. My hands slip. *Fuck.* Just an inch. Just an inch. My right foot hits something. *There it is*. The vine smacks against my leg. I wrap my ankle around it twice, and walk my hands down, letting go of the helicopter.

The aircraft rocks above my head. I slide down the vine toward the pumpkin way too fast, never really getting to enjoy my triumph. I'm prepared for death at the bottom, only to slip in mud.

Jordan follows next, like she's built for it.

Osiris swings his body out at the top and waits. Nephthys lowers into his arm. Jordan touches the end of the vine, coaxing it to grow and ease them down, closer. Once they have cleared the end, Jeff follows. The helicopter shifts with his weight. The vine swings back and forth. The helicopter above rocks. Jeff's legs hang loose from the vine up above. The branch holding the helicopter snaps. He goes flying off to the side and the helicopter comes crashing down.

"Move!" yells Jordan.

I dive out of the way as fast and as hard as I can. My arm skids into the mud. The rain-soaked soil burns.

Jeff's body hits the ground and bounces like a stuffed animal. Then the helicopter crushes him. Just like that.

My arm burns. I shoot to a stand and fling the goop off. The tips of my fingers feel like the lit ends of a match.

"Here," says Osiris.

I turn to look at him, but it's too late. Warm liquid sprays against my arm and drains the mud from my skin. Piss. He fucking pissed on me. He… I can't believe it.

"I'd close my mouth if I were you," he says.

Jordan stands nearby watching with wide eyes and a disgusted look. Nephthys is hunched up against a nearby tree, bearing the pain in her side.

The stream trickles to a stop and Osiris zips up his pants, walking back over to Nephthys like it was nothing.

"You pissed on me," I say.

"You're welcome," he says.

I storm over toward him, "You fucking pissed on me."

He pulls Nephthys' arm up around his shoulder, helping her to stand. She winces. His face turns stern and his pupils begin to dilate into their snake-like shape.

The blisters on my arm have stopped spreading, but they burn—now a little less. I turn my back to Nephthys and Osiris, taking in the scene of the crash.

"Okay you two," Nephthys says, stepping toward the scene. Osiris braces her as they walk to the edge where Jeff's corpse rests. She extends her arm out, with her tattooed wrist facing up. Jordan does too, like they are preparing for a pre-game huddle. Osiris places his hand atop of Jordan's.

"May Ra be with you," says Jordan. "Namaste."

"I will be with you soon, my love." Nephthys smiles. "Namaste."

"May you travel light." Osiris' eyes fall to the ground. A tear drips down his cheek. "Nah-mes-tay."

I step closer. They bow their heads. I slide my fingers across the top of Osiris' hand. My fingers streak across the veins of his wrist. "You saved me, made me see that people can change…"

Reverence carries. They all expect me to close it out with a salutation, so I give him the last line of Edgar Allan Poe's 'The Raven': "And my soul from out that shadow that lies floating on the floor shall be lifted—nevermore."

Nephthys closes her eyes and begins to hum, "Om-ah-hum."

It vibrates in my heart. Energy swirls from my feet, spinning up toward my fingertips. It tingles: like standing on the edge of a diving board for the first time, hesitating to jump.

Their hands sweep down to the ground. My hands fall back down to my side.

Osiris steps back, close enough to catch Nephthys if she falls.

Jordan grabs my hand and Nephthys takes the other.

A small tree grows in the center of our circle. It continues growing until we're forced to let go of each other. I step back, along with Jordan. Nephthys places her palm against its bark. The tree grows until it absorbs Jeff. Then she collapses.

Osiris catches her, carrying her back toward the house—the rubble.

The canopy leaves wave as we walk. A gust of wind pushes us faster away from the helicopter. Jordan explains something about why they didn't bury him—something along the lines of reincarnation, but I can't listen, can't get my thoughts to stop. Pieces of the house begin to line our path. The debris increases with each footfall.

The park ranger truck is charred and smoking. Hot coals and ash simmer where the helicopter had been—where Brad had been.

Brad?

I scan the rubble. My eyes fall on the man I killed. My fingers shake. *I killed Steve. What have I done?*

"Hey," says Osiris. He's standing beside the smolders with the others. Nephthys is waves me over, not looking back at the destruction—the murder I'd committed.

I glance down at my hands, my wrist. There's no mark—no tattoo. I'm not like them. There will be a time when they all turn on me, just like they did in high school.

"You coming?" Osiris' words shift the group's gaze upon me.

"What about Brad?" I say.

Nephthys leans on Osiris and turns, sucking in the pain piercing her side. "You're going to have to save him too."

Cornered

I HAVE TO FIND A BUILDING—SOMETHING WITH corners. I have to find some place before Nephthys changes her mind, before they decide to kill me instead.

The truck won't start. We take to foot. Luck has the driveway slanted in our favor. The street below is clear. We're on the outskirts of the city—within the hills. The only evidence of civilization is the sporadic driveway entrances every other half mile.

Osiris stops at the end of our driveway, handing Nephthys over to Jordan. He glances at them, and nods back at me. "You guys stay. Arden and I will find a car."

He nods in the direction of the closest driveway, not far down the road, on the opposite side.

I look at Nephthys crippled over in pain. She's bleeding internally and there isn't much time. We're wasting minutes by leaving her. Minutes we'll have to backtrack. Osiris has already started down the road.

I won't leave her. She's my only chance to get Carter back. I freeze in place as his heels dig into the sloping driveway, slowing enough to gain control over each step.

"No," I say almost in a whisper.

He stops. I can feel the group's eyes weigh on me.

"No," I say louder. "We need to find a corner. Any corner."

Osiris looks at Nephthys. She expects my words, hanging her head a little, and nods in acceptance. Osiris returns to her, scooping her into his arms, and carries her down the slope.

We make it to the neighboring driveway within minutes. Its path of gravel stretches much deeper, slinking back into the woods. A two-story cabin sits nestled at its end. The faint glow of its lights pierce through the windows.

Jordan skids to a stop.

Osiris leans Nephthys against the house's porch entrance.

Jordan hurries to brace her side.

He runs his fingers through Nephthys' hair, presses his lips to her head, and whispers, "Stay on the porch. If anything happens, you run. Got it?"

She nods, agreeing.

He kisses her head and pulls back enough to become eye level. “Got it?”

She nods, rolling her shoulders back, and digs a hand into the pouch at her side.

He looks at Jordan.

Her free hand is already stuffed inside her pouch—Jeff’s pouch. She nods—ready.

Osiris takes the lead and knocks on the front door.

No answer, just like the typical pause before the secluded mountain-man pulls a shotgun out and blasts everyone away.

He knocks again and extends his voice, “Anyone home?”

Something—possibly a plate—crashes to the floor inside.

Osiris’ hands tighten and he punches through the wood. He punches thorough the fucking door like it’s a sheet of paper.

I step back, bumping into Jordan.

“Wait here,” Osiris says, bursting through the door and disappearing inside.

Jordan helps Nephthys to a bench on the porch.

I pace at the bottom of the steps. It’s taking too long. He’s been in there too long. My heart races the seconds away. I cross my arms and force myself to stand still—sitting on the bottom step.

“Why don’t you see if I have any of those seeds?” Nephthys raises her eyebrows at Jordan.

Jordan digs around in Nephthys’ pouch, grabs a handful of seeds, and combs through them.

More dishes fall and crash to the floor inside.

The women freeze.

Osiris pops his head out of the door. "Well, what are you all doing out here?"

My shoulders drop with relief. There's no killer hiding inside.

Osiris leads us to a kitchen. Broken pieces of red plates cover the tile floor. A black cat sits on the counter above the mess. Its eyes shine as it arches its back, hissing at us.

"Stupid cat," says Osiris, reaching for it. It calms, letting him pet it. He smiles at Nephthys, looking at her like she's the only one in the entire room. "Well, girl, it's your last meal. What do you want?"

My heart aches with the words.

"Whatever you got," Nephthys says, holding a smile. I glance at her. She holds the same smile as she glances back at me.

I don't want to feel that her life is less important than Carter's, but it is—to me anyway.

She sits at a long wooden table to the left.

"Why are you doing this for me?" I ask, sinking into the seat across from her.

Her smile disappears. Her lips press together. Her hand finds the bruise at her side, pressing against it. The flood of pain passes and her body eases a little. Her eyes meet mine. "You are part of this Earth. Your baby"—she holds out her right arm with the scarab beetle tattoo—"is Horus. What I teach you, what you learn, will go to him. And I will live through that: the memory and empowerment I have passed on. I'll live on through you. Through him."

The stove sizzles and the scent of bacon reaches us.

"We are the only ones left that can ensure the next generation—his generation—survives." She rests her hands on the table, palms up like she's conducting a seance. Her eyes draw my attention down to her open hands.

I place my palms against hers, entwining my fingers with hers. She's giving up so much for me. Her fingernails grow into sharp points. I pull back, but her grip tightens and the nails pierce—slice—into my skin. I try to pull my hands free, but the slightest movement sends a stabbing pain straight to my heart. I gasp for air, trying to inflate the tightness in my chest. Tears drip down my face and splatter on the table. She squeezes harder, and then her nails re-track back to normal, leaving streaks of blood—my blood—between my knuckles.

"This..." she says, inhaling, sucking in air like it will stop the internal bleeding pain, "is going to hurt a little."

My heart swells like an inflating balloon. It fills, pressing against my lungs, pushing them to the edge of bursting. Lightning bolts of pain rush up my arms, along my neck, and pierce my eyes from behind. I close them, clench them shut to ease the burning, the scorching of their optic nerves. I stumble away from the table, toward the living room and crack my eyes. The couch is three feet away, but it's so fucking blurry. *My eyes*. Saliva thickens as it slides down my throat, strangling me.

"Just relax," says Nephthys.

A pan crashes to the floor behind me in the kitchen. Osiris' voice follows, muffled by the skillet's vibration. He sounds angry. His voice comes closer and he grabs onto my wrist.

I scream. His touch burns.

"Jesus, Nephthys. What did you do?" He yanks me through the kitchen and lets go. "Sink is to the left."

The bottoms of my feet burn. My toes rub together with each step, like matches against flint. My stomach bumps the edge of the sink and I lean over, fumbling to find the faucet.

There are voices but they are muffled by the ringing of white noise in my ears.

I wrap my fingers around the spigot and force it open, splashing my face, trying to crack my eyes enough to stop the burning. Handful after handful, I try to sink my face deeper into my palms. My shirt soaks. My eyes still burn. *What the fuck did she do to me?*

"Relax," says Osiris, coming up from behind me. His hands slide like burning embers down my arms, grabbing onto my waist.

My body stiffens. The contraction in my veins intensifies the lightning bolts of pain pulsing through me.

He grabs my face, spinning me around, saying, "Open your eyes."

I try to lift the cracks of my eyelids, try to force my eyes to take in another millimeter of light. But they won't.

He opens his mouth, extends his tongue, and licks my right eye. It is like wet sandpaper, scraping against my eyelashes, lifting—forcing—the thin eyelid up. His taste buds scratch into the thin layer of my cornea. Tears pool at the corner of my eye, trying to wash away his saliva. His fingers press into my cheeks, pushing my face in the opposite direction, licking my other eye.

I moan with the pain, waiting to feel blood dripping from my eyes like tears.

He lets go, steps back, and walks over to the skillet, picking it off the floor and starting the burner like nothing happened—like I'm not falling to my knees.

The lightning bolts of pain dissolve in my veins. My eyes cool. I blink, expecting to be blind. I close and open my eyes slowly. The room's blur sharpens with ease. I blink the tears away. His saliva drips down my cheeks. I blink at everything. It's all sharper, clearer. I can see. I can see, but a fading bolt of pain lingers in my veins, burning. My heart pounds, preparing to explode through my ribcage. I sink to all fours, dropping my shoulders, hunching over my knees like a worn-out rag doll. The tile is cold, soothing.

The freezer.

I shoot to a stand. All the blood within me rushes to my head. The room spins. I stumble to the refrigerator, pull open the freezer, and grab a bag of frozen peas, shoving my face into it. The layer of ice clinging to the plastic melts. The bag softens against my skin. I press it harder against my eyes, desperate for its last cold remnants, pushing it until I feel like I'll suffocate against its plastic. I want to drown, escape this shitty life. I push it harder. *I can't do this anymore*.

A week ago, Jackson tugged on my dress, pointing at the sky above the Atlantic Ocean. "Mom-me, look."

A large Navy ship sat off the shoreline, practicing diving drills.

I knelt beside him, letting the sand cake my damp knee, getting ready to point out the grey color of the ship and how big the boat was.

His little fingers pushed into the side of my cheek, directing my eyes up to the sky. "Mom-me, up. There."

Thick white lines crisscrossed the perfect blue sky.

We'd all been told they were contrails: water vapor lines trailing passenger planes. When I was little, I'd spend hours picking shapes from the puffy clouds of dragons and faces. I knelt beside him. "What do you see in the clouds? Snakes? Dragons? A choo-choo train?"

"No animals," he said, bending down to scoop up a wave with his little blue bucket. I'd forgotten the swim diapers on the counter and the regular one he wore was full and sagging, causing him to waddle back up to our blanket. Carter was on his back drooling all over his toes that had stuffed themselves so eloquently into his smiling lips. Jackson dumped the pile of sand almost too close to Carter's head. My little baby tightened his lips and cooed up at me, completely oblivious to the pile of sand that could have ruined everything.

Frank laid on his side beside Carter, and smiled, snapping a picture of me. It captured me all alone, with only the backdrop of the ocean.

"You hungry?" Osiris says, holding out a cup of water.

I'm back in the kitchen, clenching a limp bag of peas to my eyes. I groan at my circumstances. Drops of water drain down my face. It's not fair that this is my life. I close my eyes, trying to get back to that memory—that moment. *It's not fair.*

Jordan stands beside the table, blocking my view of Nephthys. I use the refrigerator to stand, and step around Jordan to Nephthys. She's rolling a seed around in her palm. Her eyes have dilated into vertical lines. She fists the seed and a cannabis plant explodes from her fingers. The buds look different from the one Brad chose before. A different strain perhaps.

Jordan rests a hand on my shoulder and leans in. "Congratulations. You know you could've died."

Nephthys searches her pouch and throws a pack of rolling papers on the table.

I laugh. Like smoking pot will make this world go away.

Jordan breaks the bud into pieces and sprinkles it across the paper. "You know marijuana works wonders?"

Nephthys moans, leaning into her injured side. "It's great for pain management."

"Isn't it a gateway drug?" I say.

They laugh.

I glance back at Osiris to see if his kind will join in on the amusement.

He is gone.

"We're not trying to get out of this world." Nephthys smiles for a second, then it quickly fades to a groan of pain. "We're connecting with it."

Jordan raises her eyebrows. "That's why it's been illegal."

Transformation

WE EAT IN SILENCE UNTIL THERE IS NOTHING LEFT. Jordan keeps looking at me. I don't ask Nephthys what she has done to me. I'm so hungry afterward and… well, the pot munchies have taken the rest of any control. We hadn't eaten for an entire day. And there's nothing like a warm meal for an empty stomach.

I excuse myself and move to the bathroom, glancing at the mirror, wondering if Bloody Mary will come save me if I scream her name.

I take off the shirt soaked to my body and wring it out over the sink.

A female voice comes from behind me, "You know it's not a blessing."

Jesus. I jump, clenching the soggy shirt to my breasts, concealing the milk dripping out.

Jordan stands in the doorway, leaning against its frame. "It's why he wants her. Now, he's going to want you. She knew it all along."

She steps away, closing the door.

My heart pounds. *Shit*.

It was supposed to be dark, but everything has a grey hue.

I can see in the dark. I look at my reflection in the mirror, holding my breath, expecting an evil creature to appear. And she does. She stares back at me with no pupils—not like the big beautiful ones that define a human's iris. They're thin, narrow lines, like a snake's—a dragon's. *What the…?* I grab onto the edge of the sink. *No. No, this can't be happening. Carter will never recognize me*.

My fingertips dig into the sides of my face, trying to pull the monster out. *No*. My fingers rub into my temples, pressing—restraining—the realization of what Nephthys has done to me. *No*. Bloody fingernail-lines streak up my cheeks.

The grey scene blurs.

I grip the sink harder as my weight encourages me to fall. The veins of my arms pulse with a faint green glow. I gasp and let go of the sink.

"It's not all that bad," Osiris' voice comes from the corner behind me. Not the door, but the corner of the wall.

I fall backwards.

He catches me before I hit the cold tile floor.

I want to ask where he had come from, how he transcended the corner of the wall. Instead I stare at his eyes—the vertical lines of his pupils that allow him to see me just as clearly as I can see him.

He smiles.

Before, it would have been lost to the dark. *Before… before I became… What the hell am I?*

He stands me up, drawing me much too close, saying, "You're the daughter of a God."

"No, I'm not," I say.

"If you weren't, you would've died back there in that kitchen." He grabs my chin and licks the streaks of blood with his tongue. "And even that leaves no guarantees."

The bathroom door swings open. Jordan flicks on the bathroom light. Rays of synthetic light shoot into my pupils, stretching them back to normal. It doesn't take time for my eyes to adjust. There is no need to squint or accommodate the dilation.

"Oh shit, man." Jordan chuckles. "Get a room."

Osiris realizes I'm topless. I'm fully exposed and have leaked onto his shirt. His eyes shoot to the floor to avoid staring at my boobs. He backs away and takes off his shirt, offering it to me.

I take it, trying to cover my swollen breasts by shimmying it on. His warm fingers brush my arm, guiding the fabric over my head. I lower my eyes, embarrassed. I'd been completely vulnerable in his arms. For a second I imagine his tight chest pushing up against mine. He grabs my chin and licks my other cheek. His thumb brushes the edge of the cuts.

"These might scar," he says.

I turn my head away from him, asking, "So Nephthys knew I'm the daughter of a God?"

He says nothing.

She'd known there was a possibility I could have died. "She knew? That my father was… was…"

"Was a God?" He pulls away and blocks me from exiting. "I don't know."

I push past him and storm into the kitchen. I'm sick of the secrets, sick of the waiting, sick of this fucking messed up bullshit.

Jordan catches sight of my stampede and blocks my path. I try going around her but she steps enough both ways to barricade me each time.

I stand on tiptoe, looking clear over her shoulder, yelling at Nephthys, "Did you know?"

"What are—?" Jordan starts.

"Not you." I say to Jordan, much too harshly.

Jordan looks back at Nephthys.

Nephthys nods at her and Jordan lets me pass.

I could take my anger out on Nephthys, scream until my lungs hurt, punch her until my fists are bloody, pummel her until I become the monster she has forced me to become. Instead, I sit beside her. "Did you know?"

She smiles. "No."

No. She didn't know, which means she could've killed me. *I could be dead. Carter would be left in this world—or whatever the fuck this world is—with monsters. How could she? She could've—*

"I took a chance," she says. "That's all we are afforded in this life."

I can't believe she'd take a chance, a chance on my life. But then I am the one—the stranger—the intruder sitting at her table, with her people, asking her to sacrifice herself so I can have Carter back. And why not? I hold out my hand and look her in the eyes—eyes that mirror my own. "Let's go."

She slides her hand into mine, stands, and says, "I take it you didn't know your father was a God."

My father was many things, but not a God. He would sit with me after school every day and lose terribly in chess. I blamed my mother when Dad died. They fought a lot, and it was only a matter of time before she pushed him away. He never had time to escape though, he died instead. I still think it was because good old Mom broke his heart.

If Mom is still alive, she's likely still being hypnotized by Law and Order reruns, having no fucking clue what's going on in the outside world. *No*. No, I didn't know my father was anything less than the man who would tuck me in at night, kiss my booboos goodbye, and intently listen to anything I had to say. He would've made the most perfect grandfather. Instead of knowing him, my children had known my mother. They were robbed of so much, and now… now I can never make up for it.

Osiris squeezes past me and takes Nephthys' hand, scooping her into his arms, holding her tight against his bare chest. He leans his head down toward hers, pressing his forehead against hers. "You ready?"

She nods, letting go of my hand.

He looks back at me. "When were you supposed to meet Anubis?"

"Whenever you got here." Anubis steps out from the corner of the hallway.

Jordan's the only one surprised to see a man wearing a Jackal head. She digs a fist into her pouch and clamps to Nephthys' side. Nephthys rests her hand on top of Jordan's arm, stopping the girl from doing something stupid. Jordan relaxes a little.

"Nephthys, It's been a long time," says Anubis. "He hasn't been right since you left."

Fading

NEPHTHYS SINKS A LITTLE IN OSIRIS' ARMS AT THE mention of Seth.

Anubis turns and walks into the corner of the hallway, disappearing. Or at least he would have disappeared before. Now I'm able to see it. The back corner doesn't exist. It's a portal, an arched doorway, leading straight into the world of Duat.

I look back at Nephthys.

She smiles.

I reach back, grabbing Jordan's wrist, leading her toward the corner.

She digs her heels into the floor.

I look back at her and say, "Yolo."

She snorts and rolls her eyes. "Shit."

It takes three steps to clear the portal and enter into a dark and empty closet space. The portal walls spin, intertwining together, and then fade out into separate, yet tied worlds. The closet door is closed and there's no telling what's on the other side. I have to open it. There's no turning back. Carter's in there somewhere. He has to be. I grab the doorknob, hold my breath, and twist the handle.

The door swings outward, to the white, rounded penthouse of Tekk Corp.

I don't understand. How did it lead back here? Now I have the freedom to transcend worlds. How many times can I open up this same door? How many times can I push the unknown?

I hadn't stepped out of the closet yet, when Osiris comes through with Nephthys, bumping into the back of me.

Jordan pushes me out, spinning in a circle to see the world she has only heard tales of.

"All the corners are rounded." Osiris' voice hangs heavy as he steps out, scanning the surroundings. Fear fills his face. "All the corners are round."

"How are we going to get back?" Jordan looks at Osiris in panic.

"You're not," says Seth, walking into the room with a handful of Robes. "You're going to work for me."

Osiris puts Nephthys down.

"Hello, Chastity," Seth says, walking toward her.

She bends at the pain in her side and grits her teeth, forcing herself to stand up straight, not ushering the slightest bow or curtsy to him.

Osiris steps in front of her, blocking the path between them.

Nephthys rests her hand on Osiris' shoulder, allowing him to stand down and let Seth pass.

Seth brushes Osiris' arm as he approaches the goddess. He slides his hand along Nephthys' cheek, laying his lips against hers, forcing all his weight into that one kiss.

She lets him.

He wraps his hand around her waist and she bends over in pain, pulling back from him.

A glimpse of worry fills his face as he withdraws his hand. He wanted her alive, and she's dying. He looks at me. "You didn't do as I asked."

"Seth, what are you doing?" Nephthys pushes her fingers into her side and bends a little, trying to alleviate the pain. "Give her her child."

He looks away from her, gritting his teeth, scanning Jordan and Osiris. "I see a traitor amongst you."

Osiris' face turns red and scrunches like a defensive animal. His fingernails grow an inch and his hands clench into fists. His pupils begin to dilate into lines. Spit accompanies the words, "You're the trader here—the freak."

"No need to go apeshit," Seth says, turning away from him. He grabs onto Nephthys' wrist. "You give me what I want and I'll give her the baby."

She looks at me.

I say, "You said if I brought her here, you'd—"

He laughs. The room echoes with it. "You'll do what I want, as long as I want you to."

"You can't have it," says Nephthys. "I know what it will do to you. What you'll do with it." She glances at me. "You'll be unstoppable."

He grabs her by the throat and lifts her off the floor.

Jordan goes for her, but a Robe grabs her, dragging her out of the room. Osiris runs after them but the door closes and locks. He turns, charging Seth. Seth digs his right hand into Nephthys' bag, pulling out a handful of seeds, and flings open his palm at Osiris. Various plants shoot out from his fingers and grew into a barricade—a wall.

If I intervene, I will never see Carter again. I'm no match for him.

"Give it to me!" Seth screams, throwing Nephthys to the floor.

She moans in agony and stays still, barely whispering, "You're too late."

He grunts, a low and long gorilla groan. He paces in a circle.

Osiris chips away at the stems and branches of the wall Seth has created, with no avail.

Seth stops pacing with his back to us. His head whips around and his eyes land on me, on the scratches running down my cheeks.

I step back, like it will free me from his insidious stare. I look down at Nephthys. It's all he needs as proof. The thing he wants—longs for—she has given to me. His body twists, sweeping him toward me.

"No!" Nephthys thrusts herself off the floor and into his path. "Osiris, now!"

Seth rams into her. They both fall. Her head hits the floor and her eyes roll to the ceiling. Her chest falls with her next breath.

Osiris breaks through the wall, jumping over Seth, grabs my arm, pulls me into the closet, and hits a keypad—taking a different corner—the wrong portal.

All is Lost

I PULL BACK, BUT OSIRIS' WEIGHT AND MOMENTUM forward is no match for me. We are in the musty old house around the corner from the gas station in my old neighborhood. I keep pulling back from him, but he doesn't let go until we've cleared the front porch—staring at the diner in the distance.

We're back in my world, where the sky is striped with white lines of death.

"No, you asshole." I beat my fists against his chest. "I'll never get Carter now!"

He grabs onto my wrist and jerks me around to the side of the house.

"Let go." I pull away. "I'm going back."

His grip tightens, yanking me toward him.

"Let me go!" I say.

He releases my wrist, wraps an arm around me, pushes me to the ground, and covers my mouth.

Doors inside the house bang as they search each room. Muffled voices carry out. The front door flings open, banging against the siding. All they have to do is round the side of the house to find us on the ground.

My heart races in my chest. There's still time to make things right, if I get their attention, if I sell Osiris out. I try to wiggle and shake him off, but he wouldn't budge. He pushes his weight against me, crushing my ribs, forcing all the air from my lungs. Taking in an inch of breath is painful. I rest my cheek on the ground, watching blades of grass wave with a faint breeze. I can't force my fate to change. Any pushback leads me to fighting to regain lost steps. I'm so tired of those steps. *I'm so tired.* I don't care to fight back anymore.

The Robes that had breached this world pursuing us, head for the diner across the street, kicking in the door, and breaking everything.

Osiris lets go of my mouth and climbs off. My lungs fill with air. My breasts push against the ground, dripping with milk. He grabs the bottom of my shirt, twists it, and shoves it down the front like I'm a 12-year-old-girl again. But it doesn't conceal the milk. He stands, crouching alongside the house. He doesn't head after the men, run the other way, or find a better hiding spot. He goes back inside the house.

I follow. "What are you doing?"

He pauses before the basement portal. "Saving them."

I don't want to cross back over. Not to save a bunch of strangers. But Carter is there—somewhere in that world—without me. He's without me.

I let my mother watch him once. He cried the whole time. The moment I walked through the door, he reached out his clammy little hands and nearly fell out of her arms. He gasped for a breath and nuzzled his face down, toward my breasts, seeking instant comfort and reassurance I was there. It was the sound of gasps that haunted me. The sound of not being able to breathe because your heart has torn so fast.

He's without me. So I walk down those steps. I accept my fate. I'd give my life for one more moment with him. Just one. *If I could only have one, I'd give my life for it.*

Osiris disappears in the dark.

I step to the edge of the portal. My pupils dilate and the abyss of darkness crisps to a perfect grey hue. It is three steps to change worlds. I linger in the spinning, taking in the energy of the entanglement. If I'm going to die, I'm going to do it for Carter. I take the final step and exhale so hard, the closet echoes with the noise.

Osiris stands at the edge of the doorway, staring out into the white room, pressing his back against the wall, still hidden.

Nephthys' body is gone. Poorly mopped streaks of blood stain the floor in her place.

The penthouse room is empty.

Osiris steps into the world of Duat.

"What the fuck?" comes from a voice behind me.

One of the Robes from earlier grabs my wrist, twisting it up my back. The second rams my shoulder as he charges for Osiris. Osiris turns. His eyes dilate. The Robe lunges at him. Osiris takes him down with one punch. He looks at me—past me—at the man yanking my wrist higher, twisting it harder. Then he charges.

The Robe lets go, shoving me into Osiris' path.

Osiris' hard body careens into mine. I fall to the floor. He plows on by, tackling the man, grabbing his head, pulling it back, and bashing it forward into the hard floor—knocking him out.

His chest heaves with each breath as he returns to me.

I want to move back, to get out of his path of destruction and heartache. I close my eyes, waiting for him to take all of his frustration out on me.

He grabs my arm and yanks me up off the floor, interlacing his fingers with mine, pulling me toward the stairwell that could set us free. He kicks in the door.

A stampede of Robes ascends from below.

"Run," says Osiris, letting go of my hand, pressing his palm against my back, pushing me to go back to the closet. "Run!"

I can't run. I can't leave that world. Osiris disappears from my side back into the penthouse. I stand there waiting for the mob. The sound of footfalls muffle the words Osiris is yelling at me. He rushes back, sweeping me into his arms, and runs for the closet, over the blood-stained floor.

In seconds, he has carried me through the blurred walls of darkness—back into the portal. My weight doesn't slow him, not even up the basement stairs. The door is closed at the top. He shoves my body up against its wood, turning the knob, forcing my weight against it as leverage.

The stampede trailing us will catch up soon. The guards in my world will likely be sweeping the house soon too, barricading us from leaving. We have to get out as soon as possible. He should've put me down, but he holds tighter, kicking open the basement door. He sprints through the hall, kicks in the front door, and makes for a sedan parked out front. He sets me down, jerks open the passenger door, and shoves me in.

I fall face-first. My cheek slides against the upholstery. The fresh blood clots peel from the fingernail wounds. I nudge my cheek harder against the seat, so I can force myself to sit up. Osiris takes the driver's seat.

The dreaded sound of footfalls pound their way through the house. Silhouettes flash past the windows. They're coming.

I slouch a little, not sure if I want to be in the car or not.

Osiris forces the keys and thrusts our path in the opposite direction, shooting us out of the driveway.

The faint sound of airplanes comes from the West.

There is nothing to hide us, or prevent them from firing on us and blowing the car to smithereens.

Osiris takes the beltway entrance. The aircraft will be able to see us like an elephant in a haystack.

I grab onto his arm. "We've gotta get off."

The sound of the aircraft gets closer.

There are abandoned cars on the beltway, but it's not like a huge city, despite it being the Capitol. I don't know the city very well, but I'm pretty sure I know this world better than he does.

I recognize the change of trees up ahead. It's the exit for the town of Cary—Mom's exit. I begin to point, not really wanting to go there, but Osiris takes the turn before I can say anything.

The exit leads into a strip of retail stores and large parking lots. Some are empty. Others contain the lifeless corpses of people. The street takes us like a river through an ocean of cars, an ocean of lost souls.

It isn't long before we run out of gas. Osiris stops the car in the middle of the road and jumps out, trying the closest vehicle door. It opens. A young woman lays on the steering wheel. He grabs onto her arm and yanks her from the driver's seat. Her limp hand drags across the dashboard and catches in the steering wheel, popping as Osiris throws her to the asphalt. He takes her seat and thrusts the engine on.

I don't want to move, have to do anything other than sulk in the minutes away from Carter—the suffocating memories of us: of Frank, Jackson, Carter—everything we have had.

We shouldn't be on the street, but taking sanctuary in any building in the south could be dangerous—everyone owns a gun. I step from our old car and head to join Osiris, not wanting to be alone, but not wanting to decide how to survive the next few hours.

The earth shakes like a war is coming, like they're finally depopulating us, like the whole fucking army is approaching the parking lot, preparing to pulverize us from existence. I sink into the passenger seat like it will hide me.

Osiris speeds away from our abandoned car, and the dead woman. He makes a sharp left onto a side street covered with dry leaves.

I rest my head against the window. All the houses, all the corners of my world are filled with death. It doesn't make sense why so many people had to die, why my baby boy had to die, why my husband was left rotting in our bed.

The sidewalks are sprinkled with bodies. My eyes hook on one corpse and the black heap by its side: an animal.

I sit up. "Stop!"

Osiris doesn't look over or say anything. He just does as I say: slows the car and pulls to the curb.

The engine idles while I jump out and walk toward the rear

bumper—toward a mother and her child. Exhaust blows into the pale and sunken face of a woman my age, or a little older. The boy, dead beside her, looks twice as old as Jackson—maybe six. A tiny black kitten shivers with fear at the boy's hand. It lifts its chin, meows, and puts its head back down.

I step around the mother and child, getting closer to the kitten. Envy flashes over me as I stare at the dead woman beside her son. So much envy that they'd died together. She wasn't here to suffer through the pain. To have to set the corpse of her baby boy onto his bed… and then walk away. Walk away like he was never somebody. Like he was never there.

I fall to my knees, holding the kitten in my lap. My eyes swell with the weight of my heart and tears drip down the scratches of my cheeks, stinging them. *I still have Carter.* I dig into my pocket, taking out the seed Nephthys gave me—the one with a small bulb sprouting out—the first seed I grew, brought to life. I lean over the boy and dig a hole between him and his mother, burying it, leaving the two small leaves to breathe above the ground.

The kitten purrs in the warmth of my lap.

Jackson saw a black cat in a children's book and begged for weeks to get one. Frank's allergic, so there was no discussing it.

I set my hand on the kitten's head. It pancakes itself to the ground. I lift my hand for another pet. A few more, and the kitten eases into a permanent pancake.

I used to read to the boys every night before bed. They loved listening to stories. I loved going to the library, stumbling across books we'd later fall in love with. Every Wednesday, I'd take them to storytime.

I miss reading to them. I scoop the tiny kitten up.

It meows.

"I know you want to stay, but if you do, you'll die." I press it against my chest and get up. Car exhaust spews into my mouth and lungs. I cough, and head for the open passenger door. I pass the backseat and freeze, noticing a rear-facing car seat. *Fuck.* It's a fucking baby carseat, and it isn't empty.

Secrets

I FALL TO MY KNEES AND LOSE THE KITTEN IN MY HANDS. It scampers off.

Osiris takes care of everything: getting me back into the car, disposing of the… He leaves the carseat by the curb.

The rest of the drive drifts by as houses smear past the window. The car slows and the houses crisp. It bleeds into a familiar looking neighborhood.

I sit up.

We are a block from my house—where I'd left Jackson and Frank. My toes dig into the carpet as if I can stop the car. I press my back flat against the seat and grab onto the armrest, squeezing it until my palms sweat. I feel like I'll barf. I look at Osiris.

He feels it. I can tell. He shifts in his seat, clearing his throat, then pulls into the driveway—my driveway.

Gusts of wind push against the clothesline. Wooden clothespins rock the little socks they hold so dear. They wave in the wind, tormenting me, begging me to take them down.

The breath in my chest strangles me. I barely get out the words, "Why would you do this to me?"

"If you want Carter back," his eyes fill with tears, "this is the only way."

I don't understand why we are here, but I don't understand anything anymore. I get out and make it to the front door, placing my hand against the doorknob. I've opened that door so many times, never appreciating the small fact of how lucky I was: to have a place to live, warmth on cold nights, screens to keep the bugs out in the summer, two wonderful little boys, and a man who loved me. I can't walk in there, smell the scent of my dying child and husband.

Osiris reaches around me, nudging my hand from the doorknob, and pushes open the door.

It swings inward, banging against the laundry basket.

I don't want to go in. *I just left them. Left them to—*

Osiris grabs my hand as he enters the house, pulling me in.

There is no smell of death, but one of home. I don't want to see Jackson's little body where I'd left him, alone in his bed. I should've at least put him with Frank, instead of leaving them both all alone.

"Come on." Osiris hurries up the stairs saying, "We don't have much time, if they captured Brad at the cottage."

I follow, taking each step reluctantly, waiting for each one to cave in on me and scrape out what's left of my heart.

At the top step, I can see the blue walls of Jackson's room. I stop. If I take one step, I'll be able to see straight to his bed. *Don't do it. Don't look. It will kill you.* I look.

The room is empty.

Where is he? The room was exactly as I left it—still a mess—but the bed is empty.

I step in and search the corners, the walls, the closet. He isn't there. I run into my bedroom.

Osiris is sitting on the edge of the bed. Frank's body is gone. The bed is made and its corners are tucked, something I never do. Neither one of us had time to make the bed—ever.

Tears stream down my face. I can't hold it together anymore. I can't do it. *I can't do this.*

"Where is he?" I say.

"I buried them," Osiris doesn't look at me, "together. I thought—"

"What?" I scream at him. I don't mean to, but how could he…? How the hell did he know where I lived? That they were dead …? How dare he take the burden that is mine to bear.

He nods, folds his hands, unfolds them, pats the spot next to him, then smooths it out, and stands up. "It will be easier to understand if I show you."

He walks around the bed, to the farthest corner from the door —to the corner I'd spent sleepless nights staring at—and disappears into it.

My heart jumps into a race. *If there's a portal in my bedroom, that means—*

The room spins.

It means… I grab onto the comforter, but it slides from my fingers. The walls shoot up higher to the ceiling as I fall to the floor.

"Arden!" Osiris' voice rushes back toward me. "Are you okay?"

I nod and start to sit up. It feels wrong to hear another man's voice in my bedroom.

He holds out his palm, stopping me from getting up any farther. "There's one other thing."

"What do you mean?" I push his hand out of the way. "Where the fuck does that lead?"

He grabs onto my arms, forcing my attention.

I try freeing myself from his hands—the hands that buried my son and husband.

"Do you remember Valentine's Day?" he says.

What the fuck are you talking about? I squirm. "Get off me."

"Before Carter was born," he says, holding me tighter so I can't move.

I freeze.

Frank was never good at holidays. I don't know if it was because he was cheap or if he really was hell bent on saving the world from consumerism. He hadn't thought twice when a guy at work asked him to cover his shift. It was our first Valentine's Day as an official couple and I spent it alone. I put Jackson to bed, popped in a horror movie, and finished off a bottle of wine.

By midnight, I gave up on Frank surprising me with flowers and stumbled to Jackson's room to kiss him goodnight. One last kiss before I passed out.

He was snoring away.

I'd been asleep for hours before Frank got off of work. He climbed into bed and spooned in beside me, pushing his warm body against mine.

I look up at Osiris, then past him at the corner. I swore the corners had always moved, felt like someone was watching... *You motherfucker. I thought I was just drunk.* Frank had looked different, felt different in the dark, but I thought I was just drunk. I smack Osiris across the face. "How could you...?"

"I'm sorry..." he says.

"How could you?" I feel dirty. Disgust for him crawls beneath my skin. Shame tingles like a shockwave through me. I slide out from beneath him, away from him, to the door's threshold. He had crept into my room—my bed.

"I love you," he says.

"You're a monster."

"You said yes. You—"

"I was drunk! I didn't know..."

He stands and reaches out for me. "Don't you feel it? The connection between us? You said yes because it felt right. Without your brain clouding you, you wanted me. You picked me."

"You're crazy."

"Arden..." he says, reaching for me.

"Leave me alone." I lean my head against the wall, staring at the place I'd left Frank's body—the perfectly made covers of the bed he'd fucked me on.

Osiris leans closer, reaching for my leg.

I pull it in, hugging my knees, letting my brain race, wanting so badly to stand, yet not being able to move.

"Okay." He leaves me and walks toward the portal. "Now you know he's mine. Carter is mine."

Empty

OSIRIS DISAPPEARS.

The sun begins to set and I sit in a dark, quiet, completely lifeless house. There is no one to argue with: over bath, brushing of teeth, calming down to listen to a story before bed. There are no runny noses to wipe. There are no warm bodies to lay next to at night. There is nothing left here.

I stare at the corner of the wall. Carter is in there somewhere. He is the only thing I have left in the world—this fucking world. I force myself up and walk over to my dresser. On top lays a necklace, a locket. Inside is a picture of Jackson smiling. On the other side is a picture of Carter and his big pudgy cheeks. He'd been cooing when I took that picture. I scoop the necklace up, and walk over to the portal. The grey hue of the entwining worlds comes into focus. I close the locket, clench it tight, and take a step—out of my life—into the chance that I will get my baby back.

Hope

WHITE CURVED WALLS LEAD TO A LARGE PANEL OF windows, overlooking the city of Duat. Ten-story buildings surround the emerald pyramid at the city's center. In the distance is the ocean and cottage where I'd first entered their world. A bed mattress takes up the middle of the room, laying on the floor. Stacks of books surround it, creating end tables.

Bright lights flood across the floor from a bathroom to the right. Osiris taps a razor against the sink. His voice digs like razor blades into my heart. "Nice of you to join me."

I don't have anything to say to him. I'm stuck in some fucking world where everything is wrong: the people are animals, the corners are rounded, everything is white. I step toward the window, pressing my face against the pane to look down.

"I wouldn't do that if I were you," says Osiris. "They aren't built to last."

I back away. My fingertips linger against the glass. We are several stories above the road. If the glass gave way, I'd fall to my death. It's terrifying and tempting all in the same breath. The faint reflection of myself reveals the ghost I feel like. Her eyes shimmer. I press my hand against my cheek—the claw marks. The reflection does the same. I'm like him—barely human.

His reflection comes up behind mine.

My heart jumps. I pull my fingers back from the glass, taking a step backwards, stumbling over his fucking books and falling on my ass.

"Relax. I won't..." He clears his throat. "I won't touch you until you want me to."

"Yeah," I say, looking up at him, "like that's gonna..."

His face is cleanly shaven and he smells like mint. He looks much younger, smoother, familiar—like an old story. He smiles like he's won something.

Asshole. I look away. I can't believe it. I'm laying on the floor of my rapist's bedroom. I don't want to go on—have one more thought, struggle through one more minute. My stomach growls and cramps. All I have to do is get Carter back, numb everything until I have him back.

"You hungry?" Osiris asks.

"We've got to go," I say, hugging my legs in, staring out the window.

"We need to get them out of there." His eyes move away from me, to the window, to the emerald pyramid on the other side of town: Tekk Corp. "It won't be long until they kill them."

I cover my face with my hands. "I can't go out there."

He grabs my wrist and pulls my arm toward him, scratching his claws deep down my inner arm. Five inches of fucking claw marks burn into my skin. I gag. It hurts. Just as quickly, his textured tongue scrapes against the wounds, leaving a trail of saliva.

I swing my free hand to hit him.

He catches my arm, restraining both. Then he lets go, throwing me back enough to counter any movement to hit him. "Now you'll fit right in."

I inhale. By the time I exhale, the pain has gone. *What the hell?*

He moves from the bedroom into a living room and kitchen space, heading for the front door.

What the fuck was that about? I storm after him.

He opens the door to a common corridor lined with apartment units. Everything is white. The doorways are all arched. No pictures. Seamlessly plastered white walls.

Three doors down, an elevator pings.

A man and woman stumble out. Their clothes are white, but they aren't robes. The only color in this world—his world—is the Earth. And it's creatures. The couple has no idea that my world even exists.

"Hey man!" the guy says as they approach. "You finally got a girl, huh?"

"Damn girl." The woman slides her fingers along the fresh cuts in my arm. "You're lucky." She shifts her weight and leans toward Osiris. "I could use some of that." Her fingernails slide up under his chin. Her lipstick cakes onto her teeth as she bites her lip.

Her companion fumbles with the keys in his pocket and stumbles into the apartment across from us. He pushes open the door, looking back at Osiris, "Last I heard, Nephthys never found that part"—he looks at his girl—"that we both know you crave so much."

The woman laughs. "Looks good to me."

Her boyfriend yanks her inside.

The elevator doors roll shut as their door closes. We'd missed it.

Osiris walks past me with a grin.

I join him, leaning against the wall, waiting for the elevator to slide back open. "What was that all about?"

"You wouldn't understand," he says.

"What do you mean? Why not?"

"You're human."

What the fuck is that supposed to mean? "Really? You're going to be that guy—that dick—that keeps stuff from me? You can take advantage of me, take my innocence at will—fuck me without my consent—and then not tell me some stupid shit, something mundane?" I pause to breathe. I have so much more to say—to get out—to scream at him.

He slides his hand against my cheek and steps closer.

I don't want him to be close, touch me, be near me.

His other hand brushes my arm—the fresh wounds he'd given me. "Sex you humans can only dream about."

My heart skips. My back presses harder against the wall.

He pulls away and faces the elevator doors.

"Those marks guarantee you're not human. To them anyway."

I can't help trying to remember that night—Valentine's Day. The ceiling was blurry. I'd leaned back—pushed my head against the mattress, arching my back as his lips pressed between my thighs....

I look at Osiris.

His eyes are on the floor. His chest rises and falls heavily.

The elevator pings and opens.

A woman bumps into him as she steps from the elevator. It's Bastet, carrying my baby.

Strange Encounters

"SORRY," SAYS OSIRIS AS HE STEPS PAST THE woman, into the elevator.

It's her. Carter is wrapped, secured to her chest.

All the air leaves me. I can't breathe, move, do anything but grapple for another breath.

A pacifier falls out of his mouth onto the floor.

I bend down, pick it up, and hand it to her.

"Thank you…" she says, looking down at the binky, staring at it, but not taking it.

I follow her eyes. The veins in my arm glow slightly, beneath the wounds from Osiris.

Her eyes dart to mine.

"Arden," says Osiris. The elevator doors struggle to shut as he holds them open. He looks between us. His eyes drift across the bundle in the woman's hands. His pupils dilate into the eyes of a predator.

"He…. I…" Bastet clears her throat and tries to speak, choking on the words. She unwraps the fabric that secures my baby to her, revealing Carter's little cheeks. They are so plump. His tiny fist is curled next to his chin, tucked against her chest. His eyes are closed, chasing the sweetest of dreams. She hands him to me.

I take him so fast I nearly drop him.

She fumbles with a set of keys, walking toward Osiris' apartment unit, stopping a door away. "Come in for a minute."

I should run, step into the elevator and take off with my baby, but I follow her. I'm not thinking about how her apartment unit faces the ocean instead of the pyramid. I'm feeling my heart beat against my chest with each step. I can't believe I'm holding him. He's right here. I can feel his little warm body nuzzle instinctively against mine.

"We need to leave." Osiris runs up behind us just in time for Bastet to clear the threshold into the apartment. He stares into the room. "Something's not right."

I stepped in behind her. All I wanted was to snuggle somewhere safe with Carter. I was planning on thanking Bastet for bringing him back to me, but the bathroom door opens.

Seth steps out.

My heart plummets. I squeeze Carter to my chest. He moans and squirms in his sleep. It's too tight, but I can't loosen my grip from him. *You're not taking him away again.*

Seth pulls the crystal dagger out from behind his back. Its hilt is shaped like an Egyptian cross, the Ankh—the symbol of life and death. The crystal ball at the hilt's end forms the circle of the Egyptian cross. He stares at me, speaking to Bastet, "Take the baby."

"No." I clench Carter to my chest.

Seth's eyes narrow. A grin sweeps across his lips. He steps closer, pointing the knife at me.

"No," says Osiris, stepping in front of us, nudging me back step by step.

My back bumps against something—someone. I know it's Anubis. I don't have to turn around. There is nowhere to go. I look down at Carter, bring him to my lips, and kiss his cheek.

"Don't be stupid," says Seth. "The girl gives me what I want and you can all go free."

Osiris laughs. "You're not getting shit."

Anubis slides his hand beneath my elbow and begins to pull my arm. I try to shift Carter into the opposite hand, but he's slipping. "Osiris!"

He turns.

Anubis yanks harder. A Robe comes up beside him and tears my other arm away, clamping my wrists together behind my back.

Carter's little body falls from my hands. His little fingers reach for me until his head whacks the floor.

No.

He screams a blood curdling scream.

Anubis' hands loosen from my wrists.

I begin to sink to the floor.

Seth screams, "Hold her!"

The Robe yanks my arm up, jerking me closer. I stare at my baby as he screams and cries, unable to get to him—help him—hold him—comfort him.

Osiris sinks to his knees, scooping Carter up.

Seth points the crystal dagger at Osiris.

Carter's screams echo off the walls and cut through my heart.

Osiris hands him over to Seth.

I feel like I'm going to barf. My stomach knots and my throat dries out. I've gotten so close. Seconds ago, he was in my arms, everything was perfect—only for a fucking second. The assholes knocked him out of my arms. *Oh, God. Fuck.*

I thrust all my weight forward, letting my head drop toward the floor, then swing my head back, smashing it into the Robe's nose.

He screams and lets go.

Anubis says something—some threat—and grabs onto my wrists.

If it kills me, I'm doing this. I twist my hands. Anubis repositions his, digging his nails into my skin. I stomp on his steel-toe boots with no avail. *Fuck it.* I twist until it hurts—

facing him—and head-butt him in the face. His hands loosen enough for me to twist out completely. I grab his fucking balls and squeeze until he falls to his knees.

Bastet has taken Carter. Tears drip down her cheeks as she looks down at him.

Osiris tries to knock the dagger away from Seth's hand, but Seth is faster. He punches Osiris to the ground, looks at me, smiles, and walks over to Bastet.

She looks at him, hesitating, pulling Carter back from him.

Seth yells at her, "Now!"

She straightens, letting Seth have full access to my screaming baby.

I jump over Osiris. My ankle twists as I land, but that isn't going to stop me. I keep going full steam at him. I'm going to grab Carter, save him. If I'm going to die, I'm going to do it with him in my arms. I ram my shoulder into Seth's chin. I tear Carter from Bastet's arms, and clench him to my chest as we fall to the ground. His little chest drums against mine with each cry.

Seth rolls, swings his body over us, and thrusts the blade down. The tip slices through Carter and into my stomach. I moan out, wanting to barf. Tears spill out.

Carter's chest stops breathing. He stops crying. His tiny arms lay limp at my sides. His soft cheek rests against my chest and his whole body sinks against mine.

No. My heart dies. I lay my head back on the floor, letting the tears drown out the world—my view—numb me.

Osiris screams out in anger.

The dagger's crystal fills with a green glow.

There is a scuffle.

"How could you?" says Bastet. She screams, "How could you?

The scuffle gets worse.

Bastet grabs my arm and drags me into the hallway.

Carter's tiny body shifts on my torso and my stomach cramps. I retch with the movement—the thought that his body is growing cold.

The lights of the room shift as Bastet drags me into the hallway.

Carter's head gently rolls with each step. His lifeless body slides from mine.

And I let go of the world.

Nothing

I AWAKE IN MY CHILDHOOD BEDROOM—THE LAST PLACE I want to be. I long to be six feet down, cold beneath the ground.

It is cold. I feel nothing but empty. There is a world around me, but I don't want to be in it. There is no point to living. I had everything mere days ago: Frank, Jackson, Carter. I've lost them all. I will never experience setting the table as Jackson makes Carter laugh in his swing by smashing peas against his nose. Frank will never walk through the door as the kids get their food, setting his lunchbox down and brushing my hip as he passes to wash his hands.

I want to throw-up until it kills me.

"Arden." My mother's voice comes soft from the doorway. Out of the corner of my eye, she leans in the threshold.

Frank had done that often. I knew every time he wanted me —needed me. He would lean in the doorway and raise his eyebrows.

"Honey, are you hungry?" she says.

I don't want to talk to her. She made me feel like complete and total shit when I told her I was pregnant with Jackson. She stood in that same spot telling me how horrible I was—what a whore I was—that she didn't raise me to be an easy slut.

I want to roll over, face the other wall, have her silhouette disappear from the doorway. But I can't move. I can't do anything but lay there, wishing I was dead—wishing she was dead.

She drifts out of the doorway.

The sun and moon do the same, moving into the next evening.

My mind stops talking to me, the memories cease repeating. I lay there, waiting for my body to sink into a corpse, waiting for death to free me from the ache in my heart—the breathless cries —the endless tears.

A thinner silhouette replaces my mother's where the door should be. I don't want to move, to acknowledge it, but I slide off the bed, onto the floor, landing on my hands and knees.

"Do you want to save him?" Bastet says.

I look up at the woman who took my child, who had been the cause of it all, who is the reason Carter is dead. She lured me into that apartment. Now, she stands with crossed arms, leaning against the doorframe instead of crippled on the fucking floor, drowning in grief.

My fingernails extend an inch, digging into the rug, scraping into the wood beneath. The room's dark hue morphs into a light-grey haze.

She uncrosses her arms and holds her hands out in front of her in defense. There is no doubt she knows I want to tear her to fucking pieces.

"I had to," she says. "He took my daughter."

My fingernails retract and my shoulders drop.

Bastet's chest rises and falls. She is no older than me. Her breasts are full and her blouse is wet.

I stand. The blood in my veins rushes to my feet and drains from my head. It's too much. I sink back to the floor. It's all too much.

I take the breath my lungs have been craving and let it all out, melting to the floor, broken, all alone.

She sits down beside me, takes my hand, and pulls it into her chest. The side of my hand brushes the dampness of her shirt. Her eyes hold the same longing and hope I once had. She whispers, "It's not too late yet."

I lose it. I slouch deeper, crying, taking my hand from hers. It wouldn't stop the pain from pouring out of me. I shake my head.

It is too late. I'd felt the life spill out of his tiny body. I have nothing left to lose, but myself. And I don't want that anymore. I don't want to live.

"To save him, you must obtain the dagger of Anubis, kill Set, and return the soul of Horus to your son." Bastet grabs my hand.

I get up.

She walks me down the hallway to the garage—the place my father spent most of his life. It used to scare me: the darkness, the aroma of oil, the tools that cast shadows of a torture chamber.

The door swings open. Fear sweeps away. I can still smell my father.

Bastet walks over to the old refrigerator, the one Dad warned me never to climb into—that it would shut and I wouldn't be able to open it from the inside. That going in there, could kill me.

She opens it, and there is a portal. I can see it. She crosses into the other world.

"Your father never died," says Mom from the house door. She looks at the refrigerator. "That damn thing. He couldn't stay out of there. I told him never to come back." She looks down at the wine bottle in her hand and laughs, holding it up. "Your grandmother gave him this wine when you were born. It's the last of the… It's the last bottle."

She glances in the direction of the garage door—to the road outside—realizing she'll have to brave the outside world to refill her addiction. Fear takes over, weighing the bottle in her hand.

"He loved you. He loved me too," she says, looking at the refrigerator. "But he loved them more. He said we were all going to die, that they were spraying chemicals in the sky—all over." She laughs, looking at the half full bottle, and chugs it. "Who knew he wasn't bat shit crazy?"

I don't want to hear it. It doesn't matter. I look at my mother. He chose something—someone else over her. That's what killed her. She couldn't even see that out of the world, out of all the people who died, she was still alive. I walk over to the woman who broke everything about me, who shunned my firstborn. The woman who never recovered from her heart being torn apart. I kiss her cheek, and walk into the refrigerator.

She begins to cry.

I cross the portal and look back.

I see a woman too broken to live, and too afraid to die.

Deception

I THOUGHT I WOULD BE LED INTO A KINGDOM—A Palace —that had swept my father off his feet, but it was a dump. It was a cabin. Something about the windows wasn't right. There is grass outside, but no sky. It is as if there is a wall around the exterior in the distance.

I run past Bastet, out the front door. An aircraft hangar surrounds the cabin, hiding it from the outside world. There are no airplanes, just the beat-up looking cabin.

"He's buried over there," she says, pointing at a rock by the edge of the hangar's wall.

I walk over. There is no name, no date, only a small handprint marked by pink paint.

"That's my daughter's," she says, joining me. "I found him inside this cabin, staring at the corner, rocking in his chair."

I hoped he had been driven crazy. I look at her. She looks a lot like me—like him.

She avoids my eyes, staring down at the rock, then away toward the hangar doors. "He saved me."

"What do you mean?"

Her face turns red. Her pupils narrow.

"You owe me," I say. She owes me much more than answers.

She lowers her chin. "I was a sex slave. One night I ran away. I bumped into your dad, not long after he arrived here."

"You were a prostitute?"

She bursts out with a laugh. "I wish. I had no choice. My mother sold me to this guy when I was eight." She takes a breath and stands taller, stepping toward the hangar's doors.

A chill ripples through my body. I rhythmically follow her steps, leaving my thoughts behind me—back in the cabin where my father chose to leave me. There is nothing left for me in the past. Nothing left in either world for me. If I'm lucky, death will claim me on this last journey.

She opens the hangar doors. They creak, allowing us enough room to squeeze through. She presses her back against the door and scans the open field before us. It is overgrown, but captivating, covered with butterflies and bees.

"Where are we going?" I ask.

She points down a worn path.

"What made you work for Seth?" I say.

"Your father asked me to." She pushes the aircraft hangar door closed. It clanks shut. "He said it was the only way to save you."

Me?

"Well, humans," she says. "I don't think he knew your mom's secret."

"What secret?" I say.

She starts down the path.

"What secret?" I repeat.

She stops, comes face to face with me, and grabs my wrist. "This secret. The ability to create life."

"How are we supposed to save humanity?" I say.

She lets go of my arm and shrugs. "He didn't get around to explaining that one."

How the fuck wouldn't she know? She spent more time with him than he ever spent with me—all this time—and she doesn't know?

She continues down the path, through the woods.

I grab her hand and pull her back. "Go search his stuff—"

"Don't you think I've already done that?" she yells, and scrunches her nose, trying to force away the tears pooling in her eyes. She motions to her blouse, the fabric soaked with milk.

I feel the remainder of my milk drop—rush—to spill out. There's milk, but there is no baby. I look at the ground, the brown grass. I want to believe her, to keep going. But everything in my body grounds me to stick in that place and not move.

I can't help the flood of memories. The one that sticks, brings back the feeling of summer's dried-out grass beneath my feet. We couldn't afford air-conditioning in the house, and the temperature had been rising for days. Jackson came down the stairs with an orange swimsuit in his hand, completely naked. He flung himself into my arms, not caring that Carter was already there. I expected Carter to cry and scream, but instead little laughs bellowed out. The orange swimsuit fell from Jackson's grip. I had to ease both boys to the floor to grab it, falling backwards, laughing, embracing them—the moment—taking it all in. Part of me knew that one day it would end—but not this soon—it's too soon. *It's too soon.* Jackson ran outside naked, laughing, heading straight for the sprinkler. His little toes stomped through the dried grass. I can feel it beneath my feet. Carter lets out a giggle.

It is only a memory now.

I fall to my knees.

Bastet rests her hand on my shoulder and sinks down beside me, hugging me. "If we hurry, you can still save him."

Nothing Left to Give

A MAN'S FIGURE COMES DOWN THE PATH.

Fear stops the tears.

His right arm glistens like metal in the sunlight.

Brad. I jump up, running toward him, flying into his arms.

"Arden," he says, embracing me, making life a little more bearable. The flesh of his left hand cups the back of my head, pushing my face into his chest. The smell of cannabis engulfs me.

I bury my face deeper. Death can follow.

"What are you doing with her?" he says, looking over my shoulder at Bastet. He lets go of my head, pushing me back behind him.

I rest my hand on his shoulder. "She's okay."

He glances at me. His face changes to fear or disappointment, I can't tell. He stares into my eyes, then at the scrapes running down my cheeks. "What happened to you?"

"Nephthys…," I say.

He pulls me back into his chest and whispers, "That's not what I mean. He's gone, isn't he?"

I bury my face again. This time tears choke me and wet his shirt. *He…. He… is*. I nod, not wanting to acknowledge the words that I know would have to come out of my mouth. Everything is gone.

Brad squeezes me. "Does Osiris know?"

What? I push him away. "You knew?"

"I heard," he says, refusing to look at me.

I can't believe it.

"I didn't know, per se. I overheard. Everyone kind of knew. It was the look he gave you at the cabin. It was obvious. We knew something from his past ate at him, tore at his heart. I didn't know it was…" He looks at Bastet and back at me. "I didn't think it was my place to tell you. Besides, if you didn't remember, maybe it was better that way. I don't know what I would've…"

My face burns with discomfort. Bastet looks at me, trying to figure out the riddle Brad's talking about. I look her square in the eyes. "He raped me."

Her mouth drops open. She looks away from me, into the forest.

Brad should've shut up, but he kept talking, "It wasn't like that. He's in love with you. He's been in love with you for... years."

"That's not love," Bastet says. "It's infatuation."

"Let's go." I'm ready to get out of there, away from the conversation, the remnants of my father's alternate life. I glance down the overgrown, faded path leading us out of the woods, away from the field and hidden cabin. *How'd Brad get here?* I turn around and observe him. "How long?"

"I don't know." Brad says, "He's been with us for—"

"No." I say. "How long have you known about my father's refrigerator?"

He holds up his hands. "Arden, I swear, I just found the map."

"What map?" Bastet steps past me, between us.

"The portal map." Brad digs into his pocket and pulls out a crumpled paper, yellowed with age.

Her eyes light up. She walks past him, down the path he had come, into the shadows of the overhanging trees. "Let's go."

Brad doesn't know where we're going, but he tags along anyway. He tells us his story: of running from a helicopter full of guardsmen, falling down the side of the mountain, returning to the cabin to find Ranger Steve dead. Then he went looking for us, finding Jeff crushed beneath the helicopter.

Bastet stops and glances back at me with those animalistic eyes. I can't avoid them. They're addictive. Each time I look away, I have to look back. There's no doubt, mine now look the same. What does she want from me? What's motivating her to help me? "What are you getting from helping me?"

"Revenge." She glances at Brad, then continues through the trees. The path thins more, like a worn deer trail—if they have deer in this world.

The trees end and a white sidewalk appears at the forest's edge. It follows a roundabout. A smaller sidewalk frames the small circle at the roundabout's center. A plaque is situated in its middle.

"You'll want to cover your face," says Bastet.

"I know," I say.

"Not you," she says, pulling the wrap that had held Carter from her neck, handing it to Brad.

The Green Pyramid

IT IS DAWN BY THE TIME WE REACH THE PYRAMID OF Tekk Corp. Sunrays sparkle off the green stone.

The sun has become the hand of a clock, counting down the minutes until dusk. Carter is to be mummified soon. His soul will split. Half will stay with his corpse and the other will make its way into the afterlife. Bastet said if I kill Seth before Carter's heart is weighted against the feather of Ma'at, I can save him from death. But she makes no mention of how the dagger of Anubis plays into that.

She presses her thumb over the keypad and the door to the pyramid opens.

It's too easy. My gut tells me to run, but Brad nudges me through the entrance. The plan is to sneak into Seth's living quarters and slit his throat while he sleeps.

The lobby is empty and the hidden doors behind Tekk Corp's logo are ajar. She climbs the stairs. Part of me wants to believe she is telling the truth. The other part is afraid we are being delivered to Seth on a platter. She stops at the third floor, flattens her back against the wall, and peers around the threshold, into the hallway. The coast is clear. She steps out.

I want to stay with my back against the wall, blend into it like a chameleon.

Brad grabs my hand and steps out first, shielding the path before me.

The hallway is empty.

Bastet stops at the first door on the left, leans her ear against it, and swipes her card. It blinks red twice, then turns green. The lock clicks and the door slides open. Beyond is a nursery. The walls are painted with ocean animals. A dim light illuminates its dark blue walls. An empty bassinet hugs the left side of the room. Beside it is a rocking chair and changing table.

The room is empty.

Panic crawls up my spine like a spider.

The door compresses shut behind us.

Bastet turns around, facing us, with a grin plastered to her lips.

My heart falls. *Shit. How could I be so stupid?* I let go of Brad's hand and nudge his shoulder.

His body stiffens and he digs into his pocket, scrambling for seeds.

"Bitch," rolls out of my lips. I step back toward the door we had come in, but it doesn't budge.

She heads for a door in the back, opposite us. It slides open. A wall of Robes stand ready outside. Seth steps out from between them and greets her with a kiss. He looks at me. "I always get what I want."

"The guy has the map," she says.

Seth's eyes light up. He pushes past her and charges Brad. Brad pulls a handful of seeds out, flinging them into a semi-circle before us. They grew into thick bushes of Poison Oak. Seth pushes his way through them. Brad makes the branches wrap around Seth's wrists, restraining him in place. Seth grunts. The branches twist around the snake tattoo of his right arm, then loosens. Brad is losing control. Sweat beads on his forehead. Seth gains control of the branch twisted around his arm, and shoots it back at Brad. It wraps around Brad's throat, tightening, choking him.

"No!" I scream, ramming my palm into Seth's face, sending him backward.

He lands on the bushes of poison ivy with a grunt.

Brad falls to the ground, gasping for air.

I'm going to kill the son-of-a-bitch. I step toward Seth. He had taken Carter from me. It is because of him, that my baby is dead. A sharp, stabbing pain floods my body. My arm goes numb. I look down. There is a tranquilizer sticking out of my bicep.

The ocean painted on the nursery walls swirls around me, until it all goes dark.

Abyss

"Mommy," says Jackson.

It was nighttime. Everything was dark. His voice was faint, coming from his bedroom. He's saying something, but I can't make out what it is.

I slide out of bed, stumbling from my room to his. I walk through the doorway of his room and think I see a shadow move in the closet.

Jackson looked surprised to see me.

"Hey baby," I said. "What's wrong?"

He looked down at my belly, 30 weeks full with Carter. His fingers slid across my nightgown and his thumb stopped at my stretched-out belly button.

"Who were you talking to?" I said.

"The king of the underworld," he said.

Chills crawl up my spine. "Who is the king?"

"He watches over us when we sleep," he said. "He's waiting for the baby."

My skin crawled. I rested my hand atop his and pressed it against my belly, waking up Carter, who then kicked against Jackson's hand, making him giggle. "You're safe here. I'll always be right here."

Jackson looked down at our hands and to the comforter. "He said something bad is going to happen."

That night I wished Frank wasn't working the nightshift. It felt like every window, every door had been left wide open, letting the evils of life in. I sat on the bed with him. "What did the King say?"

Jackson let go and rolled over, facing the wall away from me.

"Jackson?"

He's quiet.

"Nothing bad is going to happen." I wiped the hair from his face and lay beside him. "You're safe here. I'm here."

"He's here," he whispered. "He's always here. He said he loves you. That's okay Mom. You can love them both. He's a nice guy. I don't think Dad would mind. He watches over him too."

I didn't know what to think. Was this some kind of imaginary friend he'd conjured up? Was this some evil side of my child? I looked at Jackson and sank deeper into the mattress. That's stupid, there's nothing even slightly evil about him or his imagination.

"Love you, Mommy," he said.

I ran my fingers through his hair and kiss the back of his head, taking in the scent—the feel of his warmth.

Books fall off the bookshelf, beside the closet, behind me.

"Love him too, Mommy," he said.

Confined

I AWAKE LAYING ON A BENCH IN A PRISON CELL, surrounded by bars. Osiris is in an adjoining cell, staring at me, sitting on the bench.

"I love him, Mommy." Jackson's voice lingers in my thoughts.

I sit up. My head throbs.

The room's door opens.

Two Robes drag in Brad. His body is limp in their arms, his head hangs to the ground. They drag him into the cell across from mine, throwing him to the floor. His face hits the concrete loud enough to be heard.

The Robes face me, looking past me at Jordan who's asleep on the bench. The door of our cell slides open. The men step in, pulling batons from their belts, flicking them to extend.

I stand, stumbling backward until my back hits the prison wall.

"Get the girl," the taller of the two says, staring at Jordan. He looks at me. "She should make a good fuck."

The other guy grabs Jordan's arm, yanking her off the bench.

"No!" I grab onto Jordan like I should've in the diner.

"Pathetic," says Osiris from behind me, pressed up against the bars.

The Robe looks at me—past me—at him. "You keep your mouth shut, or your ass will be next."

The taller Robe punches Jordan in the stomach and she falls to the floor.

"No," slips out of my mouth. "You can't."

Osiris whispers, "I'm sorry."

I step away from the bars—away from him.

The Robe swings, punching me in the face, to the ground.

The room blurs and my cheek throbs. *Son of a bitch hit me*. I stand back up, holding my jaw, biting down against the pain. I'm sick of being some girl they all think they can take advantage of. I clench my fists at my side until my nails grow. The room turns grey. The blood in my veins pounds. I swing at the guy holding Jordan's wrist. My nails slice through his arm and his hand falls to the floor. He screams. The second man swings his baton. I catch it mid-air, snapping it in two.

He freezes, backing away, pulling the cell door shut to lock us in.

I charge the cell door, grab the bars, and throw it from its hinges—onto the man.

Jordan shoots to her feet.

"Hurry," says Osiris.

Jordan sprints past me, grabbing the confiscated seed bags, and searches the unconscious Robe for a key to open the other doors.

I grab the bars of Brad's prison cell first and tear the door off. The blood in my veins eases back to normal. Brad is unconscious. I try to pull him up, but he is too heavy. His synthetic arm is too heavy. I look back at Osiris. I expect him to be hovering at his cell door, begging to get out. Instead he sits on the bench with his hands folded.

Jordan hurries back with a set of keys, slowing as she glances at Brad and me. "Shit" motions through her lips before she continues to Osiris' cell, unlocking it.

He spares no time, pushing past me, scooping up Brad like he's a feather.

We sprint into the hallway.

A red light illuminates the white walls. A siren sounds, deafening the approaching Robes now making their way into the corridor.

I'm the one Seth wants. I stop. The others have their whole lives to live. Mine is done. *I have nothing to live for, no reason to keep fighting. Carter's gone.* There's no saving him anymore.

"Arden!" Jordan looks back at me. She knows what I'm thinking, it's plastered all over my face. She freezes in her escape, running back, risking capture and the destruction of her innocence. She reaches for my hand. "I won't go without you."

That means willingly sacrificing her body to those monsters. After what I've done, there is no doubt they'll seek revenge. I won't let her do that. I look back at the Robes: the guy pinned beneath the bars I'd thrown on him.

I grasp her hand and run.

Osiris is halfway down the hallway up ahead, dragging Brad over one shoulder. Brad's mechanical arm dangles at his free side. The red light reflects off its metal like a stop signal.

Osiris kicks open the stairwell door.

A man on the other side yelps, tumbling backwards.

Osiris glances back over his shoulder. "Jordan!"

She digs into her pouch, flinging her fingers out.

The seeds fall to the floor, bouncing.

She freezes, staring at them.

I sprint to her side.

Osiris charges the Robes stampeding up the stairwell, plowing them over. Jordan and I maneuver over their tattered bodies, descending behind him.

He stops at the bottom of the stairs, in front of a door that leads to the lobby. He presses his finger to his lips and leans an ear against it. Behind him, further down the stairs is an exit—a door that no doubt leads into an alleyway.

Brad moans.

Osiris leans him up against the wall. "You all right?"

"Never felt better." Brad leans his cheek in his left hand, steadying his head. His eyes shoot around the stairwell looking for something, resting upon me. He smiles. It is good to see him.

Every second counts. I sprint past them and fling open the alleyway door.

Bastet stands outside with two men.

Jordan pushes past me and throws the seeds that are still left in her hand. They fall to the ground like she's feeding pigeons.

Bastet laughs. "Get them."

I pick up a seed, roll it in my palm, and let it fall between my fingertips to the ground. It doesn't grow.

Osiris charges the first Robe and snaps his neck in one sweep. I take the sprouted seed from my pocket—the one Nephthys gave me. Its thin, green leaves grow into thick brown branches. I envision the branch reaching, shooting toward the second Robe, through his torso, and rooting to the ground, pinning him in place. And it does.

Bastet stares at me, lowering her head like she is bowing, but leaving her eyes fixated, piercing through me.

Jordan steps in front of me, blocking her path and my view.

"No, she's mine," Brad says. He bends down, scooping a handful of the fallen seeds. They do nothing. He slams them back down.

"We don't have a chance," Jordan says, grabbing my shoulder, tugging me away toward the street. One Robe is dead. Mine is now stuck standing with the blades of a tree holding his corpse up. Blood drains from his lips.

Brad charges Bastet.

Osiris stops him, nodding in our direction. "Go."

Bastet pulls out a baton. Its ends light with fire, burning through the branches I grew. They turn to ash. A cloud of black particles sparkles in the sunlight and falls over the ground.

Jordan pulls me down the alley to a busy main street. Brad is waving a hand like he's summoning a cab. The next vehicle speeds by. Its tires screech as it makes a sharp turn, not wanting to get involved.

I glance back at Osiris. Bastet shoves the baton to the ground, into his stomach. He screams in agony.

A car pulls up to the curb.

Brad takes the backseat, sliding over. Jordan hops up front, taking the passenger's side. The driver is a thin man, even for their world. He stares at me with urgent eyes—to get in the car.

Bastet gets up, towering over Osiris.

I jump into the back with Brad.

"Go!" Jordan yells at the driver. "Go!"

He does so without thinking, without knowing what he's getting himself into.

Bastet chucks the baton at the car, busting out the back window. It lands on Brad's jeans, burning through them.

He roars with pain, throwing the baton out the window.

Bastet storms after us on foot, until she reaches the baton. We are too far away. Her figure fades as the cab speeds out of town.

Jordan digs into her seed bag, sifting through the different shapes in her hand. She shoves them back into the bag and leans her head against the window.

I know that feeling: staring out the window at a clothesline filled with little socks I'll never use.

The car hits a pothole. Brad's body bounces and shifts on the seat, pinning his weight against my side.

The driver's eyes are large. His lips tremble as he whispers, "Where to?"

"The far end of the city," I say. "Where that Memorial circle is."

"You mean Anubis' Garden?" The cabby stops at a red light.

I look at Brad, but he ignores me, looking out the opposite window. I would call attention if I badgered him about the garden—the memorial—and the cabby's suspicions are already eating through the car's awkward silence.

Jordan sinks down in her seat, pulling her hood up.

The streets come alive. It will be dawn soon—in my world. I'm running out of time. Soon there will be nothing left for me to save, except for myself, and I have no interest in that.

"Just blow through the light," I say.

"You're being followed," the driver's eyes fill the rearview mirror, "right?"

Brad clears his throat.

"Three cars back," says the driver. "If I blow through this

light, you're caught."

Brad wiggles in his seat, no doubt trying to alleviate the burned flesh of his leg.

"It's gonna cost you big, though." The driver puts his hand on the back of Jordan's headrest and glances back at me. He looks like a guy who has climbed out of a dark past—a creature with sunken cheeks.

I force a smile. He holds our fate in his hands and pissing him off would be a very bad idea.

"You might want to check out that building on your right," says the cabby. "Now."

I look right and can feel the eyes from a passing car penetrate every cell of my being.

"Arden," Jordan whispers between the window and her seat. "I'm scared."

"I'm right here," flows out too fast, ripping my thoughts into the past—into glimpses of my boys. While fighting to live, I'd forgotten how much I want to die.

She leans the side of her face against the seat.

Traffic thins as we head for the city's edge. Tekk Corp vehicles still trail us. The cabby taps his fingers on the steering wheel, drumming out the nervousness, as we close-in on our destination. The road loops around a small patch of grass—the roundabout. A gold statue of Anubis is at its center. The cabby cuts the wheel right, taking a side street instead of the roundabout.

"What are you doing?" I say.

"They will kill you," he says. "I've seen it before. Driving around town for ten years. You see things, things people would never believe if you told them."

He takes another right, another block, backtracking. The sides of the white buildings light up with blue lights. A siren blasts out from behind us.

"Shit," slips out of the cabby's mouth. He cuts the wheel again, flinging the cab over a crosswalk, scattering its pedestrians. He glances in the rearview at me. "Where exactly are you going sweetheart, 'cause it's now or never."

"Take a left before the statue, through the woods. You'll see it when you get to it."

He speeds through the next turn, tipping the car a bit, then levels out, yelling back, "That overgrown path?"

"Yes!" I say.

He takes it. Tire marks burn into the grass, leaving ruts deep in the forest's soil.

The cabby grunts as he maneuvers through the trees.

The cruiser behind us smashes into one. Another closes in, but we've gained a few minutes' clearance.

"What the fuck…?" The cabby says as the aircraft hangar reveals itself.

"Through the doors," I say. "There's a cabin inside."

"No way." The Cabby slams on the breaks.

Brad leans forward, digging his metal fingers into the man's shoulder blade. His eyes met the cabby's in the rearview mirror. Brad could kill him with one twist of his neck.

The cabby shoots the car forward, covering his face as the front of the car crashes through the hangar door. He slams on the breaks afterward, but it's too late. The front of the car careens through Dad's cabin. The roof caves in, covering the front of the car. The engine seizes and hisses.

The sirens trailing us grow louder.

Jordan kicks open her door and hops out. The crash has exposed the opposite corner of the cabin that leads into my mother's garage. Jordan sprints to it and stands by, anxiously waiting for one of us to transport her through the portal.

I jump out of the cab, pushing the ceiling boards up out of my way.

Brad drags himself out of the car. His face is beet-red.

"Do you need help?" I say.

"Go!" he says.

"We're cornered." The cabby flings his door open and falls out. "There's no way out."

I grab onto his sleeve and Jordan's hand, running into the corner, yelling, "Duck!"

I kick open the small refrigerator door and throw Jordan through, in front of me.

"What?" she says as her head whacks the top of the refrigerator frame and she falls through, out onto the garage floor.

I heave the cabby through the door next and tumble in after him.

"Arden?" My mother's voice perks up as I push myself off the ground. She says, "Is that you?"

My arms buckle at the sound of her voice. Brad will be coming through soon. I yell at the cabby still lying in the path, "Roll! Move!"

He rolls all the way to the tool bench.

No one follows. No Robes. No Bastet. No Osiris. No Brad.

Where's Brad? My heart pounds. *Brad?* We cleared the spot he was supposed to tumble out onto. I stare at the open door—the open portal—waiting.

Purgatory

AN HOUR PASSES. AND THEN ANOTHER, BEFORE JORDAN scurries off to the kitchen with Mom.

I grab Dad's old chainsaw and the chair from his bench, situating myself directly in front of the refrigerator. I try the chainsaw. Smoke spits out, pluming at the ceiling, filling the garage. If Brad isn't coming, I'll at least be ready for any fucker that is.

The cabby sits in the corner behind me, beside the garage door that leads into the side yard. Its small glass window captures a moonlit night. He stands, staring out its window at the world of boxed houses—into the darkness—saying, "Where are we?"

"You wouldn't believe me even if I told you, trust me. I don't even believe it." I pick up a pair of safety glasses and slide them on, taking my attention back to the refrigerator, the grey-hued portal before me.

The chainsaw's gas fizzles out and the fumes hug the ceiling. I drift off staring at the entanglement of our worlds at the portal's center. Nothing else is visible past that.

"Hey," Jordan says, walking into the garage with a tray of food. She looks at the cabby.

He'd given up on answers and passed out in the corner.

"Did you tell him?" she says.

"No." There's no reason to. Plus, my head can't concentrate on the refrigerator if I think about the complexity of it: the ideas of this world—that world. *Carter.*

"I'll take over," she says. "You need to eat something."

I can't eat. Eating will commit me to another day of life. "I've got it. Besides... you're... you're..."

"Thirteen actually." She smiles and holds out the tray to me. It's full of cheese cubes, carrots, and apples. "It's not organic, but it's not processed."

I have no idea what she's talking about, but my body won't deny the food. I take the tray and sit beside the cabby, nudging him awake.

His eyelids flutter open and he startles. His nightmare isn't a dream. He can escape, just as much as we can.

"So what are they?" he nods toward my mother and Jordan.

I laugh and shove a piece of cheese in my mouth.

"I think you're beautiful," he says.

I snort and the piece of cheese flies out of my mouth. "What is worth money in your world?"

"My world?" he says, staring at my eyes—the eyes Nephthys gave me.

"Yeah," I say, pointing at the refrigerator. "That world, in there."

His eyes scan mine. "You're not from Earth, are you?" His eyes flash over the room, stopping at my mother. There is no doubt I'd gotten my looks from her. He looks back to my eyes. "You're… You weren't born like me?"

I laugh. "I was born—"

"I born her," says Mother standing, pacing. She's drunk. But from what? The last of the wine was… days ago.

Something feels wrong—out of place.

I shove the food tray into the cabby's lap and stand up, looking out the garage door window.

An armored National Guard vehicle is parked out front.

Shit. I whisper, yelling at Mom, "How long have they been here?"

"Oh those nice men. They've been coming here for days, off and on. They bring me food… and..." She looks away from me. They had sugared her up with booze.

I look at Jordan, "Why didn't you tell me they were—?"

"They weren't," says Jordan.

There's a knock at the front door.

Mother makes for it.

"Mom," I say.

She looks back at me.

"They'll kill me," I say.

Jordan shifts her eyes away from the refrigerator for a second.

Cabby takes to his feet.

Mom's face shifts. She realizes there is a possibility these friendly guardsmen could in fact have ill intentions, but she continues for the door anyway—for the addiction she can't shake. Before leaving the garage she says, "Everything isn't always about you, Arden."

They pound against the front door again.

We could run out of the garage, to the side yard, but then we will still be out in the open—vulnerable—in a territory I no longer know.

Cabby comes over. "You're the one all those conspiracy theorist people talk about. The one to unite worlds, give Duat back to her people—her caretakers." He laughs. A grin spreads across his face. "Oh my God, do you know what this means? Wow! Wait until Geb hears about this." His smile fades. "Shit. I'm going to owe him twenty bucks. I bet him that you weren't real. That the stories were ancient myths."

A faint male voice precedes the footfalls, running down the hallway toward the garage.

Seeds. I spin around trying to remember where Mom's spring garden shit is.

The footfalls are right outside the door.

Brad steps in through the doorway, wearing a National Guard uniform. He charges the refrigerator, slams its door shut, knocks it over, and pushes it away from the wall. His mechanical fingers pull the brim of his hat down, shielding his eyes from us.

I want to run to him, embrace the joy that he is still alive, but I pause, searching his face for evidence of trust.

He whispers my name, "Arden."

I bow my head and stand still. His reserve makes me uncomfortable.

He looks over at Jordan and laughs. "What are you doing?"

She looks quite mad in safety goggles, holding a chainsaw. At 13 years old, I wonder if she would even be able to start the thing.

"These girls have been playing this all afternoon," Mother says, entering the garage. She looks at me. I can't believe she thinks this is some game. She brushes off the look of disbelief I give her with a, "What?"

Why would I ever think she'd be any help?

"Brad was always a good kid." She pauses, noticing for the first time that my pupils are no longer human.

I thought she would try to destroy me for becoming one of the creatures she so despised. Instead, she walks over and places her cold palm against my cheek, smiling. She looks to the ground and nods in acceptance. She can't say she loves me, but it's the first time I've felt it since Father died—left us.

I forgive her for dismissing Jackson, for making him feel like less of a person around her in Carter's presence, for making my choice to keep him a nightmare. I hug her. Somehow I know she can't live in this world any longer.

"It was always about you," she whispers in my ear.

The sound of distant airplanes approaches.

She lifts her head, kisses my cheek, and holds out a handful of seeds.

I look at her. *How'd you know?*

She dumps the seeds in my hand and cups her fingers around mine.

I look at Brad. "Why didn't Nephthys' seeds work?"

He paces. "They replaced them with genetically modified seeds—engineered not to germinate."

Jordan steps closer to him. "How can they do that?"

"They've been doing it since 1973," he says, nervously scanning the garage door window for anymore cars—armored vehicles. He stops and looks at me. "That's why farmers can't collect last year's seeds. Their crop isn't viable. They have to buy seed each year. Bound like shackles. Most people think GMOs were created to save the world from starvation. But the world is still starving. They modified the seeds just in case... just in case we discovered our true power. If they flooded the market with non-viable seeds, it wouldn't matter who discovered their true power—their ability to grow things." He takes a handful of seeds from his bag with his left hand, holding them in the flesh of his palm, holding them out to me. "Nephthys picked you. And she doesn't make mistakes. That's why Osiris guarded you. Your father knew. He left to protect you." His eyes turned to the ground. "But Tekk Corp has a way of wearing people down."

Jordan pipes up, "What about the seeds? What are we going to do? How are we going to protect ourselves?"

They all look to me—like I have any clue.

Silence falls over the room, lasting a full minute that feels like an hour.

Jordan walks over, placing a hand on my still clenched fist of seeds. "You can still save him."

"You get the dagger of Anubis," says Mother. "Within his garden is the vault of Set. There you will find every seed created by man. There you will find—"

"No." Brad's face changes. It's the first time I've seen him fighting the fear swelling up inside. His lips part, but no words come out. He tries again, slowly saying, "No."

"Why not?" says Jordan.

"They'll kill us all, just for the thought," he says, looking at me, surely reading my blank expression.

"The seed vault isn't like the one in our world—"

"The one in Iceland?" says Jordan.

Brad lets out a weak laugh. "Yeah, like the one that flooded. Fucking permafrost melted, flooding the vault. Theirs houses the seeds of both worlds." He walks over to me. "They keep it in their world, away from people like me. Like you."

Jordan lets out a boisterous laugh. "Could you imagine how awesome that would be? All those seeds?"

"It doesn't matter," says Brad sitting on the stool. "We'll never get in."

"If the legend is true," says Jordan, looking at me, "then Ambrosia seeds may actually exist."

"It does," says Mother.

"Then we have to go," says Jordan.

"Why bother?" I say.

"Ambrosia..." Jordan says, "is the elixir of life. Immortality."

"Amrita," says Mother. "That is what they called it before the Greeks came and conquered Egypt." She looks at me. "Immortality has a price."

"I don't care," I say. "He's my son. I can't do nothing.... I've already done that. I've already lost one. I can't—"

"You'll die if you try to enter that vault," says Brad.

"I'll die if I don't." The smell of Dad's workbench fills the room. I wanted so bad for my boys to meet their grandfather. I slide my fingers through the dust on his workbench, watching the clumps of dead wood gather.

"What if I could get you in?" says the cabby, standing up from his place against the wall.

Car lights pierce through the garage door window.

Brad's whole body turns. "They're here."

A SWAT van has parked on the front lawn.

Jordan tugs on the chainsaw. The pull-string chokes with a sputter.

Brad holds his hand up in protest, shaking his head. He looks past her at the refrigerator. We don't know who's waiting on the other side of the portal now. He tells of another portal close by, that he'd seen on the map now in Seth's hands. Even if he remembered its location, it's not an option. We can't get to any other portal and Brad can't remember precisely where it's located.

Guardsmen kick in the front door.

Brad grabs the refrigerator, throwing it back into place.

Mom walks over and opens its door.

I stop beside her to say goodbye, say something.

"Don't forget about this world," she says, holding out a hand with a seed sprouting from its split shell.

I take it, ducking my head to enter the refrigerator, and run through the portal—away from my feelings for her.

Gunshots splatter through the garage and she screams.

I stumble, through the blurred edges of our worlds, over pieces of wood—pieces of the cabin my father spent the remainder of his life in after abandoning us. The taxi is still stuck beneath the cabin's fallen corner. The hangar is empty.

Brad grabs onto the cabby and then Jordan, throwing them through the portal. The cabby likely doesn't know his ability to transcend worlds, but Brad does. Jordan slams into my back, knocking me to the ground. The cabby comes through next, careening into the back wall, or what is left of it. Brad stands on the other side of the portal. He can't cross over without me.

Bullets fly around him and he punches a guardsman to the ground. He turns his back to me, facing the doorway to the house. Another guardsman charges into the garage. I jump into the spinning space between our worlds and dig my fingers into Brad's shirt, yanking him backwards, into the space between their world and ours.

"Thanks," he says through a lost breath. He looks at me. His cheek bleeds from a grazed bullet. He lets out a breath of relief and then a half-ass laugh.

Mom screams and the onslaught of bullets dissolve in the corner of the refrigerator. Her wine bottle smashes to the floor. I wait for her body to follow.

Brad grabs my arm and pulls me up, away from the last moments of her life.

I have abandoned her like my father had.

Illusions

BRAD RIPS A PIECE OF PAPER FROM THE CABIN WALL. The wind attempts to steal it from his fingers as he studies it.

I sprint to clear the hangar as fast as possible and hide along the footpath's forest. Jordan and the cabby follow. We clear the rubble of the cabin and make for the trees as fast as humanly possible. Night is upon us and the city will soon be bustling.

Brad lags behind in the cabin. His silhouette darkens as flames engulf the aircraft hangar in the meadow behind us.

We stop to watch it burn.

"Let's go," says Brad, stepping around us to take the lead.

We stumble over roots and sticks to the far end of the forest, zigzagging through trees, cautious of any and every noise.

When we reach the road, to the roundabout circling Anubis' Garden, there is no sign that Tekk Corp is waiting for us.

Jordan slouches down on the curb and I join her, watching the smoke rise against the navy-blue sky above the hangar, choking out the stars.

Brad walks across the asphalt to the garden of Anubis.

Cabby stands in the middle of the roundabout. Instead of looking at the shrine, he stares at the blazing fire we've left.

They'll be here soon.

Fuck: that's what he's thinking, that's what we're all thinking.

The caddy was doomed the moment he pulled up to the curb and picked us up. His eyes search the city lights in the distance for something. Then he starts off down the sidewalk, power-walking toward downtown.

"Where are you going?" Brad asks, following him.

Jordan and I hurry to catch up. He leads us to the side of town where the walls are not power-washed white, but soiled with soot.

A homeless man sits on the ground, not far away. He holds out his hand, looking for empathy, lowering his head closer to the ground in shame when he asks, "Spare some change?"

Brad digs into his pocket and places a seed in the man's hand. We need all the seeds we can get and he's handing it off like candy.

Cabby stops outside an iron backdoor. A small square peephole opens. Dragon-eyes glance over us. "Tell Belch, Notts is here."

The eyes behind the door squint into tight vertical lines, until they're almost closed, showing no pupil.

Cabby twists a section of his hair into a knot against his head.

The Dragon-eyes widen and dilate, easing back to normal—into fatter vertical lines.

Notts releases his hair and it returns to a flat position. "Tell him…," he looks over at me, "Ambrosia."

The dragon-eyes shift to me.

Brad's fingers curl into fists.

The peephole closes.

Brad grabs Notts' wrist, forcing it behind him, pulling it up the small of his back: law enforcement style. "What are you trying to pull?"

"You want into Anubis' Garden?" Notts looks past me, at the beggar, lowering his voice, "This is your best bet."

"But the garden was back there," I say, motioning at the distance we had walked—the statue and the roundabout.

Notts laughs. "That's not the real garden. The real garden is in a pyramid." He looks at me. "Forgive me."

The alley door creaks open.

The dragon-eyes behind the door belong to a bodyguard. His broad shoulders match the magnitude of his irises. His posture is hunched like a gorilla, as one would expect from the guard of a backdoor establishment.

Behind him is a dark hallway decorated with dusty, faded pictures of flapper girls: feathers and silk. Each woman is staged beside a man much too wealthy to consider her anything other than a throw-away sex toy.

The hallway opens into a strip club. Cigarette smoke hangs like a heavy cloud above the seated onlookers. Men with dragon eyes, are dressed in white business suits, all mesmerized by the woman on stage. She twists her legs around a pole, in a way that I'd never be able to.

Notts walks up to the stage.

The woman untangles herself from the pole and slides like a tiger across the stage floor toward him.

"What's a 'Belch' costing these days?" says Notts.

She rolls onto her back, thrusting her silicone breasts toward the ceiling. Some of the crowd stirs, excited by it. She spins her legs over the stage's edge, reaching for Notts' hand.

He helps her slide off stage.

Her miniskirt drifts up her thighs, revealing a penis. "What's up Notty?" she says in a deep voice. "Where them dreads?"

"My partying days are over. Got a wife and kids now." He looks back at me.

"Whatcha doing in a place like this?" Belch says.

"I need the corner suite," Notts says.

Belch looks me over and moves onto Jordan, lingering on her eyes. "It's gonna cost you."

"You owe me for that..." Notts sways, "you know...."

"Give me the girl and we call it even."

Notts looks back at Jordan. "She's too young."

"Even better," says Belch. "There are a lot of sick fucks out there in the world, and they pay big."

I step in front of Jordan. "You'll take me instead."

"I like you." Belch grins, smacks my ass, and steps into my personal space, sliding a hand down my breast.

It fucking hurts. Enough milk leaks out that my shirt dampens, painting a bullseye on my breast.

"Tell you what, you keep those babies full and I won't hand you over to the Robes. Our entire world is looking for you." He gestures to the bar's television, displaying my photograph.

Brad's weight shifts, "She stays with us."

Cabby shakes his head for Brad to stand down. Somehow he's going to get us into Anubis' Garden, and this is it.

I shake Belch's hand and restrain Brad with the other, lowering my eyes. It's Jordan or me, and something tells me this is the only way. I look at Brad. Not all of us can go.

His face turns beet red. He can't bear the thought of leaving me alone in this place, but he has to.

I lightly shake my head, encouraging him not to do anything stupid.

Belch notices. He slides his acrylic nails down the bony skin of his fishnets, and pulls a knife from his knee-high hooker-boots, pointing it at Brad. "No fast moves, lover boy."

"Why don't we continue this upstairs?" says Notts. His eyes narrow at me, as if he knows something I don't.

A paper-thin girl enters the stage and the music changes. The front door opens, letting a moment of moonlight through as new customers enter. Time is slipping. There's no way Carter can be saved. Unless I can find the garden.

Belch leads us up a set of stairs, overlooking the stage. The steps creak as our party ascends them. Five glass rooms with sliding-glass doors overlook the stage. Each has a sheer curtain that can be drawn, but each is open.

The paper-thin woman twirls around a worn-out pole, throwing pieces of bright scarves across the stage. Nineties music blares through the club. Her velvet green bodysuit has buttons at the bottom that she rips open.

I look away.

"Coming?" Belch bellows from the third door—the center room.

The others have already entered. The building is as old as the dusty flapper photographs mounting its walls. The room's corners are curved, yet inside room three the corners are boxed. Cowboy pictures cover the back wall that frames the building and room. A faded handkerchief thrown over the rooms only lampshade creates an intimate atmosphere despite the sheerness of the walls.

Belch shuts the glass door behind me, closing us all in. He faces the group and grabs my arm, yanking me with him across the room toward the farthest corner. I have lost everything and now a pimp in his whore house drags me across the room. He pulls me past the lamp and into the corner—through a portal—into a room where it's walls are striped in floral wallpaper. Victorian furniture and elegant oil paintings form a bedroom.

"Bobby?" an old woman's voice rises from the bottom of a wooden staircase just outside the bedroom. "Bobby, is that you?"

Belch lets out a sigh, "Yes."

A withered old woman pops her face in the doorway. The angle of her glasses captures sunrays, blinding me.

Earth. I jerk my arm away from Belch, shielding my eyes. Ra made it into my world, bringing the sun with him. I begin to sink to the floor. *What's the point? There's no point to go on.*

Belch grabs my arm, yanking me back up.

"Bobby," says the old lady. "What are you doing to that poor young woman?"

"He's holding me hostage," I say. "What's the plan again? Oh, that's right, pimp me out in exchange for passage through your house?"

"It's her, Mom," says Belch. He holds the knife against the fresh cut along my collarbone.

His mother takes her time making her way over to us, smiles at me, and smacks me in the face. The momentum knocks me to the side and Belch lets go, laughing. She appears human and she's still alive, which means she's one of us—she has the power to grow things. But I can see it in her eyes, she slept with one of the shadow people, either willingly or forced. It changed her. She pushes her glasses further up her nose and stands as straight as her hunched back will allow. "Sell her to Geb."

"No!" yells Brad, pushed through the portal behind us by Notts with Jordan.

Belch pulls me back beside him, holding the knife as ransom against my throat.

"That's not part of the deal," says Brad.

"Change of plans," says Belch.

The old lady grabs a handful of my hair and throws me onto the mattress, withdrawing a gun. "Better get going."

Notts drags Jordan down the stairwell.

Brad crosses his arms and stands guard at the top step, unmoving.

Belch slices into my collarbone. It isn't deep, but it burns like a motherfucker. I clench my teeth, trying to bear the pain, but I can't. Tears pour from my eyes. I'd wanted so bad to feel death. Now, I'm not sure I can bear the pain.

I had Jackson by C-section, with no support person there—except for the anesthesiologist. Carter's birth was the complete opposite. He came strong and fast, pushing into this world 100 percent naturally. I never felt so much pain. When he was in my arms, that pain disappeared into the past. Love replaced it within a single moment. I open my eyes.

Brad goes for Belch, but the old lady cocks a gun. "Now, now dear. I believe you boys had a deal." She aims it at him. "Be on your way."

Belch grabs onto my hair, pulling me closer to him.

I slide my fingers into my pocket, where Mother's seeds ended up.

"I wouldn't do that if I were you." The old lady redirects the gun at my head.

"Relax." I continue to reach for the seeds, pulling them out. I look at Belch. "They won't have a chance without these."

He nods in approval.

His mother lowers the gun.

I step toward Brad, and Belch lets me. Brad doesn't move, doesn't offer out a hand. He stares at me. "I'm not leaving without you."

"You don't have a choice." I grab his hand, pry his fingers open, and dump the seeds into his palm. "Use them well."

The old lady presses the gun into Brad's back, directing him out of the room.

I have done the right thing. At least for their sake. This is my sentence.

Transcend

DAY TURNED TO NIGHT AS WE TRANSCENDED WORLDS—back into Duat.

The room is cold and I sit on the hooker-stained bed, staring at the portal. Belch has made his way back into his whore-house and his fucking mother has forced me to follow. My father's portal is gone and the only other I know of is the one in Tekk Corp.

I tear a piece of fabric from the bed skirt and wrap it around my wound. Thankfully it isn't too deep, but it burns. With each beat of my heart, the pounding of my veins throbs against the cut, infuriating me.

The thin stripper from earlier runs down the hallway, into the adjacent room. The walls that separate the two are glass, covered with sheer curtains. A man in a business suite hurries after her. She sits on the bed. He enters, taking no care to close the door behind him.

"Emily," he says, loosening his tie.

"Get out of here," she says. "I don't want to see you."

He steps closer and I can't help myself from closing the distance between me and the curtain, pulling it back a little.

The girl's eyes grow wild, her pupils dilate into vertical lines. She springs from the bed, charging him, throwing her fists at his chest.

He catches her wrists, throws her to the floor, grabs a handful of her hair, and forces her to her feet—chucking her anorexic figure toward the glass wall separating us. She must have seen me, but doesn't care. Her body hits the glass. Defeat fills her face. Any security, any hope for the future melts down that pane of glass.

She closes her eyes as the man yells, reminding her that she's a piece of trash. The glass fogs beneath her breath. She opens her eyes, staring into mine. Her pupils relax into circles and then tighten to vertical lines again. She pulls away from the wall to face him.

I stand straight up. There is no telling how many years she's been captive, how many times she's been thrown around. I stand a little straighter, because I need her to be everything I cannot be.

She faces him completely.

I pull back the curtain more.

She grabs a lamp from the end table and swings it—hard and fast. The handkerchief falls.

The man goes down, cupping his cheek. Blood drips between his fingers. "You bitch!"

She swings the lamp back over her shoulder like a baseball bat.

He waves his palm in the air in defense, but the metal lamp whacks it back down. She pounds it against his skull. He stops moving and her body drops to the floor in sobs by his feet.

Music from the performance downstairs floats up to the second floor.

I step into the hallway. There is a guard at the bottom of the steps, but none at my door. I walk into her room and slide my hand over her shoulder.

She gasps, looks back at me, and sinks into my arms.

I don't know her, but I know what she needs—what I need: someone to be there.

The man is still breathing, barely. His lips leak carbon dioxide, sputtering blood. She lets go and grabs his tie from the floor, wraps it around his throat, and pulls it tight until his breath stops.

A grin sweeps across her face and a sigh of relief fills the air. The tightness of her arm muscles loosens and the man's body goes limp. She begins to laugh. I sit there beside her until the laugh tapers to an exhale. She looks at me, heaving it out in delight—relief—a sense of freedom.

"Who is he?" I ask.

The smile disappears from her face. She looks at him. "My brother."

What?

Her voice goes sour, "He wants to straighten me out, clean me up." She wipes a line of snot running from her nose.

I look down at his mangled face.

She stands up, grabs a pack of smokes from the side table, and lights a cigarette.

I stare at her. How could she?

"What?" She sucks on the drug and blows it out. "Don't look at me like that. Okay? He raped me since I was four. How about that?"

I don't believe her.

A knock comes at the door.

"Time's uh..." Belch steps in. He looks at me, the bloody mess on the floor, and then at her. "Fuck, Emily. You're cleaning this shit up."

"What are you doing about this one?" She pulls the cigarette away from her lips, pointing at me. Its smoke drifts, disappearing as fast as life.

Belch smiles at me. His eyes lift to his hairline as he digs a hand into his pocket. "How about a kick?"

Emily laughs, taking another drag. A clump of spent cigarette ash falls to the floor. She lets the rest of the cigarette-butt follow, grinding it into the rug.

I stand up, stumbling backwards as fast as I can for the door.

Belch moves faster, scoops me up with one arm, and chucks me onto the bed.

My body bounces against worn springs.

Emily jumps on top of me, pinning my wrists and legs.

Belch jams a needle into my arm.

The walls rush into a blur.

She releases me.

I draw my knees into my chest, curling into a fetal position like it will help, like it will protect me.

She laughs, "How's that feel?"

Her hand slides up my leg. It feels so good. Blood rushes through my veins. I flop my head to the side trying to force my eyes to focus. I can't see the corners of the room, the threads of the comforter, or the faces of my captors.

A male voice shouts into the room, "Serena called out again."

Belch grunts. "Drive over to her place and drag her fucking ass down here. I am not dealing with this shit today."

"Who's going on stage?" the guy asks.

"Get your ass up there," Belch says to Emily.

Her fingertips slide up my inner thigh. All the blood in my body rushes to feel them. The covers feel so soft, so good against my skin.

She pushes my shoulder enough to roll me onto my back. I try to lift my head and stand, but the room spins. It's all a blur.

"Move," says Belch. His voice amplifies with each syllable. "Go get changed."

Emily's fingers retract from my pants and her weight lifts.

"And pick out something for our very own goddess," he says.

The door slams behind her.

Belch's sweaty palms wrap around my arm, yanking me off the bed. I fall to the floor. My backbone feels like it's shattered into a million pieces upon impact. After that, I can't feel anything but the carpet scraping into my spine. He drags me out the door, to the stairs, hoisting me over his shoulder to be carried down the steps.

I watch my arms flap loose, dangling behind him. The air rushing between my fingers is so refreshing. It's like I'm dead. I can't feel anything at that moment. The walls blur into lines of light. The drug pulsating in my veins floods my brain with euphoria.

Belch carries me backstage, unloading me onto a metal chair. Emily comes over with a handful of string and thin pieces of silk: a costume.

"Put it on," Belch says.

I smile. He's so funny standing there, demanding me to wear some stripper's outfit. *Whatever.* I reach out and take the damn thing.

"What are you waiting for?" he says.

"Privacy," I say.

Emily bursts with laughter.

"Now." Belch grabs my hair and rips me off the chair. He pulls the knife from his waist again, like I need a reminder. "We have a special guest coming any minute now."

Asshole. I take off my shirt, letting it float to the floor. I stand, to slide down my pants, but fall back down, missing the chair.

Emily laughs.

I run the silk between my fingers. Crusty blotches stain the crotch area, so I pull the strings of lingerie overtop my underwear.

"What the fuck are you doing?" says Belch

I have no idea what he's talking about.

He looks down at my underwear.

"I'm not wearing this without underwear. It's disgusting."

Emily lets out a grunt of offense.

Belch looks at her. "Get a new one. It's only the God of the universe. And get me some…" he glances back at me, "some of the good stuff."

Emily disappears behind a curtain. I watch a heavyset woman twirl in a thong on stage. Sweat beads on her skin and glistens in the spotlight. Emily returns with a school-girl outfit and lingerie that I would have never bought, throwing it at me.

I look at the pile of clothing at my feet.

"If you don't do it," says Belch, "I'll undress you myself." He steps closer, bends down and grabs my face to meet his eyes. "And trust me. You won't like that."

I pull my underwear down, leaning on the chair, dressing myself in the paper-thin fabric.

The bartender comes running into the backstage area.

I try to ball the clothing in front of me, cover myself, but it's no use.

The guy is out of breath, "They just pulled up."

"Start with something classy. Give them a drink on the house. We're running late." Belch shoos the guy off and glances at Emily.

She hands him a syringe.

I clench the ball of clothes in front of me and back away. "No. I don't need anything else."

Pieces of the outfit fall from my grip.

He steps closer and grabs my arm, yanking it toward him. The rest of the clothes fall to the floor.

"No." I kick at him.

Emily approaches, forcing me down long enough for Belch

to stick me again. "I can't have you growing shit."

I sink into the floor as she dresses me. The ceiling looks like it's twinkling with stars. Nausea gargles in my stomach and I roll onto my side. She nudges a pair of fuck-heels out of the way. "There's no way you're going to be able to walk in those." She jerks me up and whispers in my ear, "Don't fuck this up baby girl. That's our biggest client out there."

I want to spit in her face, but I can barely keep my head up.

She pushes me through the curtains, out onto the stage. A slow crescendo of music begins as I step into the spotlight.

A group of men in white business suits cluster, front and center. An older man sits in the middle, but the lights shift, blinding me from seeing his face.

I walk toward a pole at the stage's end, dropping pieces of the school girl outfit as I go. I reach for the bar and fall.

The spotlight spins. Male voices shout curse words. It's all muffled by the fact that I don't give a fuck what they're saying. It feels so good to lay down—right there in the blaring light. I blink and find myself in a room, lying on a bed. The walls are a soft blue. Photographs of black and white trees decorate the room. It's clean and sophisticated. The walls aren't glass.

Someone kisses my stomach.

My heart jumps. I try to sit up, see whose lips are touching me. My eyes drift over the face and to the white business suits guarding the door—watching. He kisses me again. *Fuck it feels so good.* My breath deepens. He kisses my stomach again and I rest my head back. I can't move, don't care to move. His lips reach the top of my panties. *I can't*. I use all my energy to grab onto his fucking hair and yank him away from my body. Time had wrinkled his face, but I recognize it. His name rushes through my lips like a ghost: "Dad?"

Surprise seeps across his face and shock lights up his eyes. He stands up, backing away. I can't see what he does next. The room starts spinning. The silk underwear shifts between my legs. My body wants more. *Fuck*.

"What the fuck, Arden? How are you...? What are you…? Belch!" His voice moves in and out of my consciousness. He continues blabbering things to try and make sense of the whole thing, followed by a string of profanity. Then the door slams. He is gone. They are all gone. And my world—their world—is still spinning.

I move, trying to see what's going on, but the silk rubs my nipples and the panties twist between my thighs. *Shit*. A moan escapes me. What the fuck did they give me?

The door opens. Dad is yelling at Belch, trying to get answers, wipe the taste of me off his lips.

"If you don't," says Belch, "then it is just going to be more painful for her."

The silk of my underwear is wet and the cool flow of air brushes against the thin fabric covering my now hard nipples.

Father yells, "Get Set!"

The stairs creak.

My heart pounds, beats through my veins, begging to be released in orgasm.

"Look who it is," a male voice comes from the doorway. I know that voice. Seth walks into the room.

Father says something, but it cuts off when Seth slams the door shut.

The room grows hot. There is no air flow. I feel like I'm suffocating, helpless on the bed.

"You're quite the dancer," he says.

He killed Carter. *I'm going to barf.* I roll a little, letting my panties taunt the flow of blood building in my veins. I squint my eyes.

Seth comes into a crisp view. His shirt is off. His fingers wrap beneath my chin and pull my face to his, forcing me to sit up.

Beneath the tattoo wrapping his shoulder, is a scar, like his whole arm had been cut off and sewn back on. In the same place as Brad's mechanical limb. "You didn't tell me Geb was your dad." He runs his finger down the strip of satin covering my breast, continuing to my waist.

Blood rushes to the satin and my milk lets down, leaking out.

His fingers slide down to my thighs and brush between them. Whatever fabric was still dry is now soaked. His nails scrape the top of my panties and slide them down, stopping at the indent of my C-section. He climbs on top of me and looks down at my neck—the heart locket—and yanks it, tears it away.

A tear drips down my numb cheek. I can't feel the scraped line left by the torn necklace.

He climbs off.

I sit up, my breath forcing me more than my muscles. The room spins faster.

He digs his nail along the side of the locket, opening the heart. "Tell you what." He closes it. "I'll take this instead. Whore."

"No!" I reach for it, but my depth perception is all messed up and I miss.

He heads for the door.

I get up after him, falling—stumbling—to the floor.

He passes through the threshold and two Robes barricade the exit behind him. His voice trails into the room, "Take her to Lazarus."

"Sir?" says one of the Robes, turning his head at the request.

"You heard me," Seth says.

The Robe's weight shifts. He looks at his partner and they both look down at me.

Lazarus

THE MEN SCOOP ME UP. I MAKE IT EASY FOR THEM. MY body's spent and my mind is still fuzzy. They bind my hands behind my back and throw me into the back of an SUV.

The seat bounces beneath my hips and my knees knock together. I lay on the seat, drifting in and out of consciousness. Clouds roll in overhead, dampening the sky. Real clouds. Gravel crunches beneath the tires and the vehicle sways. My knees rub together again. My panties dampen more.

"Lazarus," says one of the men.

His partner shushes him.

"If she's who they say, why don't you and I take her?"

His partner smacks him.

He moans, "Shit man, what's that for?"

"You wouldn't know what to do with that power," says the other.

The vehicle stops.

The men jump out, open my door, and tug me to a stand.

An ancient pyramid stands before us. Instead of a desert, there is forest. Instead of a crumbling stone wall, there are clumps of flourishing moss.

Stars twinkle overhead. They'd never looked so bright. The night sky glows above the pyramid's tip, reminding me for a moment, that there is still beauty left in the world.

One of the guys flings me over his shoulder. His finger brushes my panties and a moan escapes my lips. The shit they pumped into my veins pulsed through me the whole car ride. I longed for the release of orgasm. With one touch, one accidental brush of his finger, I'm limp in total ecstasy.

"Oh my God, dude," says the other guy.

"Shut up, dude." He grabs my arm and slides me off his shoulder to a standing position.

My inner thighs swish against each other with each step. My head is still foggy. The lights of the pyramid windows blur with the stars above as I stumbled into the inside.

Elegant marble walls create a spacious living space. Hieroglyphics painted in golds and blues line the room. A red velvet throw rug connects the entrance to an altar, covered in lit candles.

The two men scamper off back through the heavy wooden front door, leaving me alone.

"You're very powerful, Arden," Father's voice comes from behind me, from a kitchen that leads to a dining nook. "Come have dinner with me."

He moves into the next room, expecting I'll follow. He had left me with my mother—abandoned me. He wasn't there when I needed him, when I was pregnant with Jackson, when I was struggling to survive every goddamn moment of my life.

He looks back at me.

He wasn't there when my baby was dying, when I was fighting to get Carter back. He wasn't there when Seth was getting ready to fuck me. He served me up, like I was some cheap whore.

"Are you coming?" he asks. His voice drifts like a ghost.

I drop to my knees in front of the man who had his lips pressed against my thigh mere moments ago. He'd left me like this—half naked—a prey to strangers.

"For Christ's sake, Arden, get up. I leave you with your mother for a few years and you turn into some pathetic—"

I unhooked the back of my bra and let it fall to the ground.

"What are you do—"

I slide down my panties.

"For fuck's sake…" His face turns red.

"What's the matter, Dad? You don't want to fuck me now. Is it this...?" I push back the scar tissue around my C-section.

His eyes race to it, he attempts to look away, but glances back. His eyes met mine and his lips droop. "Arden..."

"Fuck you, Dad." I walk across the altar-room, hoping there's a bedroom—bathroom—something on the West side of the pyramid. I'd just cleared the room, into the hallway, when the front door flings open.

A woman's voice bellows, "You son of a bitch!"

The Robe's protests are cut short as she curses them.

I step into the concealment of the hallway's shadow. If I go any further, I'll be out of earshot.

"Who the fuck's panties are these?" she screams, picking up my underwear.

Father mumbles something.

Hard footsteps come my way. Bastet sees me and freezes midway. She looks back at him. "So, what, you're fucking your dead daughter now?"

"She's not—" he says.

She comes at me, nails drawn, eyes narrowed. Her claws cut into my shoulder as she knocks me to the floor. I roll. Her nails slice into my hip.

"Bastet!" Father yells. "That's enough."

She straightens up, looking down at me, then walks away.

He comes to my aid, reaches down, and grabs onto my hand.

I pull away, pushing myself up. “Get away from me. I don’t want anything to do with you.”

I run farther down the hallway, stopping at the next door. It’s an empty nursery. Silent. I walk in, sinking into the rocking chair at the far end of the room. Outside the room’s window is the most beautiful garden I’ve ever seen. White roses with black tips hug a bed of oregano, and things I’d never seen in my life.

I sink into the rocking chair and it sways with one push. My arms are empty. I’m naked and cold, nearly dead, nearly there with my boys.

Inevitable

SUNLIGHT WARMS MY FACE AND BLINDS MY EYES. A blanket covers me and a pile of clothes waits on the changing table beside the rocker. I stand, running my fingers over the baby's crib, spinning the mobile. Four stuffed animals dance in a circle as I dress.

There is a knock at the door.

The nursery is not mine, but the garden beyond calls to me.

The door opens.

It's Seth. He's the reason Carter's dead. He's the fucking reason I lost everything: Jackson, Frank. I grab the mobile of stuffed animals, tearing it from its place, and clench it to my chest in defense of whatever is next.

"Relax," he says, holding up his hands.

I clench the mobile harder, looking at the empty mattress below—the unused changing table. "You…" squeezes out of my lips. I throw the animals to the floor.

He holds out his hands further, like they will protect him.

"You!" *I'm going to kill you.* I charge. My nails stretch and my vision changes—narrows.

He digs into the back of his pants, pulls out a gun, and takes a shot.

I fall to the floor. Warmth floods through my veins. The room instantly feels cozy and safe. My eyelids fall shut—even though I don't want them to.

Someone smacks the side of my face.

I shake my attention back to this world. Everything has a grey hue. My pupils are still dilated.

Bastet is holding my head up, slapping the side of my face. "Sorry about that," she says. "We guessed Seth would be the easiest to see in the morning."

Her finger brushes over the top of my C-section scar. I shoot up and a chill floods my spine.

"I see they still butcher women in your world," she says. "Pity."

My head is so heavy, it weighs me back down. The headache and swelling in my arm is proof enough that Seth shot me with a stun gun—full of sedative.

"Your father wants to make things right with you. You'll stay here until your head is fixed."

Fixed?

"Those plant kids really fucked up your brain. Don't worry we'll help you." She slides off the bed and makes for the door. "Get dressed."

The room they'd put me in is a tomb: no animals painted on the walls, no crib, no windows. There is no nursery. A thick blanket and pillow make up a bed on a slab of marble.

Bastet stops in the doorway and glances back. "You missed a few meals. Why don't you come eat dinner with us?"

I pull on a pair of lace underwear, clearly chosen from her garments. The only clothing provided is a white robe, like the one Seth's Robes wear. I lean against the wall, trying to sink into it, trying to clear the fog from my head.

Bastet exits the room, allowing me a moment's peace.

"Hey babe," Seth says, stepping into the doorway. "You need some help?"

Who the fuck is he talking to?

Before I take another step, he is by my side, supporting me.

What the fuck?

"Oh, I think we better get you some food," he says.

I don't want him to touch me. Why is he touching me? It

feels so disgusting, dirty. I want to shake him off, but when I wiggle, his hand tightens around my arm.

Nausea stops me dead in my tracks. I brace my hand against the wall.

He lets go, waiting beside me.

Once the feeling passes, I lift my head, focusing on the perfectly carved stone walls.

"Come on, you'll feel better once you eat." He lightly presses his hand against my back, nudging me forward to the dining room that's down the hall. It's on the opposite side of the pyramid. I wouldn't have made it without his help. My heart yearns to find that nursery.

When we reach the dining room, he pulls a chair out at the table for me and I sink into it, still dizzy. He leans over, kissing my cheek.

Disgust fills me for a moment, but it fades quickly. It's too much work to hold up my head. I plant an elbow on the table and rest my head down against it, pushing the empty plate before me out of the way.

Father is in the kitchen, humming to himself. He'd done that when I was little. I would sit at the table and draw, humming along with him.

Seth takes the seat to my right.

Bastet sits across from him.

Father turns around.

I don't want to look at him, so I look down.

"Oh, looks like you were being bad again," he says. "Jesus, Arden."

Fuck you, Dad.

He approaches, scoops two pancakes onto my plate, and makes his way to his slut next.

"Just like old times, huh, Dad?" I say.

He stops mid-serve and chucks the frying pan on the table. "We are not going to do this now."

I laugh. "Then when?" Adrenaline starts to pulse through my veins. I'm sick of the games, all the fucking games that only end with me being torn to pieces. I push my head up, force my legs to stand, and throw my fists upon the table. "When? Because I've been waiting a long time for this!"

Father looks at Seth, raising his eyebrows for help.

"Honey, sit down," Seth says, reaching for my arm.

"No!" I yank it away. "You killed my baby." I look down at my wrists, the blood pounding through my veins. "Stay away from me. I hate you!"

Seth stands.

I try to back away, but the chair doesn't slide like expected and keeps me pinned in place.

Bastet jumps out of her seat, rounds the table, and jams a needle into my arm.

The walls spin.

Bitch.

"Easy," Seth's voice fades, "too much and you'll kill her."

Hell

"You can either fight this," Seth's voice comes strong, "or you can learn to accept it."

I'm back in the windowless room. I roll my head.

Seth is standing beside the bed. "This is your life now." He walks out, slamming the door enough to jolt my nerves.

A knock at the door follows.

Before I have a say, Father enters the room.

I roll away from him, facing the wall.

His hand brushes my hair as he sits. "I'm sorry. I should've never left you. I thought you would be more comfortable in your world. I never expected you to become… one of them."

I roll over to look at him, analyze his every manipulation of emotion. He had left me in my world, knowing full well that at some point we'd all die—that I'd die.

His eyes squint, like he notices something about me that he hadn't seen before. He catches me scanning his eyes and draws them down to the bed, pushing a large white box toward me.

"What's this?"

"A gift," he says.

"I don't want anything from you." I roll away from him.

"You can only choose one." He gets up and walks out.

"One what?" I sit up and stare down at the box. He has left me all alone. My head hangs heavy, but it's clearing. My fingers shake as they rush along the edge of the box. It's big enough to fit Carter inside. I can't breathe. My heart throbs. I yank the top off, letting it fall to the floor.

Inside is a crystal ball laying on a bed of velvet. It's the shape of an upside down tear drop—the same shape as the top of Seth's crystal dagger. It glows a deep emerald color. The ancient Egyptian eye of Horus is etched into its surface.

My hand shakes as I pick it up. My fingers tremble, nearly letting it slip to the floor.

Voices trail down the hall and into my room.

I pocket the crystal and follow the voices to another room down the hallway. Its door is cracked, but blocks all view.

"How long have you known?" Father says, barely restraining a yell.

"Not long," says a man.

I lean further in the doorway, peering through the cracked door, risking exposure.

"How did this happen?" Father says. "Who choose her? How did this happen!"

"It was Nephthys," says the man.

Father lets out a loud grunt. "Are you sure you can handle it?"

"Yes," says the man, "but I'm afraid drugging her will weaken the transfer."

Father laughs. "Don't worry about that. But you remember who you work for, boy."

The man turns away from him and heads for the cracked door—straight towards me. I move to the side of the door. I want to find out who this man is, why his voice seems so familiar. Instinct thrusts me in the opposite direction, but it isn't fast enough.

The door opens. It is Brad.

How could you?

His eyes mirror the shock I feel.

I run from him—from having to face the fact that he's betrayed me. He is my Judas and I never saw it coming. I sprint for the altar room—the front door.

Bastet rounds the threshold and I plow into her. She falls to the floor. Maps go flying into the air. My tracks tear them to pieces. She yells obscenities as I push myself harder, faster toward the exit. Before she can get back up, I thrust the door open.

A worn-out dirt road stretches for miles. I sprint down it. Every step is painful. The forest alongside the path blurs. The end of the road has to be in sight, but it isn't. There is nothing at the end but a meadow. There is nothing: no escaping. I throw my knees to the ground, sinking into the dirt—into the earth. I attempt to push my cheek through the grains of sand, wishing quicksand would swallow me whole. The sun beats down upon my back.

I can hear Jackson laughing. And then Carter. The blinding sunrays bring back the memory of a white crib sheet hung on my clothesline. Jackson used to pop his head around the edge of it. Carter could see Jackson's silhouette behind it, but that didn't dampen his excitement when his brother popped out from behind it, yelling, "Peek-a-boo!"

I pinched another clothespin to the sheet and chucked a pair of Frank's shorts into the laundry basket, taking the time to watch the boys and absorb the fleeting moment. If only I had taken more of those moments and not rushed through them.

The sun shifts in the sky overhead, pulling me from my memories.

A hand slides over my shoulder.

It is my father's voice that speaks. "Do you remember when we pitched that tent in the backyard? It was sunny like this, warm. After we got it all set up, a thunderstorm rolled in and the sky poured. The tent shrunk down on us."

Exasperation is my next breath, pushing the dirt into dust. My mind lingers in the images of the long white sheet being tugged on by little fingers.

Sunlight absorbs the memory.

More dust disintegrates into the air as I let out the words, "Where's Jordan?"

"Who?" he says.

I draw in a breath, taking in the taste of dirt. He knows who.

"The goth twerp?" he says.

My fingers press against the dry earth. The grass between my fingers grows a little. I flatten my palm and my whole body turns rigid. I can't force the grass to grow. "I'll give Seth whatever you want. Just let my friends go."

"What friends are they to you? They left you in that whore house."

"No." I push myself up, leaning on one arm. "You left me in that whore-house, five years ago. I choose to stay in the hell that you have created for me. I choose to let them live. Because my life..." my heart pounds and my voice rises to a roar, "isn't worth anything anymore."

He tries to brush my hair, refrains, and pulls his arm back to his side. “You can only choose one,” he says. He stands up and offers his hand down to help me up off the ground.

I knock it away.

“I will release her,” he says.

I sit up.

He leans in, kissing my head before I can back away. His exhale is of satisfaction. His hands rise up in the air.

I let the tears swell in my eyes, absorbing the sunrays that could white out the moment.

He takes another glowing-green crystal ball from his pocket, sets it on the ground beside me, and heads for the cottage.

Cumbersome

I THROW MYSELF ONTO THE GROUND, WANTING TO CRY—bawl my eyes out until completely exasperated, but all I can do is stare at the ground.

"Hey," Seth says as he opens the door, sitting, joining me on the ground.

He looks at the ball. "I wanted to..." he clears his throat. "I want to tell you I'm sorry. I didn't mean for this to happen, for you…" He moves closer. His words choke in his throat. "For you to lose…." He scoots closer, brushing his hand against the side of my face.

I move away, falling back onto the ground, staring up at an empty blue sky.

He leans into my view, blocking the thoughts that drift by like clouds. His lips rest two inches from mine. "If you only knew your true self."

I can feel him inhale.

His lips press against mine.

I hadn't felt that in so long. It had only been days, but it was so long ago, such empty time, pointless time. Blood rushes in my veins whether I want it to or not. His deep exhale yearns for mine to follow.

He pulls away, this time closer than before. "I wish you could remember."

"I'm not who you think I am," barely breaks free from my lips. I close my eyes, longing for it all to be a dream. I open them, but Frank still isn't here. I take the crystal of Horus from my pocket. Its glow is dark in comparison to the pale-green one Father left beside me on the ground. Whatever he took from Carter was now in the crystal in my palm. And based on Dad's reaction, I guessed part of Jordan was in the other.

"What are these?" I say.

"Souls." Seth leans, whispering in my ear. The warmth of his breath blows against my neck sending a shiver through my body.

It's not possible.

He offers his hand out so that I'll take it and he can lead me back into the altar room.

My heart aches, toying with the thought that Carter might somehow come back to me. All I want to do is die here, seep into the ground. All I want is to be with my boys, and for my heart to stop hurting.

His fingers slide across the soil, extending out to mine.

I roll over, turning my back to him.

He jumps on top of me, flattening my back against the ground, and pins my arms.

"What the fuck?" I attempt to sit up, unable to move. The world flashes grey.

"You give me what I want, and I'll revive him," he says.

"What does that mean? He's dead!" I sink into the earth, staring at the glowing crystal balls beside me, refusing to look at him. The world's color eases back to normal. "It's too late. I wasn't there for him."

"You give me the gift Nephthys gave you. I'll take that burden from you. You shouldn't have to bear it." He rolls off, sitting beside me. "And I'll give you a gift. I'll give you back your baby."

That's not possible. There's a reason Nephthys didn't want him to have it—the ability to transcend worlds. "What do you want with it?"

He straightens up, gazing down the long road ahead. "Why do you even care, Arden? This is your baby's life we're talking about here." He faces me, holding out the heart locket he had stolen from my neck. "What kind of mother debates this?"

He's right. How could I not give him whatever he demands? Anything—everything—for Carter. I take the locket, sliding my finger along its seam.

"Are we ready?" Father's voice bellows from the doorway. "It's time."

I crack the locket open enough so I can see the faces of my boys.

Seth reaches for the crystal balls. I throw myself onto him, roll on the ground so he is pinned beneath me. My thighs squeeze around his hips. The drugs pulsing through my veins have subsided and the thoughts running through my head return. It was Seth who plunged the dagger through Carter's little body. The wound it gave me burns with pain. The world turns grey.

"Arden!" Father's voice is loud but muffled.

I dig my fingers into Seth's wrists. If he wants the gift, I'll give it to him. My nails cut through his flesh as Nephthys' once did. Every thought, every emotion is sucked out of my brain. As the life force is pulled out of me, Seth's memories pour in.

He is a young boy in the first memory, elementary-school age. An older man and woman converse on the far side of an ancient Egyptian temple. Their clothes are deeply dyed with color and weaved with extravagant gold detail.

The sound of another young boy giggling with a girl comes from behind him. The jealousy I feel is overpowering.

"Still stuck up Dad's ass, brother?" the frolicking boy says.

"One day you will bow to me, Osiris," Seth says.

The young Osiris turns to his girl and they both start laughing.

Seth pulls the dagger of Anubis out, looking at the girl. "And that day, you will be mine."

They stop laughing and Osiris steps between the dagger and his girl. "Father! Set has the dagger! And he's threatening us again!"

The conversation across the room ceases and the older man storms the children, ripping the dagger from Seth's hand. It's my father, not exactly the same looks, but his soul energy is the same as my father.

"Isis," Osiris says, grabbing onto the girl's hand. "Let's go to the garden."

The memory bleeds into another. Set is with Nephthys, in the awkward stage of zits and puberty. He holds her hand, walking down a forest path. I feel the sun shining. It smells of flowers all around. He spins her, leaning her against a stone wall, kissing her.

Her lips curl at the edges with a smile. "What's that in your pocket?"

He steps back, looking at the ground.

The smile fades from her lips. "Set, what's in your pocket?"

He digs further and pulls out the dagger. Its top crystal glows green. She moves away. "What did you do?"

Tears flood down his face. "I killed her."

He sinks to the ground, wrapping his arms around her legs.

She pulls back at first, and then slides her fingers through his hair, bending down to comfort him. "You can make this right," she says. "If no one has seen you, you can bring her back."

Osiris comes barreling down the path. He holds a blade at his side and heartache within his chest. His voice quivers with furry, "You son of a bitch! You murderer!"

"Father told me to," Set says through deep breaths and tears. He holds out the crystal dagger, offering it out to Osiris.

Part of Osiris dies seeing the glow of the ball. He swings his blade at Set. Nephthys conjures up a vine from the ground with a wave of her hand, blocking the assault.

Set looks to Osiris—broken. "You would kill me, brother?"

"I would do anything for her," says Osiris. He grabs the dagger loosely hung at Set's side. The blade slices into his palm and blood drips down the crystal.

So many memories flood my mind, I can't ground myself in just one anymore. They flood in crashing, suffocating, easing into the final one.

Set stands before an entire closet full of crystal balls—all glowing green. He unscrews the top of the dagger and places it on the shelf amongst many, replacing it with a new, clear and empty crystal that has the eye of Horus etched into its side.

Nephthys enters the room from behind him. "What are you doing?"

He shut the doors, concealing his trophy-case of souls, and stows the dagger as he faces her.

"We're going to be late for the baby shower," she says.

I let go.

I let go of Seth's wrists. I can feel his blood drip down my fingers. I can breathe.

He screams in agony and my father runs to his side. I want to run away, but I can't even sit up.

"It will all be perfect," I hear Father say to Seth. "In just a few hours we will get everything you've ever dreamed of."

"What about my dreams, Dad?" I say.

"Darling, you'll get everything you've always wanted. You'll have everything you could imagine, never have to worry about money, hardship, cleaning the dishes," he laughs. "You'll be royalty."

"I want my son," I say. I shouldn't have the energy to move, but I'm not going to let them take him from me.

"There will be no disobedience," Father says. "Do you understand?"

"I understand that you're nothing like I remember. My father died years ago. You are nothing to me." I don't want to say it. My heart still aches to love him, try to understand what had happened, why he had left, but I'd been through that grief years ago. *Fuck if I am going to relive it now.*

I try to stand up, falling like I'd been shot with a sedative, stumbling back to the ground. "Where is he?" I try to get up again, heading for the temple door. He has to be in there somewhere.

Father kneels beside Seth as he screams in agony.

The abandonment pins me back to the ground. I look away from my father—away from his voice.

"My son," he says.

My eyes fill with tears that burn.

There is a stone wall leading toward the backyard garden. The same wall in Seth's memories.

Anubis' Garden! I shove my hands beneath me. Blades of grass shoot up between my fingers as I stand, sprinting for it. I stumble after two feet.

Father's too busy with Seth to notice my shift in direction. He's mumbling something. Before I am out of earshot, I hear him say her name, "Isis..."

I stop and glance back.

Father lets go of Seth's arm, turning all his attention to me. He shouts, "All this time I've been looking for you!"

I turn my back to him and sprint for the garden.

"Isis!" he yells.

Contract

I WIPED THE BLOOD FROM JACKSON'S STUFFED *beetle, Atum, only days ago*. The thought brings me to my knees before the garden's gate. Tears wash away the dirt from my cheeks. I close my eyes to shake the blur from my head, but it wouldn't leave. I try searching for something to ground me. My eyes drift back to the gate and its symbol—Atum. The beetle's wings expanded to form the gate doors, but the beetle itself is no larger than my hand. Its keyhole is the shape of a heart. Hieroglyphs spiral towards its center.

My necklace. I rip it from my neck, shoving it into the hole.

Gold runs into the seams of the hieroglyphs and a breeze catches in the air, pushing the metal bars open.

Beyond is a garden rich with summer's harvest.

Father's footfalls stamped for me.

At the center of the garden is a small pyramid—a tomb. But there is no way in. There is no entrance at its front or right side. I check the back and then the left.

The gate closes.

There is no entrance at all. I hide behind the tomb.

"Your mother was always such a bitch," Father says. "She'd told me she threw out that necklace. Destroyed it with her magic."

A branch snaps to my right. He's coming around the side, but his voice hasn't changed direction.

The vine of a squash plant shoots toward my head. I duck. It cracks a brick in the pyramid. It is Father. He waves his right hand, conjuring the plants around him to rise like a tsunami. My heart swells. He's set on killing me. This time will be different. Mother drank her life away after he'd left. She had stollen his heart—his heart locket.

We were standing at his graveside when she gave it to me. I was in eighth grade, four years before having Jackson.

She'd started drinking then. I thought it was because Father died. But it was because he had lived.

"Arden," she said, wrapping her arm over my shoulder, bringing me close.

No one had come to the funeral. We never had many close friends.

"Arden," she said. "One day this will make sense. One day this sadness will turn into rage." She bent down, looking into my eyes, draining a tear of her own. She cupped my hand and with the other placed the locket in my palm. "Feel the energy. But remember to control it. For if it controls you, you'll lose it."

I could feel it.

That was the last time she had shown any affection. Perhaps I was too much like my father for her to bear.

I look into his eyes. It is time for my grief to mean something.

He shoots a finger at me and another squash-vine flings toward the pyramid—toward my face. I duck. He shoots another, this time with a zucchini attached to it. It slams into the edge of the building. Sandstone brakes away upon impact, leaving dust in the air.

And then another explodes.

I catch the squash-vines and yank them toward me, imagining them whipping back towards him. And they do. They twist around his arms, pulling him to the ground like an alligator readying to roll, to suffocate its prey.

"Arden, please," Father says through winded breath. "Arden, you're killing me."

The world stops. The vines tense, cease in mid-air. Father wiggles within them, though they do not budge.

"You know once you kill him," Brad says from behind me, "you can't bring him back."

I face him, turning my back to my father. Brad betrayed me. He had been in the room with my father. The crystal ball holding Jordan's soul weighs heavy in my pocket. I fling the vines toward him.

He waves his hand and the vines disintegrate, falling like dust to the ground. His smile takes me back to the day he'd given me Jackson's only gift. It was the smile of a boy who was too sweet, kind, and thoughtful to be your boyfriend. I don't know why or how Brad got there in the house with Dad, but I know I can trust him with all my life.

Father grunts from behind me.

Brad swings his left arm up above me. The thick stem of a tomato plant snaps into pieces, falling beside me. I turn to face my father. He had been freed from my vines while dealing with Brad. He gained control of the garden again. He draws his arms back—to thrust his power—to swing the foliage forward to crush us. His arms thrust forward.

I raise my hand. I believe I can be more than just a helpless, weak, insecure girl. *I am a goddess*.

His abandonment crumbled the small girl within me, and Shawn took the rest.

The vines hover in the air.

Father digs into his pocket, pulling something out, and throws it. Streams of branches spring from seeds, wrapping around Brad's wrists and ankles, knocking him to the ground.

Vines twist around my wrists, pulling my hands to the ground, making me kneel before him.

Seth joins us, out of breath. He rips his shirt off, throws it down, and steps up to me, spitting in my face.

His non-tattooed left arm is black, hanging unmoving at his side. On the other arm, I can see the seam along his shoulder—identical to Brad's—where flesh had been molded together. He shoots his right fingers toward the ground, turning his wrist as if digging into the ground, yet four-feet above it. An underground root shoots up through the soil. He aims at me and the root hairs grow to the size of branches—flying straight at me. There isn't time to move—to duck.

Brad steps in front of me. The root pierces through his torso, then withers to ash. He falls to his knees.

"No!" I break free from the vines and sink to his side.

"It was the only way I could save her." Blood seeps from his lips. "You have no idea who you are. How powerful you'll become."

I lean my forehead against his, closing my eyes.

His body jerks as Seth retracts what's left of the root for a second kill.

I pull my head away from Brad's, before opening my eyes.

Seth charges, breaks off a piece of root, and swings it over his head, like a spear.

"No!" Father yells. "No."

I imagine the vine twisting back, wrapping around Father's wrist and pinning him like Jesus on the cross for all to see. And it happens.

He screams as I twist the vine around his neck and shoot it down his throat. I twist another vine tighter and tighter around his body, squeezing—squeezing so fucking hard till his ribs pop. Tears of pain drip from his eyes. His gasps for air, drowning in choking noises. His skin fades pale and he stops moving. He stops ruining my life. Blood drains out of his mouth.

The man who taught me to ride a bike, read to me every night, and left me all alone in this cruel, dark world lay dead against the floor.

"Not bad, Sis," says Seth.

Family

My nails retract and the blood pulsing through my veins eases.

Seth passes me, runs around the side of the tomb, and disappears.

What have I done? The world is spinning. I sprint to follow him. *I'm going to kill him.*

I grow the forest larger around the edge of the tomb and charge. I throw the branches of nearby apple trees, bending them to spear the back area of the tomb. He isn't there. I do the same with the other side. He isn't there either. I round the tomb again. He's gone. He had run to the back before disappearing so I follow his empty footsteps.

The back of the tomb is stone. A bloody handprint is smeared over a quarter-sized scarab beetle carved into its side. I can see an old memory. I can see the dagger of Anubis slicing into the palm of a hand and the blood being smeared over the beetle. It is Seth's memory, but it feels like my own, like a memory long forgotten and caved in.

A rose bush grows at the corner of the tomb.

I wave my hand, begging the thorns to grow into swords. They grow into knives and I break one off, cutting into the flesh of my palm, smearing my blood over the scarab beetle, waiting for anything to happen.

I fall through the wall, through a portal, landing at the floor of an enormous gold statue of Anubis with his jackal-head. He looks like a God. Three mummies rest on granite slabs at his feet. The center one is a full grown man. To his left is a smaller body. *Jordan*. On his right is an infant. *Carter.*

My arms give out. I hit my face on the ground, letting the pain linger in my bones. I could've stayed there on the ground, never knowing if I could save him, so I get up. I shove my hands beneath me and charge Seth.

He scoops up Carter's mummy, and clenches it in his arms.

I stop.

He pulls out the dagger of Anubis. "You kept your promise." He offers out the dagger to me. "I will keep mine."

I don't trust him. But I waited too long for this moment, I cannot wait anymore. I grab the dagger, but he doesn't let go. The cut of my hand opens up. My blood drains over the dagger, dripping into the gauze wrapping my son.

His grip loosens and he turns the blade on himself. The dagger and the mummy drop at the same time.

I dive for Carter, but without the dagger, there's no way to save him. *The dagger!* It's too late. It shattered into a million pieces before I realized I made a wrong choice.

But there is no sound. No pieces shatter. I pull Carter tight. The gauze is still soft. I look for the dagger on the floor.

Anubis sits beside me, twirling the crystal in his hand. He had caught it mid-air. "She will be mad," he says, twirling the dagger on a finger. "You've killed her husband and son." He looks back at Seth.

The crystal ball glows.

Anubis clenches the dagger.

"I wouldn't trust him." Brad falls through the portal's entrance face-first.

Anubis unscrews the glowing crystal ball and heads toward an old wooden cabinet. I know that cabinet. He pulls open the set of doors. The inside glows with the faint green glow of hundreds of crystal balls.

Anubis reluctantly places the crystal on the shelf with all the others, grabbing an empty one, and screws it to the dagger. He passes me, heading for Brad, who's still on the floor.

My heart races. I should intervene, but I can't put Carter down.

Anubis kneels beside Brad, places both hands tightly around the dagger, and thrusts it down into his back.

No. I gasp. All the air expels from my lungs.

A green glow drains into the ball and Brad's body goes limp on the floor.

"What did you do?" I say.

He walks over to Seth's lifeless body, kicks him until his body rolls facedown, then plummets the dagger into his back.

Seth's lungs fill with air and he spills a cough all over the floor.

"What did you do?" I say, stepping backward, banging into the center mummy beside me.

Candle Light

THE EGYPTIANS WOULD REMOVE THE ORGANS OF THE body and place them in jars. The body was mummified, preserving it long enough for the spirit to travel through the gates of hell.

I wasn't there when they took out Carter's heart. And I wasn't there when he took his last breath.

Anubis offers me the dagger.

Seth's lungs gasp for a breath, heaving his chest into the air.

"Have you found yourself?" Anubis says, setting the empty dagger upon Carter's cast. He motions for me to hand him Carter, and I do, grabbing the dagger and pulling the glowing crystal balls from my pocket.

I look at my baby's mummified body resting in Anubis' arms and then at the 13 year old body wrapped opposite me. *Jordan*.

I have a crystal for Carter and Jordan. As much as I want to hold Carter, I have to be sure it works first. I unscrew the empty crystal ball as quick as I can.

It falls from my grasp and shatters to the ground.

I take the dimmer of the two balls from my pocket, screw it on, and thrust the dagger into the medium-sized mummy.

All the light flows out of the ball, down the dagger and into the corpse.

Seth rips the dagger from my hands. I go for it. He shoves me to the ground, barreling the dagger down upon the mummy, cutting through the wrapping.

Gasps of breath came from the mummy.

Seth scoops Jordan into a sitting position, tearing the gauze from her mouth. "Are you all right?"

She sits up, catching a breath, digging her fingers into his shoulder, where Brad's robotic arm would have been. She nods her head yes. How could she trust Seth?

It's a trap. It's always been a trap. I look at Carter and clench his glowing crystal.

I dive for the dagger, grab it, and fall to the floor beside the altar.

"No," screams Seth, letting go of Jordan.

One mummy separates us.

I shove Carter's ball into the place of the hilt and twist it onto the dagger.

"Arden," says Seth. "You'll kill him!"

"You lie!" I say. The ball screws tight.

Seth reaches his left hand into Jordon's wrapping, pulling out a handful of dried flowers. Their petals turn bright white and alive. Their withered stems fill with life and grow, wrapping around the dagger, pinning my hands in place.

Jordan's still sitting in the bouquet of dead flowers, trying to catch her breath, but she isn't scared of him.

And neither am I.

I thrust the new plant growth from my wrists and send it back at him. The stems thicken, catch him by the throat, and lift him into the air.

I imagine reaching deep into the earth of the garden's root system. Root hairs grow in the tomb, crawling up the walls, sprouting from the floor, covering the interior with vines of fruit and vegetables.

Jordan raises a hand in defense, rolling off the altar to take cover.

I stop and the world freezes. The vines loosen from Seth's throat. If he is part of me—my brother—what would I be if I killed him? I let him down.

His feet weakly hit the ground and he falls to his knees. His next breath is raspy but spoken with conviction, "You'll kill him"

I bring the dagger down, looking at it.

"A piece of you is missing," says Seth.

"Why should I believe you?" I say.

"Because," he says walking toward me.

I hold up my hand to block whatever arsenal he is plotting.

He steps closer. "Because you trusted me when we were in my treehouse."

Treehouse? I look at Anubis.

He lowers his eyes and kneels before me. "Your highness."

"Brad?" Spills from my lips, though I refuse to believe it.

He nods yes, never taking his eyes from mine, stepping closer until my palm collides with his chest. He runs his fingers down my torso, stopping at the cut in my stomach. "Part of you was taken when his soul was. To replace his, you must"—he looks back at Anubis.

Anubis walks over, unclenching Carter from his chest, offering him to me.

Seth offers out a hand for the dagger.

I watch the green swirl within the crystal ball. I can't exchange the dagger for Carter's corpse—it's the only thing that can bring him back. *I can't.*

"I promise, you won't fall down into any tree houses," says Seth. A smile fills his lips.

I look into his eyes. *Brad?*

His smile deepens.

I give him the dagger and take Carter, clenching him to my chest. Anubis approaches. "You must untangle the souls."

Within the crystal ball of Horus, you can tell the green is

darker. A smaller ball of light-green entangles the other.

"Part of you was taken when Seth took Horus—Carter's—soul," Anubis says.

I feel for the wound in my torso. My stomach pits at where the conversation is heading.

"To release one soul, the other must stay," he says.

"No," says Brad.

Jordan lets out a breath of defeat.

"You expect me to believe that?" I ask. "To give up everything to save my son and not be able to hold him ever again? To be filed on a shelf in a fucking tomb in the middle of nowhere?" I look at Carter's wrapped body and cradle him like I did every time he nursed.

I can't leave his soul trapped on that same shelf. I won't take the risk.

I take the dagger from Brad and cut open the mummified gauze of my baby. Dried flowers that still smell frame his pale little body. I pull his corpse onto my own, taking his place on the altar. Anubis helps position his tiny body where he'd been when life left us both. His limp arms drape both sides of me. My heart pounds against my chest—attempting to wake him.

I can't do it. I hold the dagger over his back. I'll have to jam it through his back and straight down, until it cuts deep into my torso.

Defeat

TIME SLOWS. NOT BECAUSE I WANT IT TO, BUT BECAUSE Brad has wrapped his hands around mine and shoves the blade into my torso—through my baby's body and through the stitches of my wound. Blood drains from my stomach. The green glow of the crystal begins to flow through the blade. Carter's body warms against mine. His fingers begin to twitch. I'm beginning to believe it could work.

Brad gives me a look, like he'll never see me again. He leans above me, jamming the blade further—deeper into me.

I lose control of myself. Darkness takes over. Dreams of moments comfort me. I can almost feel the heat of summer coming in through the window. Carter's little lips are pressed up against my breast. Jackson's small voice saying, "Mom-me. Me not feel good."

The memory drifts into a baby's cry. I can hear Carter crying. I can feel the warmth fills his body and the fist of his tiny hand grasp onto the side of my breast, as everything goes dark and cold around me.

Acknowledgements

To my kids, for giving up on my dreams would be to great a risk for yours. To my dad, for reading when it felt like no one else was. To Lisa W., Carla O., Suzanne, Joanna B., Stephanie M. for reading when no one should have and giving me essential tools to craft with. To Partners in Crime Book Service for finding the little things and smoothing the story.

To the readers and the dreamers.
We are still here.

About the Author

Julie Embers graduated from Stockton University with a degree in Biology. Writing ignited her journey into enlightenment. In a constantly changing world, she writes full-time. She recently traded the Pacific Northwest for the Gulf beaches of Florida with her kids and french bulldog.

www.ingramcontent.com/pod-product-compliance
Lightning Source LLC
Chambersburg PA
CBHW022243020726
47496CB00004B/1042
* 9 7 8 0 9 9 6 2 7 9 5 7 4 *